Here's to the Ladies

Stories of the Frontier Army

Here's to the Ladies

Stories of the Frontier Army

Carla Kelly

TCU PRESS ❧ FORT WORTH

Library of Congress Cataloging-in-Publication Data

Kelly, Carla.
  Here's to the ladies : stories of the frontier army / by Carla Kelly.
      p. cm.
    ISBN 0-87565-270-0 (trade paper : alk. paper)
    1. Indians of North America—Wars—Fiction. 2. Officers'
spouses—Fiction. 3. Women pioneers—Fiction. 4. Western stories. I.
Title.
    PS3561.E3928 H47 2003
    813'.54—dc21

                                        2002010196

Cover and text design by Bill Maize; Duo Design Group

COVER PHOTO: First Sgt. Richard Flynn, D Company 4th Infantry, and his wife, Marilla, with their children, Elizabeth and Frank, at Fort Omaha in Nebraska in the 1870s.

This camp follower/ranger dedicates these stories
to her comrades and fellow rangers of Company K,
Second Cavalry, garrisoned at Fort Laramie
National Historic Site in 1974-1975:
William Dobak, Bill Henry,
Paul Hedren, Randy Kane,
Tom Lindmier, Gaithel Gilchriest,
and post sutler Lewis Eaton.
You were dear to me then,
and nothing has changed.

Table of Contents

❧ Introduction ❧

When Judy Alter, director of Texas Christian University Press, invited me to write the introduction to *Here's to the Ladies: Stories of the Frontier Army*, I began to ask myself why I wrote these stories in the first place and why they have such a hold on me. I have written many books since I wrote some of these stories, but none that I hold in comparable affection.

I can trace where and how it began. In 1974 and 1975, I worked as a seasonal ranger at Fort Laramie National Historic Site in eastern Wyoming. It's a remarkable site, one which has seen the ebb and flow of American history for a lengthy time, ranging from the fur trade era to the western migration, the Indian Wars, and into the homesteader phase. Through it all, Fort Laramie played a prominent role.

Like some on the staff, I worked as both a uniformed ranger and an interpreter of the fort's history. Once a week, dressed in National Park Service gray and green, I answered visitors' questions and gave twenty-minute history talks under the cottonwood trees in front of the commissary storehouse, which served—then and now—as the administrative center/museum/bookstore.

On other days, I participated in the fort's living history program. I wore period clothing and assumed various personae, depending on where I was stationed. One day a week, I sat in the rocking chair on the porch of the 1876 duplex, talking with visitors as though I were the wife of a captain garrisoned at the fort during the height of the Great Sioux War. I told them of my life as an officer's wife, far from the more genteel society I was accustomed to "back in the States."

On another day, I stationed myself upstairs in the sewing alcove of the post surgeon's house and interpreted a slightly later period of the fort's history. I spoke to visitors of the difficulty of raising children in a garrison and the gloomy prospect of having to send them back East to live with relatives so they could get a proper education. I also advised visitors that if they were traveling north and needed medical care, they could stop at Fort Robinson, where Captain Walter Reed was the post surgeon. "He's a young fellow," I would tell them, "but my husband expects great things of him."

Sometimes, I was a servant in the lieutenant colonel's quarters during the mid- to late-1880s, when more garrison comforts were evident. (One of my colleagues calls this the "country club era" of military forts.) I churned butter on the back porch, washed clothing in the 1880s rocker washing machine, and gave visitors a glimpse of life for a domestic servant during those waning days of Fort Laramie's usefulness.

One summer, we decided to set up a tent on the edge of the parade ground and install a cot, trunk, and folding chair. There I sat and represented a lowly lieutenant's wife, bumped into a tent because someone who outranked her husband had joined the garrison and claimed her home. This little domestic drama was an excellent springboard to discussion of that unpleasant reality of military life.

Living history interpretation was—and is—a positive way to introduce visitors to garrison life in a frontier army post. It was an excellent opportunity to point out the similarities we share with an earlier age and also the differences. To say that people living a century ago think as we do today would be to err. On the other hand, to infer that we have nothing in common would be an equal mistake.

How then, to strike a balance? As park rangers—custodians of our nation's history—we had a story to tell at Fort Laramie; living history was one way to do it. For me, another way was writing short stories. After only a short time at Fort Laramie, I became deeply aware of the vast amount of story material at my fingertips. I decided to write the truest story I possibly could in order to combat those movies and potboiler novels of an earlier age that contained stereotypes and blunders about the frontier army. I would tell the truth, as much as it was in my power to do.

Stereotypes can be daunting. One of our standing amusements at Fort Laramie was to tally how many times visitors asked, "Where is the wall?" Generations of people have been raised on motion pictures where all western forts were walled to prevent Indian assault. In reality, only a few western forts had walls. Wood was scarce, and Plains Indians were not inclined to attack forts, anyway. We would explain this, but I sometimes suspected that visitors were disappointed. When myth smacks against reality, it's hard to discard the myth.

That's what I have tried to do with these stories: entertain readers with fiction but educate them about life in a garrison at an army post after the Civil War. As a historian, I am interested in military life. As a woman, I like to know more about women and children, invariably overlooked in official records. As a fiction writer, I know a fertile field when I see it. The drama can be as large and painful as waiting for the return of soldiers who are long overdue or as small as coming West to help tend a sister's twins.

Each story has its own background. Two of them came directly from historical research, coupled with the writer's eternal and necessary question: "Well, what if?" During two Wyoming winters, I volunteered each week to review and catalog Fort Laramie's microfilm collection. One day, I came across a census listing the garrison's residents and their occupations. There it was: a company laundress, age twenty-eight or so, and her one or two dependents, with no husband listed. From this sketchy beginning came "Mary Murphy," a personal favorite.

"Casually at Post," a term describing officers and men passing through a garrison on their way to another duty station, was based on official correspondence at Fort Buford, Dakota Territory, to the post adjutant from the post surgeon. The doctor had been directed to decide if a man calling himself Augustus Gustavus God is sane or not.

Some stories came from personal experience. During my last summer at Fort Laramie, I asked for and received permission to spend the night on the parade ground in my tent, the one where I interpreted the lieutenant's wife bumped out of quarters. "Such Brave Men" was the result.

As any fiction writer knows, the oddest tidbits can spark stories. An elderly friend of mine had told me about her father who had a glass eye. He never could get a good fit and accumulated a box full of glass eyes. "Season for Heroes" has such a moment. The story must have struck a chord with readers; it earned a Spur Award from Western Writers of America.

My own grandmother gave me the idea for "Kathleen Flaherty's Long Winter," also a Spur Award winner. After my grandfather's death, she had told me that early in their marriage, Grandpa promised her that he would always have savings set by, so that if something happened to him, she wouldn't be forced to remarry, just to eat. My writer's "What if" took over from there and created a woman whose husband wasn't so provident.

Friend's stories are fair game, too. A lady of my acquaintance told me of an embarrassing incident that happened to her and her husband when she came to Las Vegas during World War II to see him, after a lengthy absence. I moved the basic idea back to Cheyenne just after the railroad has gone through and wrote "Fille de Joie."

"The Gift"? Sometimes it's just fun to write an unabashed love story. No one should need a reason for that. "We Shall Meet, but We Shall Miss Him," is another love story, but this one on two levels: the love of a man for a woman he has not seen in years and his own affection for a fort that is closing and the life he is leaving.

"Jesse MacGregor" is a direct result of my years spent working in hospital public relations, where I came to know a little about medicine and its practitioners. Motion pictures and literature have often portrayed army surgeons as incompetent, hopeless drunks; hardly anything could be farther from the truth. Most physicians of the U.S. Army Medical Corps were skilled, well-educated men who preferred the active life of an army post to a safe, stodgy (and better-paying) medical practice in the East. If "Jesse MacGregor" reads a bit like a Grade B movie, then I did my job, because that's what I wanted: a swashbuckling physician in spectacles.

Most of my colleagues have more knowledge about the frontier army than I will ever acquire. I have probably used them shamelessly in my quest to get the stories as right as I can make them, but they are kind, obliging friends. For example, when I was writing "Kathleen Flaherty," I needed to set the story in the worst garrison imaginable. I suspected that was Camp Ruby, or Fort Halleck—both in Nevada—during the days when the transcontinental railroad was under construction. To confirm this, I called Paul Hedren, one of my useful, all-purpose ranger/friends, and he agreed. I used Halleck. Paul and Randy Kane have given me advice on other aspects of soldier life. William Dobak and Bill Henry have shared official correspondence from their own research and advice of a sound nature, some of which I take. Where the details are right, I give these friends the credit. Where they are not, the blame is mine. My special thanks go to Wright Publishing Company of Costa Mesa, California, for permission to reprint some of these stories that earlier appeared in *Far West* magazine.

So *Here's to the Ladies*. It's not a standard textbook of the Indian Wars but a glimpse of life as it might have been during a colorful era of our not-so-distant past. If you enjoy reading them as much as I enjoyed writing them, we'll both be satisfied.

Carla Kelly

Such Brave Men

"A little paint will make all the difference," Hart Sanders said as he and his wife surveyed the scabby walls in Quarters B.

Emma stood on tiptoe to whisper in her husband's ear. She didn't want to offend the quartermaster sergeant, who was leaning against the door and listening (she was sure). "Hart, what are these walls made of?"

"Adobe," he whispered back.

"Oh." Perhaps she could find out what adobe was later.

Hart turned to the sergeant in the doorway. The man straightened up when the lieutenant spoke to him. "Sergeant, have some men bring our household effects here. And we'll need a bed, table, and chairs from supply."

"Yes, sir."

Emma took off her bonnet and watched the sergeant heading back to the quartermaster storehouse. Then she turned and looked at her first army home again. Two rooms and a lean-to kitchen, the allotment of a second lieutenant.

Hart was watching her. Theirs wasn't a marriage of long standing, but she knew him well enough to know that he wanted to smile but wasn't sure how she would take that. "Not exactly Sandusky, is it?" he ventured finally.

She grinned at him and snapped his suspenders. "It's not even Omaha, Hart, and you know it!"

But I have been prepared for this, she thought to herself later as she blacked the cook stove in the lean-to. Hart had warned her about life at Fort Laramie, Dakota Territory. He had told her about the wind and the heat and the cold and the bugs and the dirt. But sitting in the parlor of her father's house in Sandusky, she hadn't dreamed anything quite like this.

Later that afternoon, as she was tacking down an army blanket for the front room carpet, she noticed that the ceiling was shedding. Every time she hammered in a tack, white flakes drifted down to the floor and settled on her hair, the folding rocking chair, and the whatnot shelf she had carried on her lap from Cheyenne Depot to Fort Laramie. She swept out the flakes after the blanket was secure and reminded herself to step lightly in the front room.

Dinner was brought in by some of the other officers' wives, and they dined on sowbelly, hash browns, and eggless custard. The sowbelly looked definitely lowbrow congealing on her Lowestoft bridal china, and she wished she had thought to bring along tin plates like Hart had suggested.

She was putting the last knickknack on the whatnot when Hart got into bed in the next room. The crackling and rustling startled her, and she nearly dropped the figurine in her hand. She hurried to the door. "Hart? Are you all right?" she asked.

He had blown out the candle, and the bedroom was dark. "Well, sure, Emma. What's the matter?"

"That awful noise!"

She heard the rustling again as he sat up in bed. "Emma, haven't you ever slept on a straw-tick mattress?"

"In my father's house?" She shook her head. "Does it ever quiet down?"

"After you sleep on it awhile," he assured her, and the noise started up again as he lay down and rolled over. He laughed. "Well, my dear, be grateful that we're not in a connecting duplex. This bed's not really discreet, is it?"

She felt her face go red, then laughed, too, and put down the figurine.

She had finished setting the little house in order the next morning when Hart came bursting into the front room. He waved a piece of paper in front of her nose.

"Guess what?" he shouted. "D Company is going on detached duty to Fetterman! We leave tomorrow!"

"Do I get to come?" she asked.

"Oh, no. We'll be gone a couple of months. Isn't it exciting? My first campaign!"

Well, it probably was exciting, she thought, after he left, but that meant she would have to face the house alone. The prospect gleamed less brightly than it had the night before.

D Company left the fort next morning after Guard Mount. She was just fluffing up the pillows on their noisy bed when someone knocked on the front door.

It was the adjutant. He took off his hat and stepped into the front room, looking for all the world like a man with bad news. She wondered what could possibly be worse than seeing your husband of one month ride out toward Fetterman—wherever that was—and having to figure out how to turn that scabrous adobe box into a house, let alone a home.

"I hate to tell you this, Mrs. Sanders," he said at last.

"Tell me what?"

"You've been ranked."

Emma shook her head. Whatever was he talking about? Ranked?

"I don't understand, Lieutenant."

He took a step toward her, but he was careful to stay near the door. "Well, you know, ma'am, ranked. Bumped. Bricks falling?"

She stared at him and wondered why he couldn't make sense. Didn't they teach them English at the academy? "I'm afraid it's still a mystery to me, Lieutenant."

He rubbed his hand over his head and shifted from one foot to the other. "You'll have to move, ma'am."

"But I just did," she protested, at the same time surprised at herself for springing to the defense of such a defenseless house.

"I mean again," the lieutenant persisted. "Another lieutenant just reported on post with his wife, and he outranks your husband. Yours is the only quarters available, so you'll have to move."

It took a minute to sink in. "Who? I can't . . . ."

She was interrupted by the sound of boots on the front porch. The man who stepped inside was familiar to her, but she couldn't quite place him until he greeted her; then she knew she would never forget that squeaky voice. He was Hart's old roommate from the academy, and she had met him once. She remembered that Hart had told her how the man spent all his time studying and never was any fun at all.

"Are *you* taking my house?" she accused the lieutenant.

"I'm sorry, Mrs. Sanders," he said, but he didn't sound sorry at all.

"But . . . but . . . didn't you just graduate with my husband two months ago? How can you outrank him?" she asked, wanting to throw both of the officers out of her home.

He smiled again, and she resisted the urge to scrape her fingernails along his face. Instead, she stamped her foot, and white flakes from the ceiling floated down.

"Yes, ma'am, we graduated together, but Hart was forty-sixth in class standing. I was fifteenth. I still outrank him."

As she slammed the pots and pans into a box and yanked the sheets off the bed, she wished for the first time that Hart had been a little more diligent in his studies.

Two privates moved her into quarters that looked suspiciously like a chicken coop. She sniffed the air in the one-room shack and almost asked one of the privates if the former tenants she ranked out had clucked and laid eggs. But he didn't speak much English, and she didn't feel like wasting her sarcasm.

Emma swept out the room with a vigor that made her cough, and by nightfall when she crawled into the rustling bed, she speculated on the cost of rail fare from Cheyenne to Sandusky.

The situation looked better by morning. The room was small, to be sure, but she was the only one using it, and if she cut up a sheet, curtains would make all the difference. She hung up the Currier and Ives lithograph of sugaring off in Vermont and was ripping up the sheet when someone knocked at the door.

It was the adjutant again. He had to duck to get into the room, and when he straightened up, his head just brushed the ceiling. "Mrs. Sanders," he began, and it was an effort. "I hope you'll understand what I have to tell you."

Emma sensed what was coming and braced herself, but she didn't want to make it easy on him. "What?" she asked, seating herself in the rocking chair and folding her hands in her lap. As she waited for him to speak, she remembered a poem she had read in school called "Horatio at the Bridge."

"You've been ranked out again."

She was silent, looking at him for several moments. She noticed the drops of perspiration gathering on his forehead and that his Adam's apple bobbed up and down when he swallowed.

"And where do I go from here?" she asked at last.

He shuffled his feet and rubbed his head again, gestures she was beginning to recognize. "All we have is a tent, ma'am."

"A tent," she repeated.

"Yes, ma'am."

At least I didn't get attached to my chicken coop, she thought, as she rolled up her bedding. She felt a certain satisfaction in the knowledge that Hart's roommate and his wife—probably a little snip—had been bumped down to her coop by whoever it was that outranked him. "Serves him right," she said out loud as she carried out the whatnot and closed the door.

The same privates set up the tent at the corner of Officers Row. It wasn't even an officer's tent. Because of the increased activity in the field this summer, only a sergeant's tent could be found. The bedstead wouldn't fit in, so the private dumped the bed sack on the grass and put the frame back in the wagon. She started to protest when they drove away, but remembering the shortage of useful English, she saved her breath. They were was back soon with a cot.

She had crammed in her trunks, spread the army blanket on the grass, and was setting up the rocking chair when someone rapped on the tent pole.

She knew it would be the adjutant even before she turned around. Emma pulled back the flap and stepped outside. "You can't have it, Lieutenant."

He shook his head and smiled this time. "Oh, no, ma'am. I wasn't going to bump you again." He held out a large square of green fabric.

She took it. "What's this for?"

"Ma'am, I used to serve in Arizona Territory, and most folks down there line tent ceilings with green. Easier on the eyes."

He smiled again, and Emma began to see that the lot of an adjutant was not to be envied. She smiled back.

"Thank you, Lieutenant. I appreciate it."

He helped her fasten up the green baize, and it did make a difference inside the tent. Before he left, he pulled her cot away from the tent wall.

"So the tent won't leak when it rains," he explained and then laughed. "But it never rains here anyway."

Since she couldn't cook in the tent, she messed with the officers in Old Bedlam that night. There were only three. The adjutant was a bachelor, Captain Endicott was an orphan who had left his family back in the States, and the other lieutenant was casually at post on his way from Fort Robinson to Fort D.A. Russell.

The salt pork looked more at home on a tin plate, and she discovered that plum duff was edible. The coffee burned its way down, but she knew she could get used to it.

She excused herself, ran back to her tent, and returned with the tin of peaches she had bought at the post trader's store for the exorbitant sum of $2.25. The adjutant pried open the lid, and the four of them speared slices out of the can and laughed and talked until Tattoo.

Captain Endicott walked her back to her tent before Last Call. He shook his head when he saw the tent. "Women ought to stay in the States. Good schools there, doctors, sociability. Much better."

"Don't you miss your family?" she asked.

"Oh, God . . ." he began and then stopped. "Beg pardon, Mrs. Sanders." He said goodnight to her and walked off alone to his room in Old Bedlam.

Emma undressed, did up her hair, and got into bed. She lay still, listening to the bugler blow Extinguish Lights. She heard horses snuffling in the officers' stables behind Old Bedlam. When the coyotes started tuning up on the slopes rimming the fort, she pulled the blanket over her head and closed her eyes.

She knew she was not alone when she woke up before Reveille next morning. She sat up and gasped. A snake was curled at the foot of her blanket. She carefully pulled her feet up until she sat in a ball on her pillow. She was afraid to scream because she didn't know what the snake would do, and, besides, she didn't want the sergeant at arms to rush in and catch her with her hair done up in rags.

As she watched and held her breath, the snake unwound itself and moved off the cot. She couldn't see any rattles on its tail, and she slowly let out her breath. The snake undulated across the grass, and she stared at it, fascinated. She hadn't known a reptile could be so graceful. "How do they do that?" she asked herself, as the snake slithered through the grass at the edge of the tent. "I must remember to ask Hart."

She took the rag twists from her hair, pulled on her wrapper, and poked her head out of the tent. The sun was just coming up, and the buildings were tinted with the most delicious shade of pink. She marveled that she could ever have thought the old place ugly.

Her first letter from Hart was handed to her three days later at mail call. She ripped open the envelope and drew out a long, narrow sheet. She read as she walked along the edge of the parade ground.

> *Dearest Emma,*
>
> *Pardon this stationery, but I forgot to take any along, and this works better for letters than in the sink. Good news. We're going to be garrisoned here permanently, so you'll be moving quite soon, perhaps within the next few days. Or it could be a month. That's the Army. Bad news. Brace yourself. There aren't any quarters available, so we'll have to make do in a tent.*

Emma stood still and laughed out loud. A soldier with a large P painted on the back of his shirt stopped spearing trash and looked at her, but she didn't acknowledge him. She read on.

> *It won't be that bad. The commanding officer swears there will be quarters ready by winter. Am looking forward to seeing you soon. I can't express how much I miss you.*
>
> *Love, Hart*

She was almost back to her tent when the adjutant caught up with her.

"Mrs. Sanders," he began. His Adam's apple bobbed, and he put up his hand to rub his head, she was sure.

"It's all right, Lieutenant," she broke in before he could continue. "I've already heard. When am I leaving?"

"In the morning, ma'am."

"I'll be ready."

As she was repacking her trunks that evening, she remembered something her mother had said to her when she left on the train to join Hart in Cheyenne. Mother had dabbed at her eyes and said over and over, "Such brave men, Emma, such brave men!"

Emma smiled.

We Shall Meet, but We Shall Miss Him

Lieutenant McIver stood in front of the window, rocking back and forth on his heels. He looked over his shoulder at the sergeant straightening some papers on his desk. "Better take a look, sergeant. There they go."

Sergeant John Cole put down the papers and walked over to the window. C Company was leading out across the parade ground, Captain Burnett hunched over in his saddle. The wind was blowing as usual, and the men rode with their collars turned up and their caps pulled low. E Company followed, and the string of Dougherty wagons and ambulances brought up the rear.

"Doesn't seem like so much to show for forty years, does it, sir?" Cole asked, his eyes on the troops as they headed south on Cheyenne-Deadwood Road.

The lieutenant didn't answer. He was at his desk again, rummaging through some papers. He found what he was looking for and held it out to the sergeant. "I almost forgot about this. Here, take it, sergeant."

Cole knew it was his discharge before his hand closed over the paper. He glanced at it and smiled at his superior, then handed it back. "Not much to show for almost thirty years, is it, sir?"

The lieutenant grinned. "Well, no matter how you look at it, you'll be a free man as soon as we close up this post. Shouldn't take more than another couple of weeks."

Sergeant Cole worked in the Admin Building until noon, sorting out forty years of endorsements, inspection reports, dispatches, and all the bits and pieces—important and otherwise—that had crossed any commander's desk at Fort Laramie. There wasn't a bugler left to blow Mess Call, but a glance at the clock sent him down to the cavalry barracks, leaning against the Wyoming wind and holding the top of his overcoat tight against his throat.

The Seventh Infantry had left behind a detachment of ten men from Company B to assist in packing up and dismantling all military equipment at the fort that wasn't to be auctioned off to the homesteaders in the area. Since the troopers had vacated their barracks, the infantrymen left behind had spent the morning moving their gear into the newer building. Their own quarters had been leaning at an angle and creaking for almost ten years.

The men were already eating in the cavalry mess hall. There were only a handful of them left, so everyone sat close together by the pot-belly stove. John sat down near them. Ordinarily, he liked to preserve a little dignity as regimental staff sergeant, but he felt it would be pretentious to isolate himself, under the circumstances. The food tasted a little better than usual, maybe because the one remaining cook wasn't dealing in quantities of one hundred any more.

It was slumgullion again. As John ate, he smiled to himself, wondering how many meals just like this he had downed since his enlistment on the Christmas of '61. *And I owe it all to Martha Taylor*, he thought as he gnawed at a piece of gristle with a scrap of meat clinging to it. He raised his coffee cup and toasted her, then gave up on the stew and went back to the office.

He sorted correspondence year by year that afternoon, all the time listening for Drill for Target Practice, Fatigue Call, Recall, and Stable Call. The bugler may have left that morning for Fort Logan, but the habits of a lifetime kept Cole's ears alert. The only sound he heard was the whirring of the clock as it prepared to strike and the clicking of the grommets against the flagpole. McIver popped in and out all afternoon with more papers he had dug up from Lord-knows-where.

After Stable Call that never came, John Cole put down the letters he was filing and stood up to stretch. He knew the papers would all be there in the morning, and he felt that he was going cross-eyed from trying to decipher a half-century's collection of the worst handwriting in the United States and her territories.

Instead of walking across the parade ground to the barracks, he went behind the Admin Building and crossed in back of the old guardhouse. It had been used as an ordnance storehouse for the past few years, and now it was empty like the rest of the buildings.

He walked along the Laramie River, looking over at the deserted houses on Suds Row. A shutter on the end quarters had come unlatched and banged back and forth in the wind. He made a mental note to send a private over there after supper to secure it. As he stood there, a cat rubbed its way around the corner of the building. Someone must have abandoned it. Cole shook his head and walked on. He had seen kittens sell for as much as ten dollars in gold at Fort Riley, right after the war. Mice were legion then, and cats were worth every bit of that extortionate fee. But that was twenty-five years ago—maybe homeless cats were a sign of civilization.

Supper was sowbelly and beans. Cole ate without thinking about it much, but a couple of the younger privates complained. It was on the tip of Cole's tongue to tell them to shut up and be glad it wasn't horsemeat, but he sensed that the young ones wouldn't appreciate his old-time tales of starvation marches, half rations, and Civil War hardtack, ten years after the fact. He didn't feel up to wasting his stories on pups who would only laugh at him after he went to his room.

And that, he decided, was the chief advantage of being a regimental sergeant—his own room. He had moved his gear over from the infantry barracks that morning, and everything was still in a jumble on the floor. He closed the door. Now no one could come in without knocking. After years and years of listening to soldiers gamble, pray, belch, and pass gas, it was nice to shut it all out.

He groped to the packing box by his cot and lit the kerosene lamp, then walked over to the pile on the floor and toed around in it. There wasn't much point in unpacking the dress uniform. Cole stowed the gear he would need in the next month and stacked the rest of it in the corner. He sifted around for his shaving supplies and set them on the packing case next to the lamp. He was about to close his footlocker when he saw Martha's picture.

He took it out and held it up to the light. For years, he had leaned the picture up on the shelf over his bunk. When he made sergeant and got his own room, he had propped the picture on the chest of drawers that held his clothes. A few years back in Omaha, he had picked up a silver wire frame for it.

There was a nail by the cot, so he hung up the tintype. "Martha, how nice you look tonight," he said out loud and smiled at the image. Martha smiled back at him, and he sat down on the cot, watching her.

She continued to smile at him. Her hands were folded in her lap, and they were covered with the lace half-mittens women wore back then. He remembered that her dress was taffeta and it rustled when she walked. Her hair was pulled low over her ears. As he looked at her, John tried to recall if he had ever seen her ears. Back then, nice girls didn't show their ears, and if Martha Taylor was anything, she was a nice girl.

She had pressed the picture into his hands before the troop train pulled out of Gibson, Ohio. "So you'll remember me," she whispered, and then she kissed him. On the lips.

John lay back on the cot and put his hands behind his head. *Boy, howdy, what a fool I was*, he thought, and closed his eyes.

He had met Martha Taylor at a Fourth of July picnic. He had been reading law that year in Cincinnati with his uncle and only went to the picnic because his mother needed someone to haul the milk pan full of pork and beans she had fixed for the big event. He was planning on leaving right away and going back home for some more studying when he heard someone singing "The Battle Cry of Freedom" at the bandstand. The voice wasn't loud, but it carried because it was slightly higher than the accompaniment.

She sang with her hands clasped in front of her and with such a pleading look in her eyes that some of the mothers with sons already in the army were reaching for their handkerchiefs. The sniffing and nose blowing grew louder as she finished, then carried on with "The Vacant Chair." She had just sung the line, "We shall meet, but we shall miss him," when the mayor stood up to announce the events of the afternoon and waved the band into silence.

It hadn't been hard to get to know her. He had tripped over what turned out to be her little brother's feet and dumped the pan of beans all over her dress. Cole whipped out his handkerchief and started blotting off her dress, all the while babbling apologies until he heard her laugh and looked up.

She took the cloth from his hand and began to dab at the flounces. "Please don't worry about it," she said and batted her eyes at him. Cole was in love even before she picked off all the beans.

That summer, the summer of Bull Run and Wilson's Creek, he spent each evening in her parlor, trying to get up the nerve to hold her hand. He told her outrageous lies about his winter in Cincinnati, and she believed every word of it, punctuating his remarks about his law career with "Do tell," and "Well, did you ever?" and flicking the air with the ivory fan she carried. He tried to kiss her once, and she slammed that same fan so hard on his wrist that he winced and begged her pardon.

Together they watched Gibson's finest march off to the soldier camps around Washington, D.C. The local church circles and ladies' aide societies made the uniforms, and each soldier who got on the train looked like a special edition.

Cole had thought briefly about joining up right after Fort Sumter and mentioned it to his father, who promptly vetoed the idea. Pa couldn't see any point to his only child marching off somewhere and getting blown to bits. John could see the wisdom in that, especially when Pa vowed to sever the family ties if his son ever put on a uniform.

It wasn't just that his father was unpatriotic. Amos Cole hadn't voted since the Polk election and didn't give a damn about the government or its present difficulties. Reading newspapers gave him the hives. His father didn't hanker to be part of any scheme to enrich moneylenders and politicians, so he looked on war as a pain to be tolerated but not encouraged.

Toward the end of August, Martha began to drop hints. When Cole insisted that he wasn't going to join up, she had a way of pouting and running her tongue over her lips that made him want to grab her and take his chances with the fan. But she sat farther and farther away from him on the settee and only gave him the tips of her fingers to shake when he said his goodnights.

Her little brother, Clarence, started eyeing him, too. Asael Clarence (he was named after both grandfathers) had a way of flicking his eyes around like a lizard. All that was missing was for the kid to dart his tongue out once in a while. Cole had already earned his undying ingratitude by calling him "Asshole."

Cole went back to Cincinnati the first of September, but the whole business of reading law was even duller than usual. He was glad to use Christmas as an excuse to return to Gibson.

Martha looked just the same. She spent most of her spare time rolling bandages and knitting socks for the Presbyterian Ladies Circle. She said she was glad to see him, but John observed how she avoided the mistletoe her brother had hung inside the front door.

As they sat in the parlor on Christmas Eve, Martha went on and on about the gallant boys in blue who were serving their state and nation, until he had a headache and wondered why he had ever been so eager to leave Cincinnati.

Clarence Taylor didn't help matters. When Cole came up the walk the next morning to deliver a present, Asshole followed him to the front steps, prancing around and chanting "Yellow belly, yellow belly!" Cole picked up the boy by the collar and the belt and threw him into a snowdrift.

He leaned over the hole in the snow where Clarence had gone in, noting with some satisfaction that the snow was yellow and that there were dog tracks all around. Clarence sat rubbing his eyes and crying.

"You know something, Clarence?" Cole said, "You really are a first-class asshole."

Clarence blubbered louder at that, then got up and ran into the house yelling, "I'll get you for that, Cole; you just wait and see if I don't!"

He stayed at the Taylors' for Christmas dinner and endured one more afternoon of Martha's tales of gallantry at the front, Mr. Taylor's thoughtful stares, and Clarence's unspoken menace. When they gathered around the piano and Martha played "Just Before the Battle, Mother" and "The Vacant Chair," Cole knew he was licked.

The next morning after breakfast, he went to the recruiting office and signed up. As if from across the room, he watched himself sign the papers, laugh at the recruiting officer's jokes, raise his right hand, and swear the oath.

He waited until after supper to tell his parents. His mother was sitting down with her mending, and his father was clearing his throat for his nightly reading of the Bible. John knew he would always remember that moment. His mother stared at him, and his father clapped the book shut.

"You did what?"

"I joined up."

Cole could see several topics running through his father's head: Filial Duty, The Folly of War, The Foolhardiness of Youth, but the man didn't say anything. He only opened and closed his mouth a couple times, which reminded Cole of a fish hooked and tossed up on the riverbank.

"Well, I thought I ought to serve my country," John explained, trying to fill the silence that was making his ears hum.

"You're a damned fool," his father said.

Mrs. Cole gasped and left the room. John Cole spent the night at the railroad depot, his head on his carpetbag.

Martha and her brother were there in the morning to see him off. She pressed the tintype into his hand and stood on tiptoe to kiss him on the mouth. It wasn't much of a kiss, but since he had joined the army to get it, Cole hugged her to him and ignored her brother, who was crossing his eyes at him and making a vulgar gesture with his fingers. All in all, it wasn't a happy beginning.

He spent the first few months in his Ohio volunteer regiment drilling and peeling potatoes. They spent the early spring and summer months marching about to no good purpose, drilling some more, and engaging in an occasional skirmish. He wrote to his parents but received no answer. Martha Taylor replied to all his letters, but he was hard put to find anything interesting to tell her. The food was bad, the uniforms didn't fit, and his bunkies were fellows like himself. The only gallantry he had witnessed was the time Lieutenant Smathers came across a Secesh girl about to drown a sack full of kittens and volunteered to do it for her.

That was before Antietam. His division was in reserve, and they watched the shattered remains of men like themselves being carried to the rear. He remembered Antietam as one long scream.

Fredericksburg was a different story. Something in his law training made him see the inherent silliness of trying to take Marye's Heights after five other attempts had failed, but apparently precedence didn't count for much in the army. He found himself pushed along by the men behind him. As they ran across the field, tripping over dying men and skirting around blasted horses, he found himself yelling along with the rest of the boys in blue.

They were mowed down like all the other charges. John crept behind a dead body. He lay eyeball to eyeball with the corpse and marveled how the dead eyes jiggled every time a bullet smacked into the body.

When his cover started shredding away, he managed to crawl over to a group of soldiers who had erected a whole barrier of dead men. Lieutenant Smathers was there, his right arm gone, his uniform front covered with vomit. He stared at John with his mouth open. The pain in the officer's eyes made John look away. When he could turn back, the lieutenant was dead. The cold was already freezing him into part of the barricade.

The firing stopped at dusk, but, as no order had been given to withdraw, the men spent the night on the battlefield. The living huddled together behind the wall of the dead, slapping their arms to keep warm or stopping up their ears to block the cries and screams of the wounded in the darkness around them.

The dead grass had been put on fire here and there by the cannon barrage. John shuddered and hunched down in his coat, trying to drown out the crackle of wounded men burning alive. The smell drifted over the battlefield. As tears froze on his cheeks, John wondered what Martha would say if he wrote to her that a real battle was a bit different than "We'll Rally 'round the Flag, Boys," as interpreted on pianos all over Ohio.

The order to withdraw came next morning as the sky lightened, but rebel fire from Marye's Heights pinned them down for another day. One of the men crouching behind the corpses stood up and ran laughing and screaming across the field. He didn't get twenty feet before the guns opened up. His body bounced and jerked for another ten feet, then fell in a heap like a pile of old rags.

No one talked much; there wasn't anything to say. When night fell, the men stood up straight for the first time and helped each other off the field.

He could have gotten furlough in January, but he didn't relish the idea of lying to Martha Taylor about the war, or listening to her bang out another one of those awful patriotic songs on the piano. He couldn't see himself balancing a plate of goodies on one knee, drinking tea, and looking her in the eye. Besides, there was that ivory fan, and after Fredericksburg, he didn't feel up to it. He stayed in winter quarters instead and let someone else go in his place.

John almost didn't mind losing at Chancellorsville. He was getting used to the cold lump in his stomach and the dryness of his mouth. The army was defeated so cleverly and soundly at Chancellorsville that if he hadn't been so involved in staying alive and inflicting maximum damage, he might have enjoyed a bird's-eye view of the whole sorry event.

He took a ball in the arm during the battle. He was too excited to notice at first. During a lull, he tried to wipe the blood off his sleeve, thinking it was someone else's. The more he rubbed the redder it grew, until the soldier next to him told him to cut it out and get to the rear.

He helped a man with an ear and other accessories missing get back to the dressing station. They got there in time to watch the surgeon's orderlies set up the amputating tables. He decided that his wound wasn't worth the bother, wrapped a piece of long underwear around it, and went back to his unit. He didn't return to the dressing station until the battle was lost and the surgeons were exhausted. His lieutenant swore at him for being so careless with his person, but he got to keep his arm and still earned one month in a Washington hospital.

So he missed Gettysburg. His bunkies—the ones left alive—told him about it when he rejoined his outfit. It sounded a great deal better than Chancellorsville. Martha wrote that she was sorry he missed the action and went on for two more pages about the newspaper accounts of Culp's Hill, Little Round Top, and Pickett's Charge.

Sergeant Cole rolled over on his cot and sat up. His lamp had gone out while he was reminiscing. He thought about hunting up some more kerosene but lay back instead and stared at the ceiling. He knew it was past Extinguish Lights, but he heard men still laughing and talking. He probably should tell them to pipe down, but he didn't feel like it. He didn't really want to think about the War of the Rebellion anymore, but his thoughts were leading him to the Spotsylvania Courthouse, as sure as if he were there again. He couldn't think of any way to avoid it, same as there had been no choice thirty years ago.

The months following Gettysburg had been a time of march and dig and fight. All the little hamlets began to resemble each other: the burned-out buildings with their empty window frames looking like eye sockets, the tight-lipped Secesh women, the lean children, and the bare-branch look of December, even in August.

He did something valorous he had since forgotten at a river he couldn't even remember, and his colonel tried to commission him a lieutenant. Remembering the look on Lieutenant Smathers' face as he froze into the corpse barricade at Fredericksburg, John stayed a sergeant.

Martha wrote regularly. She sent him packages of socks, tobacco, soap, needles and thread, plus fudge and breads that were usually melted or moldy. She said she missed him, and John began to think that maybe she did. With every day that passed, he knew he wanted to see her, and soon.

Her little brother Clarence wrote, too, badly scribbled, much-erased letters that called him all sorts of names and promised painful and agonizing tortures if he should ever dare to return to Gibson, Ohio. John read the first two letters and threw away any others without opening them. He tried writing to his parents again, but his letters were never answered. He quit.

Sergeant Cole swung his feet off his cot and got up. He put on his overcoat and went outside in the dark. He waved to the sentry sitting on the barracks porch and walked past the post trader's store. Snow was falling. For a change, there was no wind, so the snow dropped straight and silent. He walked around the parade ground, past the captains' duplex, and between the buildings to the bluff overlooking the Laramie River. He squatted there and chunked rocks into the water, seeing nothing but listening for the splash.

He liked to go down to the river in the evening. He had done it many times during the years he had served off and on at Fort Laramie. He liked to sit out of everyone's sight and listen to the family sounds that came from the quarters nearby. Sometimes, if he was lucky, he could hear a mother humming in the kitchen or singing to her children. Once he sat and watched one of the captains playing ball with his sons. They even asked him to join them, and he did, tossing the ball around until it was too dark to see anything. He remembered that evening for years, coming back to it in his mind in the deep of winter when the men in the barracks complained about the food and the cold and the fact that there weren't any Indians to harass.

The quarters were empty now, even a bit spooky. It seemed a pity to Sergeant Cole that the families were gone. He would miss them. He sat there on the bank in the cold and gave up the effort of trying to remember only what he wanted to remember.

☙

In 1864, Grant had the Army of the Potomac, and they finally started moving south. They had done that before, but something in Grant made John think that perhaps this time they would stay and win.

Even now, he remembered the Wilderness as a weeklong nightmare of forest fires and burning men. The artillery was nearly useless in the dense growth of trees and brush. The men cursed Lee up and down for leading them into such a pit. The two armies slugged it out like drunks in a bar. Cole remembered tattered bits of men and uniforms hanging in strips from the trees. He trudged on through that maze of briars and forests so thick the sun never got through and swore that when it was all over, he would never get near a recruiting stand again.

There was a breathing space after the Wilderness; not much, but enough time to eat something warm and change socks. The mail caught up with them, and there was a letter for John. He looked at the return address and nearly threw it away. It was another of Asshole Taylor's letters. He grinned in spite of himself and wondered when the boy would learn to spell Corps.

He didn't know why he bothered to open it. Clarence was a piss ant and always would be, but it had been a month since he had heard from Martha, and he was lonely.

"Dear Mr. Cole," it began, which surprised him. Clarence had never been so polite before. He put down the hardtack he was gnawing, leaned back against a tree, and read,

> *Mother couldn't bring herself to write, so I have taken upon myself the sad duty. We buried Martha yesterday. She died suddenly of a fever, and we thought you would like to know. Her last words were, "Please*

write to John for me," so I have fulfilled the promise I made her.
Yours respectfully,
Clarence Taylor

John stared at the letter. Tears welled up in his eyes, and he didn't care who saw them. He crumpled up the paper and threw it into the campfire. He had forgotten that other people died besides soldiers.

Sergeant Cole stood up and pitched one last rock into the Laramie. He started back toward the barracks but stopped in the middle of the parade ground and stood there, his face turned up to the sky. The snow drifted down on him, and his face was wet.

Grant started them moving in a race to get between Lee and Richmond. They marched for hours by the left flank, and John was grateful he didn't have to think about anything more important than putting one foot in front of the other.

Lee beat them again. By the time they drew up to Spotsylvania Courthouse, he was already there, dug in with his Army of Northern Virginia. There wasn't anything to do but fight. They threw themselves at the Rebs over and over, reeled back, and tried again.

Artillery blasted away, and visibility dropped to the hand in front of the face. It rained. John had campaigned through mud before, but there was no comparison with the mud of Spotsylvania. He watched the artillerymen try to bring up the field pieces. The mules were useless and were turned loose, to be replaced by the gunners, who pushed and tugged on the limbers. He watched a gunner lose his balance and fall in front of a wheel, just as the men behind him managed to roll it forward. The gunner disappeared in the mud. John ran to him, threw himself on his hands and knees with the others and pawed at the ooze. The soldier raised himself once, clutched at John, then sank down again and drowned, his back broken.

They were held in reserve for the first part of the action and watched the wounded coming back from the battle. Covered with mud and holding his stomach, a soldier staggering to the rear looked at John. "Hey, mate," he called out. "Guess where you're going?" He started laughing and shrugged off a sergeant who tried to move him along. "To hell!" He laughed louder and louder and let the sergeant push him away.

Some of the men looked at each other. No one spoke, but one of them took out a scrap of paper and a pencil, wrote his name and regiment on it, and pinned the note to his fatigue blouse. John found an old letter from Martha in his pocket. He ripped off a corner of it and wrote his name, regiment, and hometown. He found a strand of thread and needle and sewed the paper to his coat.

They moved closer to the front. Smoke from the field pieces hung stinking over the battlefield, and the rain poured down. John's colonel rode up and down in front of the regiment, shouting at them to tighten up their line and get ready. John checked his musket, then looked down at the paper sewn to the front of his blouse. Before they started across the field, he thought that he should have sewn it to the back. Then he was yelling and running with the rest of his bunkies.

He hoped he would be shot down before they vanished into the fog. He wasn't too curious to find out what was going on behind that grey curtain, but he ran on and on, splashing through mud, stepping over bodies, tripping, and getting up again.

He was about twenty yards from the entrenchment when someone slapped him on the shoulder. He looked over his shoulder to see who it was, but no one was there. He felt a pain in his shoulder then but kept running.

He reached the breastworks and stopped. The ground oozed and moved under his feet, and he realized he was standing on soldiers who had been shot down and who were struggling to get out of the mud. Horrified, he stepped aside, but everywhere he moved were the wounded and the dying. He ran forward then and fired his piece at the men on the other side of the breastworks. There wasn't time to reload, so he grabbed his gun by the barrel and swung it at the head of a Reb in front of him.

He dropped his gun, and a Rebel grabbed him by the hair and tried to gouge out his eyes. He fought back with his good arm, slipped, and fell in the mud at the foot of the entrenchment. He tried to get up, but someone jumped on his back, and he slid deeper in the mud. He screamed in panic, and then couldn't remember anything else.

It seemed years later when he opened his eyes. He was lying on his back, looking up at the stars. The rain was gone, the guns were silent, and he could see dawn coming in the distance, timid almost, after such an apocalypse. He wondered how he even knew about dawn, since he was dead.

Someone prodded him. He tried to say something, but there was a gob of mud in his mouth. When he tried to swallow it and speak before the man moved away, he gagged instead.

"Wait a minute, boys. This one's still with us."

A man holding a torch bent down and peered at John. He slid his hand under Cole's neck and raised him up. When John kept gagging, he stuck two fingers in his mouth and scooped out a wad of mud and teeth. He took a cloth and wiped off John's face. The man smiled when John blinked in the light of the torch and tried to speak.

"Look here, you just hold still. We'll get you out."

Three men lifted him out of the mud. His body came away from the ooze and the slime with a sucking noise. They carried him several yards away from the entrenchments and set him down. John struggled into a sitting position and looked around.

Little bits of flame dotted the ground in front of the earthworks as soldiers dug for survivors in the mud of the Bloody Angle. The men worked quietly, stopping to listen every now and then.

John shivered and felt his left shoulder. He knew he had been hit during the charge yesterday, but he was so muddy that he could not feel a wound. He pulled off his fatigue blouse, trying to hold his left side still.

The soldiers carried over another man and put him down next to John. The man's uniform must have been torn off him during his premature burial yesterday afternoon, and he shook in the predawn chill. His body was covered with bruises and lacerations made by the boots of the men who had stood on top of him; the side of his head was caved in. He looked at John, and his teeth chattered.

John leaned over and covered the soldier with his own coat. It wasn't nearly enough, but it was all he had. The man drew up his legs close to his body like a baby and closed his eyes.

Somewhere out on the plains recently (it may have been Fort Totten), Sergeant Cole had read an article about Heinrich Schliemann's excavation of Troy. Schliemann described the different layers through which he dug. Cole had no trouble picturing Schliemann's venture. He had only to recall the early morning at Spotsylvania as he watched soldiers dig through layers of mud to uncover men ground into the mire by a day's fighting. Some of the soldiers near the top layers still lived, while those on the bottom were not recognizable.

A few years before Fort Totten, when his own Seventh Infantry under Gibbon came across the bodies of Custer's men, John discovered that the burying scarcely troubled him. He had seen worse at Spotsylvania.

The ball he took in the shoulder at the Bloody Angle landed him in another Washington hospital. He was eligible for discharge, but because Martha was dead and there wasn't anything in Gibson to go home for, he went back to the army and spent the next months in a trench at Petersburg. They pounded and shelled the city day and night until it finally fell and with it, the last railroad into Richmond.

The end came soon. They followed Lee's skeletons to Saylor's Creek, where the Rebs turned and fought, then stopped them at Appomattox Courthouse. After Lee signed the papers, John and others in his regiment were detailed to distribute rations to the late Army of Northern Virginia, which had been subsisting on parched corn and branch water for the past two weeks. After the supplies were handed out, John turned away, unable to bear the sight of men pawning their pride and tearing at the food. He remembered the young Secesh soldiers, just children really, sitting and crying.

He received his discharge shortly after the Grand Review in Washington, spent the night wandering the streets of the still-celebrating federal district, then enlisted in the regular army the following morning. His bunkies chided him about re-upping, and he laughed along with them, but he couldn't think of what else to do.

It was so long ago. As Sergeant Cole stood on the parade ground at Fort Laramie, he watched the last light go out in the cavalry barracks. The snow had stopped falling, and the wind was picking up, so he raised his collar and walked back to his quarters. He undressed in the dark, with a glance at Martha Taylor as he took off his pants. She continued to smile at him.

Cole spent the rest of the week classifying the fort's correspondence. Since the commanding officer had left, John took the pile of papers into his office and sorted them in mounds all over the floor: inspection reports, morning reports, boards of inquiry, garrison and regimental courts-martial, endorsement after endorsement for the most trivial of equipment.

It pleased his clerk's heart to portion the years into neat piles, to see time so conveniently filed away and packed in crates, to languish—unread, he was sure—in a more eastern venue, likely some federal attic in Washington.

The following week, Cole led the soldiers from building to building, writing down the contents of each in preparation for the auction of government property that was to take place as soon as personnel arrived from Fort Robinson. Already, settlers were gathering from miles around. The military reservation itself would be open to homesteading, and citizens camped close by to be in on the kill.

Cole's little detachment sorted out the effects remaining in the commissary storehouse. A private came across two bottles of Kentucky bourbon stuck in a recess under the cellar stairs. Since the finder was Private Flaherty, Cole figured he had waged a mighty battle with his conscience before surrendering the bottles to McIver.

While Cole watched, hiding his smile, the lieutenant looked at the dusty, cobwebbed bottles and back at Private Flaherty. He told him to get the men together after supper. With everyone lined up and trying not to appear over-interested, McIver divided the liquor. Each man got several good swallows, except for Corporal Dugan, who had taken the pledge after a two-day spree at Fort Hays and had been up the pole ever since.

The bourbon went down with a pleasant burn that settled on top of the evening's government beef and plum duff. Cole was hard put to remember the last time he had dealt with bourbon. In his nearly thirty years on the plains, he'd contented himself with warm beer, when it was available.

The auction crew from Fort Rob was due any day. Cole and his men marked time by emptying out the root cellars and burning tumbleweeds they pulled off the corral fences. The crowd of homesteaders kept gathering. Several of the men sat on the ground near the stables and offered advice and suggestions until McIver ran them off.

On April 3, the men from Fort Robinson arrived, Buffalo Soldiers of the Tenth Cavalry, led by Lieutenant Ace Taylor. Cole bunked the troopers in the other half of the two-company barracks and directed the officer to the Admin Building, where McIver was cleaning out his desk.

Cole walked with the officer across the parade ground. Lieutenant Taylor was a bald, middle-aged man with a paunch that hung over his belt. He had an unruly red moustache that curled in several directions.

John discovered with a start that while he was sizing up the officer out of the corner of his eye, the lieutenant was doing the same thing. He wasn't used to being under an officer's scrutiny, and it bothered him.

He led the man to the Admin Building and paused at the entrance. "Lieutenant McIver's office is the first door to your left, sir," he said, then saluted and stepped back.

The officer put his hand on the doorknob, then turned back to Cole. "Thank you, Sergeant." He cleared his throat. "Say, Sergeant, have you ever served at Fort Halleck?"

"No, sir."

"What about the Presidio?"

"No, sir."

The officer opened the door, then looked back one more time. "You look familiar. Can't quite place you, though."

John couldn't think of any reply, so he saluted again and went back to the commissary storehouse. He was pretty sure he had never seen Lieutenant Taylor before.

During supper, he had second thoughts. In order to simplify the duty, McIver had been taking his meals with the men in the mess hall. He sat alone, usually with a book propped open on the salt and pepper shakers. Tonight, he had Taylor to keep him company.

John was finishing a dish of stewed prunes when the two officers started laughing about something. Taylor tossed his head back and let go with a barking guffaw, and John paused with his spoon halfway to his open mouth. He'd only known one person in his life who laughed like that, and it was Martha's little brother Clarence. He remembered the time he had escorted Martha to a musicale, and Clarence had carried on so with his braying laughter that Martha ran home in tears.

It couldn't be Clarence. Cole leaned over to one of the troopers from Fort Rob. "Corporal, about that lieutenant. Do you know his full name?"

"It's something Asael Taylor, I think, sergeant," the soldier replied with a smile. "Ain't he got the damnedest laugh?"

"He certainly has," Cole said. He got up, threw down his spoon, and left the mess hall.

Ace Taylor, Asael Taylor, Asshole Taylor. John went to his room and slammed the door. He leaned against it and looked up at Martha on the wall. "Imagine that, honey," he whispered.

John spent the next day supervising the removal of all government furniture from the officers' quarters to the unused half of the barracks mess hall. He glimpsed Taylor when the officer walked back and forth from the Admin Building to the storehouses and again at meals.

By the next morning, Cole had almost convinced himself that he was mistaken. It wasn't impossible that he could run across an officer named Asael Taylor. Even more to the point, he couldn't imagine Clarence Taylor being commissioned an officer in any army anywhere. The laugh was just a coincidence. On the other hand, he had been used to thinking of Asshole as a little boy, when obviously he would be about the age of the Fort Robinson Taylor now.

He was going over the inventory with Lieutenant Taylor after breakfast and trying not to make his darting glances too obvious, when the officer put down the list and sighed.

"All right, sergeant, what's so incredible about me that you have to keep sneaking peeks?"

John stepped back, and he felt his face go red. "Well, sir, I . . . I think I knew an Asael Taylor before."

The lieutenant chuckled. "Well, I think I knew another Cole before, too. Where're you from?"

"Gibson, Ohio, sir."

Taylor stared at him. "I'll be buggered," he murmured. His eyes narrowed, and he leaned back in his chair. "But you're dead."

"No, I'm not, sir," John said. It had to be Asshole Taylor. No one else would make such a stupid remark.

"Yes, you are," Taylor insisted. "Right after the Wilderness, May of '64, I guess, your father got a telegram from the War Department." He shook his head. "Your father pulled all kinds of strings to bring your body home. He went to Washington to get you."

"I wish you would stop talking like that, sir," John broke in.

"Well, we all thought it was you. Some medical officer said the body was identified by a note with the same name and rank sewed to the front of the uniform."

John sat down in the armchair next to the desk, not bothering to ask permission. He remembered the naked man shivering beside him at the Bloody Angle, but he hadn't ever thought about the note he had tacked to his uniform. It was a long moment before he said anything. "You mean . . . you mean . . . my father went to all that trouble to bring the body home? My father?"

Ace Taylor grinned. "Yep. Who would've thought it? He was right busted up, too. Cried and cried at your funeral."

John closed his eyes.

Ace Taylor went on. "Lord, how he carried on. Used to visit you . . . the grave every day. Planted flowers, even. Can you beat that?"

When John just sat there with his eyes closed and didn't say anything, Taylor went on. "Of course, that wasn't nothing compared to the way Martha carried on. She . . ."

John stood up and leaned over Taylor so quickly that the officer nearly went over backward in his chair. "What do you mean, Martha?" he asked in a quiet voice.

"Hell, you remember Martha."

John moved closer. "I got a letter from you saying she was dead."

Taylor tipped back his chair against the wall and laughed. He laughed until McIver poked his head in from the next room. McIver frowned, then closed the door again.

John stepped forward, wanting to grab Taylor by the shoulders and shake him until his neck snapped. He sensed what was coming, and he was helpless to brace himself against it.

Taylor stood up and leaned forward over the desk, his weight resting on his knuckles. He and Cole were almost nose-to-nose. "Told you I'd get you back, Cole," he said softly.

"It was all a lie, wasn't it, Taylor?" John asked. He added "sir" a beat too late.

Ace frowned. "Watch yourself, sergeant," he warned. "Yes, it was all a humbug, and then when news of your . . . death reached us, I never had to tell Martha the truth. You couldn't have made it more convenient."

John sat down again. For thirty years he had thought Martha dead. Thirty years. He stared at his hands, unwilling to look at the lieutenant. "Did she ever marry?"

Ace barked out his laugh and shook his head. "No. In fact, she wore black for over ten years. After your father died, she took care of the flowers on your grave." He laughed again. "Oh, God, they were forget-me-nots!"

John almost hated to ask the next question, but he had to know. "Is she still alive?"

Ace shook his head and grinned. "She died last summer. Some female complaint, I gather. Kind of rotted away from the inside. You should have seen her. Whatever it was ate up her liver, and damned if her eyes didn't turn yellow. Craziest sight you ever . . ."

"Stop it," John pleaded.

Taylor ignored him. "And damned if she didn't die with your name on her lips, just like I wrote in that letter."

John shook his head.

"Kinda theatrical, I think, but you know Martha. She rose up off her pillow and said, 'I'm coming, John.'" He stopped, put his hand to his heart, and started laughing again. He laughed until Cole didn't think he could stand one more second. "God Almighty," Taylor sputtered, when he got his breath again. "Don't you think she got one hell of a jolt when she found that other soldier waiting for her at the Pearly Gates?"

Without a word, John wrapped his hand around a government-issue paperweight and stood up. Taylor stopped laughing and backed away. He wiped his mouth with the back of his hand and swallowed. "Drop it, Cole," he ordered and backed away another step. Taylor backed up until he was wedged against a filing cabinet. The sudden contact with the wood brought him up sharp, and that light came into his eyes again. John watched him and wavered.

"That's right, Cole. Put it down. You so much as touch me, and by God, even if you do have only a couple days left in the army, I'll see that you spend your retirement in a four by six in Leavenworth."

John dropped the paperweight, turned on his heel, and started for the door.

"Sergeant . . . ."

John turned around.

"You forgot to salute."

Taylor grinned at him again, and John felt the shudders run down his back. He saluted.

All he felt as he stumbled across the parade ground toward the barracks was a great need to run away. He wanted to run from Taylor and his revenge, run until he came to a place where no one knew him, and where he didn't even know himself. The thought that a boy of eight could have ruined two lives so completely sickened him. He waved his hand in front of his face, as if to brush off the idea. His mind was full of the sight of Martha dying, loyal to the end. He sobbed out loud. A private loading furniture glanced at him, then looked away quickly.

Back in his quarters, he couldn't bring himself to look at Martha's picture. He didn't have a thing to say to her, either. For the first time in a lifetime of loneliness and isolation, he was truly all by himself.

The next two days before the auction crawled by. Cole stayed as far away from Lieutenant Taylor as he could, but it was not possible to avoid the man. Taylor would holler for him to bring coffee, or recopy some paperwork, or perform any number of senseless little errands far beneath the purview of a regimental staff sergeant. Cole did what Taylor told him to do, hating the look in the man's eyes and the grin on his face.

His discharge was in effect the day before the auction. He had originally planned to hang around until it was over, then travel with the Seventh Infantry's detachment to Fort Russell near Cheyenne. He knew now he could not stay, that nothing on earth would keep him there.

Cole dreaded the thought of another day under Taylor's scrutiny. He also didn't think he could bear to see the fort picked apart by people who only wanted the boards and windows and the leftover iceboxes and scrap iron. The people just drooling for the auction to start would only have laughed if someone tried to tell them what a great heart beat under the wood, adobe, and concrete. It was almost like murder, and Cole wanted no more of it.

McIver gave him his discharge papers that last night in the mess hall. He shifted his feet, obviously wanting to say something to the sergeant with a ladder of duty stripes on his sleeves and scars from more than one war. Instead, he stepped back and saluted the sergeant, then shook his hand.

"We'll be at Fort Logan several months, sergeant," he said, still gripping Cole's hand. "Write to us."

Packing that night was an easy matter. He had already sold his old uniforms to another sergeant in the regiment, except for the dress outfit he planned to be buried in someday. He stowed his books and other heavy gear in his footlocker, and there was room to spare.

He put the tintype of Martha between his two good shirts in his carpetbag. He toyed with the idea of leaving her hanging on the wall but couldn't bring himself to do it, not after all these years. She would likely follow him from boardinghouse to rented room, to smile down on him, and listen to him when he talked to her.

The Cheyenne-Deadwood stage pulled out from Fort Laramie at eight the following morning, and he was ready. While the driver was strapping his footlocker on top, Cole looked around at the soldiers working to dismantle the sheds and outbuildings before the auction. As he watched, Lieutenant Taylor strolled up. John braced himself.

"Going now, Cole?" he asked.

"Yes, sir." Cole opened the door and put his foot on the step. Taylor cleared his throat, and John looked around.

"Cole, good luck to you." Taylor grinned. "Just remember not to believe everything you read." He laughed and then turned and strolled back to the cavalry barracks, where a crowd gathered for the auction.

Cole slowly let out his breath. He settled himself in his corner of the stage, then felt the inside of his coat for the two thousand dollar bank draft on Cheyenne Thrift and Savings. It was his savings over thirty years. He settled lower in the seat and hunched down inside his coat.

"Where're you heading?" asked one of the men in the stage.

"Nowhere in particular." John yawned. He hoped the traveler would take the hint, but as the coach swayed and took the bend by the sawmill, the man looked back at the fort. He turned to John again.

"Almost wish we could hang around for that auction. A fellow could pick up some real bargains."

John closed his eyes, but the man went on. "Fort Laramie, Queen of the Plains. Think you'll miss her?"

John opened his eyes. "Yes, I'll miss her," he answered quietly. "Every day of my life." He stared out the window. The driver was slowing down for the iron bridge, and everything was blurry. He was through, and the fort was through. Maybe even the frontier was through. For the first time in his life, he had nowhere to go.

They started across the bridge. When no one was watching, John wiped his eyes and looked back toward the fort. He couldn't see it from the bridge, but he knew Taylor was there, selling it all.

It was too much. He stuck his head out the window and hollered to the driver. "Hey, stop this thing."

"What's the matter? You gotta heave already? We haven't even started yet," the driver called down. He did slow the horses, and John opened the door and jumped out.

"Just leave my foot locker alone. Ten to one, I'll catch you before you get too far."

"All right, mister, all right."

The stage left him there in the middle of the bridge. He put his hands on his hips and watched the stage until it was out of sight, then started back across the bridge at a jog. He knew he was three miles from the fort. He would probably get there after all the big stuff had been auctioned, but he didn't care. What he had his mind to bid on wasn't high on anyone's list.

He walked fast at his usual swinging infantry gait, whistling to himself. The more he thought about what he was going to do, the better the day looked. He stopped whistling and started smiling. "Oh, you Asshole," he said out loud, and laughed.

It was a pleasant walk on a spring morning, reminiscent of many such walks he had taken in over thirty-odd years, and yet different. No Secesh trash was shooting at him. There weren't any Indians or road agents poking around. He wasn't burdened by a pack or carrying a rifle. Perhaps retirement would be something worthwhile after all, if it felt as good as this.

The crowd was still thick in front of the cavalry barracks as John Cole strolled around the east end of it, his hands in his pockets, humming to himself. Taylor stood on the porch, and John could tell he enjoyed being the focus of everyone's attention. He had a list in his hand, and he was drawing lines through it as John approached.

"Howdy, Taylor," John called out.

The lieutenant looked up and frowned. "I thought you left on the stage," he said.

"Taylor, I just couldn't bear to miss this auction."

The sergeant stood with the crowd, his hands still in his pockets. Taylor watched him for a moment, then read another item off the list. After several minutes of spirited bargaining, the item was sold, and Taylor crossed off another line.

After a few more flour bins and barrels, Taylor motioned to some of his black troopers to pull forward the tables covered with small household goods. The homesteaders moved in closer and bargained for china, washboards, and other clutter left from forty years of military occupancy.

Then it happened. Taylor held up a chamber pot. John took his hands out of his pockets. "What am I bid for this . . . fine item?" the lieutenant asked. Some of the ladies in the crowd tittered. Taylor winked at one on the front row.

"Two bits," Cole said, stepping closer to the porch.

"Four bits," someone else said.

"Six bits," Cole said. The men in his former company laughed and poked each other.

"Do I hear anything else?" Lieutenant Taylor asked. John noticed that he was clutching his clipboard tighter than he needed to.

"Guess that's it, Taylor," Cole said. He put the change on the table and took the chamber pot out of the officer's hands. "See you in a minute, Taylor," he said as he walked across the barracks porch, chamber pot tucked under his arm, and went around the corner of the building.

John regretted that it was such a slapdash job. If he'd really had time to concentrate, he could have done justice to the occasion. As it was, he asked some of the boys from B Company to lend him a hand. No one turned him down, especially those who had watched how Taylor had treated their sergeant in the last few days. There was a certain anonymity to their contributions that pleased everyone. John thought about asking Lieutenant McIver to add his ounce, but he reconsidered. After all, his lieutenant was just beginning his career, not ending it.

The auction was almost over when Cole came around the corner again. He walked slowly, careful not to spill anything. Taylor stopped in the middle of a sentence, his eyes on the chamber pot. It pleased John to notice how quickly the blush spread from his neck up to his bald head.

He held out the chamber pot to the lieutenant, who took it. That was better than Cole had hoped for. Taylor had a dazed look on his face. At that moment, he probably would have dropped to all fours and barked, if the sergeant had requested it.

The people in the crowd looked at each other. The more sporting among them started to laugh. Some of the ladies covered their mouths with their handkerchiefs and make choking noises behind them.

"Lieutenant Taylor, it's a custom to make some sort of presentation to one's final commanding officer," Cole began. "I know you outrank Lieutenant McIver by a year or two, so never let it be said I was remiss. Gotcha, Asshole."

The lieutenant slammed the chamber pot down on the table and the contents washed all over his hands. He jumped back and wiped them on the seat of his pants.

The crowd roared. Women leaned against each other and dabbed at their eyes. The children shouted with laughter and rushed off to tell their friends who missed the fun. The soldiers from Fort Rob laughed until they had to hold up each other.

John watched the crowd, approval in his eyes. There was no question that anyone would ever forget this occasion. The story would follow Lieutenant Taylor from post to post, all over the country. He would never be free of it. People would whisper behind his back, laugh when they thought he wasn't looking. Taylor didn't know it yet, but his army career was over, as surely as if he had already resigned his commission.

The lieutenant just stood there, his face white now, wiping his hands on his pants.

"Asshole, maybe you'd better sit down and prop up your feet," Cole suggested.

Taylor looked at him, tried to speak, then sat down hard on the porch steps. He landed on a wet spot, and the crowd snickered its appreciation.

John drew up in front of the lieutenant and executed his fanciest salute, then turned on his heel. He pulled his watch out and looked at it; the time lacked just five minutes to twelve. He knew he could borrow a horse from one of his friends and meet the stage before it traveled too many more miles.

Seated a few minutes later on an obliging mare of some antiquity—the perfect venue for an infantryman—he started up the hill by the cemetery, past the boarded-up hospital and the empty non-com quarters. He had a train to catch in Cheyenne. He wasn't sure where it would take him, but he thought he would enjoy the ride now.

Fille de Joie

Pure and simple, it was a case of acute necessity. If Hugh Marsh had to wait one more week for his wife to show up at Fort Fetterman, he knew he would explode. Little pieces of him would careen off and fill the air between the Platte and Powder Rivers like so many cottonwood seeds. The army would be short—but probably not missing—one second lieutenant.

"Sir, except for trail and escort duty, I have not been off this military reservation in almost eighteen months. I really would like to meet my wife in Cheyenne."

His commanding officer smiled at him in that benign way he had with junior officers and then further rattled Marsh's composure by winking at him. "Got the can't-waits, Mr. Marsh?"

"My God, sir, you don't know."

"Begging to differ, Mr. Marsh, I *do* know." The colonel leaned back in his swivel chair and his smile broadened. "I may be fifty years old and with one foot in the grave—now don't deny it; I know you pups think I fought with Hannibal—but I'll have you know that my vigor didn't vanish with my hair! Permission granted."

I should be embarrassed, Hugh thought as he closed the door and resisted the urge to sprint across the parade ground. *Guess that shows how desperate I am.*

He yearned for Millie, pined for her, tossed and turned at night because of her, took cold hip baths because of her, dreamed of her. It scorched his Yankee economy to its bedrock at the thought of someone else escorting his wife to Fetterman while he paced up and down in the duty room biting his nails to the quick. Surely he could con some other greenie—*Good Lord, did anyone owe him a favor?*—to play adjutant for a week and a half while he got between real sheets in a real hotel with his very own wife.

He knew he wasn't the only one who felt this way. Millie's last few letters had taken on a subtle note of longing that was not lost on him. The farthest she ever went was to write how she longed for his arms around her, but that was enough. As he read and then reread her letter four weeks later in his chaste room in the bachelor officers' quarters, he knew that Millie Marsh was doing her own nail biting.

The marriage had begun with the greatest expectations. He had been luckier than most army lovers, in that he was on detached duty from his regiment at the recruiting depot in Boston and was able to get to Lyme every weekend or so for some strenuous courting.

Millie's father had married them in the Lyme First Congregational Church. Both mothers sobbed into their inadequate handkerchiefs, his own father harrumphed and blew his nose several times, the bridesmaids giggled, and the flower girl threw up all over the chancel. He didn't remember anything of the ceremony, except that his collar was too tight. He had put the ring on Millie's finger, she had put one on his, and when he looked into her lovely eyes, he was sure his heart pounded loud enough to be heard on the third row.

Their wedding night had been a bewildering experience, compounded as it was by the fact that a blizzard stranded all out-of-town visitors at Millie's home, and he and Millie were afraid to breathe for fear that someone would overhear their amateur tableau in her room at the head of the stairs. He had blown out the lamp, and they fumbled around in the dark.

I've never even seen my wife naked, Hugh thought, and then looked over his shoulder. He didn't think he had spoken out loud, but he had started talking to himself lately, and he couldn't be sure. A jailbird with a large P on his uniform blouse stood nearby, but his attention never wavered from the trash he was spearing. Hugh sighed and shook his head.

The snow stopped the morning after the wedding, piling up deep against the house, but not deep enough to prevent the local messenger boy from banging on the door at the God-awful hour of seven o'clock. It was a telegram, an edict, a call to arms for Lieutenant Hugh Marsh entreating him—nay, commanding him—to rejoin his regiment immediately.

He remembered pulling on his drawers and opening the door a crack to receive the glad tidings from the maid who thrust it at him and ran tittering down the stairs. Hugh read the telegram, and then glanced over at Millie, who was sleeping with her back to him. Her shoulders were deliciously bare, and only a couple years of military discipline kept him from leaping back into bed and having his way with her.

But duty called and could not be ignored, especially as his regiment was pulling out for Dakota Territory from Omaha Barracks in four days. If the trains were running right, he would be there just in time. He abandoned all thought of a morning romp.

It had been so hard to leave Millie. He promised over and over to send for her as soon as the regiment was settled somewhere. She only sobbed louder as she nodded her head, shaking those brown curls that only the night before he had buried his face in.

Everyone gave him good advice as he threw his gear together. Both mothers told him to dress warm and look out for Indians; his father reminded him that he was a Marsh; and his father-in-law glared at him as if wondering what he had done to his little daughter up there in her own bedroom.

He gave Millie a kiss to remember, then felt like a cad as he leaped through the snowdrifts to the postman's cutter. That worthy had been commandeered to haul him to the nearest depot, and the old letter carrier seemed to relish the whole tearful scene by the front door. He told Hugh that it reminded him of his own military days during the Mexican War when he left his wife behind. "But Jee-rusalem Crickets if my wife wasn't as wide as a barn door and uglier than a well-chewed seegar butt. *I* didn't mind leaving!" To Hugh's discomfort, the postman regaled him with stories about the athletic "sennerittas" of Vera Cruz until Hugh longed to leap from the cutter and make his way through the drifts back to Millie's bed.

He made it to Omaha Barracks with half a day to spare, only to spend the rest of the winter sitting around with the regiment in drafty quarters. When he thought what he had left behind in Connecticut for the privilege of playing cribbage with his comrades in arms and enduring their rude noises, he wondered for the umpteenth time why he had chosen the glamour of a military career. Each time he petitioned the colonel to allow him to send for his wife, he was assured that they were pulling out in two days' time. So passed January, February, and March.

When the regiment finally shipped west that spring on the uncompleted Union Pacific, the men were informed that they would be constructing a fort on the south bank of the North Platte to protect pilgrims on the Bozeman Trail. The post was to be named Fetterman, after the asshole that got himself and eighty men killed up near Fort Phil Kearney a couple years back.

Amid numerous complaints from the troops about being detailed to damned ditch-digging duty, Fort Fetterman went up and stood sentinel on the bluffs overlooking the Platte to defend any chance travelers on the trail. Naturally, there were few. At his leisure, Hugh Marsh had ample time to contemplate government efficiency.

His first wedding anniversary came and went. He spent most of the winter of 1868 on patrol in the Powder River country, attempting to keep an eye on hostiles who heartily wished him to the devil. He developed lively reflexes and a wariness that kept his hair on his head, not dangling from some scalp stick.

When the treaty was signed at Fort Laramie in 1868, the colonel gave permission to send for the regiment's wives. Hugh wrote Millie right away, only to be informed in a tear-splotched letter than she had the measles, and the doctor wouldn't let her travel. Had Hugh been a drinking man, he would have rushed over to the sutler's store for the dissipation of a warm beer. He went to his quarters instead and threw darts until the officer on the other side of the wall hollered at him.

Two months later, he received a more promising letter from his wife, stating that she would be in Cheyenne September fifteenth. That letter coincided with a directive from the colonel informing Lieutenant Hugh Marsh that he was the regiment's new adjutant. In small print, that meant that his life was no longer his own—hence the session with his colonel.

Here he was now, on his way to Cheyenne. With the signing of the treaty and the closing of the three forts to the north, Fetterman sat in uneasy isolation. Fortnightly, a detachment rode south for mail and other incidentals. By tossing a couple shirts into his saddlebag and really hassling the quartermaster sergeant for rations, Hugh caught up with the detail before it was too far away from Fetterman for protection.

They had a skirmish, which amounted to nearly nothing, with some of Red Cloud's finest about twenty miles from Fetterman. The troops dismounted, fired a round or two, and then continued toward Fort Laramie. The dogfight was of such insignificance that it warranted less than a line in his journal.

Not until he got to Laramie and took his pants off to crawl onto a spare cot did Hugh realize he had forgotten to bring his wallet. He ordinarily kept his money, wedding ring (the commanding officer said it was not prudent to wear rings), and his identification in his footlocker. In his hurry to leave, he completely forgot that this trip was different from the tedium of others.

He lay awake for the space of a few minutes cursing his forgetfulness, then consoled himself that Millie would at least be traveling with money and could pay the hotel bill. The thought soothed him to sleep, along with the realization that soon he wouldn't be sharing quarters with someone who snored and left whiskers all around the washbasin.

He spent a sleepless night at Chug Station, wrestling with the effects of five days of undercooked sowbelly and War of the Rebellion hardtack. He dozed in the saddle most of the way to Lodgepole Creek, where they camped on the last night out from Cheyenne.

On the early afternoon of September fifteenth, after separating from the detail at Fort Russell, Hugh rode into Cheyenne alone. He covered the three miles between the fort and town with the same mingled terror and delight of his wedding night. He wondered if she had changed; he knew he had. He wondered if she still loved him. He wished he had time for a soak in a tub before bouncing into Millie's life again.

Although he was almost dizzy with yearning for his wife, Marsh noticed something different about Cheyenne as he rode down Front Street in the hot sun of early autumn. His last time in town the railroad had been going through; Cheyenne had been a tent city of Irish railroaders and prostitutes, a hell on wheels. That was eighteen months ago, and now with the track laid and pushing out across the Red Desert, Cheyenne appeared to be attempting respectability. Hugh counted three churches and what looked like a schoolhouse going up.

He stabled his remount in the livery behind the hotel and found the lobby with amazing speed. The room clerk sat drowsing behind the desk, and a couple of drummers conversed in loud voices at a writing table. Hugh turned the register around and scanned the guest list. There she was, Millie Chase. He chuckled as he signed his name next to hers. She still had trouble remembering to write her married name. Time to change that, he thought.

He rapped on the bell, and the clerk nearly fell out of his chair. "Yes, captain," he gasped, promoting Hugh. "What can I do for you?"

"I see you have a Millie Chase registered."

"Yes, sir. She came in this morning on the westbound."

"She's my wife. What room?"

The clerk handed him the single key and nodded toward the stairs. He took them two at a time and knocked on 208. "Millie?" He turned the key in the lock and opened the door.

Millie sat in a chair near the window where she had been reading. She stood up quickly, her eyes on his face. He knew he looked different. He was leaner and browner, and he had neglected to mention the moustache that he figured made him look at least ten years older. There was something of surprise in her eyes, and he knew he was a different man from the pale Yankee she married going on two years ago.

"Hugh?" she asked, as if she needed confirmation from an outside source.

"No, Phil Sheridan," he joked, holding out his arms to her.

She tossed the book into the chair, came to him, pulled his head down toward her and kissed him. His arms latched around her, and he kissed her until she started squirming for breath. She laughed and protested as he spun her around and started down the row of mother-of-pearl buttons on the back of her shirtwaist. He had never been any great shakes with precision dexterity, so his proficiency amazed him.

To his gratification, Millie wasn't particularly shy about shedding her clothes. Before he was all the way rid of his uniform, she had shucked off shirtwaist, draped overdress, underdress, small wire hoops, corset cover, corset, petticoats (he lost count), camisole, chemise—the sight of her beautiful breasts stopped him cold for a moment—garters, black stockings, underdrawers, and was pulling back the bedspread when she looked at him. "Dear, perhaps you should pull down the shade while you still have on your pants."

He did as she said. He could have sobbed with frustration as he fumbled with his belt clasp, but it yielded finally, and he stumbled out of his trousers and stripped down to his long johns.

Millie watched his antics from the bed. She gasped at the bruise on his chest. "What happened to you?"

He wished he could have told her it was the result of a fight to the finish with Red Cloud himself, but his mind was occupied with the casual way Millie sat with her legs crossed. *Were her legs always that long?* he asked himself. A month back he'd gotten pranged with a roof joist while supervising construction of their own quarters. "I'll tell you later, Millie," he said, his eyes still on her magnificent legs. "Move over, eh?"

His lovemaking had none of the hesitancy of his wedding night. He knew he hadn't acquired any more skill in the intervening months, beyond an active imagination that didn't fail him now. *I hope she doesn't mind that I smell like my horse,* he thought. Five minutes later, he didn't care if he smelled like a blue-assed baboon.

At one point in the following madness, he hoped fervently that there weren't any patrons in the adjoining room. A few seconds later, when Millie was running her tongue inside his ear and doing amazing things with her legs, he didn't give a damn if the whole Ladies Aide Society of Cheyenne had their ears pressed against the wall. Millie didn't seem to care, either. She murmured his name over and over and really dug in her fingernails at appropriate moments.

When the floor leveled again, they lay close together, his arm cradling her shoulders, her fingers softly rubbing the bruise on his chest. There was definite blush on her cheeks and breasts, and Hugh could almost tell what was going through her mind, bless her Yankee heart. He considered getting one of the towels draped over the rack next to the washbasin to wipe off the sweat they had worked up, but the towel looked so far away, and his eyes were closing or glazing over. He lay there in quiet contentment, pleased to let the breeze that ruffled the curtains cool them. He closed his eyes, listening to Millie tell him something about her purse.

"Open up! This is a raid!"

Hugh opened his eyes, then closed them again. "There must be some shady people in these environs," he murmured.

"Open up, I say! I have a pass key!" The doorknob jiggled, and the door slammed open.

Millie shrieked and lunged for the sheet that was somewhere at the foot of the bed. Hugh sat up, wider awake than he had been in a week. The two men glaring at them both wore tin stars. One of them looked right at Millie, who was trying to wrap as much of the sheet around her as she could—no mean feat, since she was a cuddlesome woman. "You're under arrest!" he told her.

"What?" Hugh shouted. He reached behind him and pulled the pillow onto his lap.

"You heard me. Now get your duds on and hurry up about it, sister, before I run you out like that."

Millie burst into tears, and Hugh wanted to join her. He thought better of it when the lawmen continued to glare at his wife. A crowd gathered in the doorway, and Hugh could see no tactical advantage, sitting there stark naked with a pillow over his privates.

"Look here, lieutenant," the sheriff said, his voice surprisingly patient, "we have a new ordinance in this town against *filles de joie* servicing their johns in our best hotel." He pronounced it "fillies dee joy," but Millie obviously knew what he meant because she sobbed harder.

"Be reasonable," Hugh began, wondering if the world had ever known a dignified naked man. "You are greatly mistaken. This is my wife."

The sheriff burst out laughing; as if on cue, the people in the hall did, too. He laughed for a long moment, then wiped his eyes. "Do you honestly expect me to believe that a respectable female would spread 'em in the middle of the afternoon? You've got to do better than that, sonny boy."

Bristling with importance, the desk clerk pushed his way through the crowd and into the room. He shoved the hotel register under Hugh's nose. "It says here, 'Millie Chase and Lieutenant Hugh Marsh.'"

The sheriff brayed with laughter again. "Are you sure that isn't 'Millie *Chaste*'?" The Greek chorus in the hall did what was expected, rejoicing in the sheriff's wit.

"Millie, show them some identification," Hugh commanded, desperation making him sound as sharp as though he were addressing his troops. She cried harder. Hugh repeated himself more calmly, shaking her gently by the shoulder. "Millie, where's your handbag?"

She stopped sobbing long enough to pierce him with a glance that could have blasted granite. "That's what I was trying to tell you," she hissed at him. "Someone robbed me on the train!"

She melted into tears again, and Hugh threw up his hands. "Run us in, Sheriff. But for God's sake, close the door so we can get dressed!"

The sheriff closed the door, pulling his deputy inside with him, but not before some wag in the hall hollered for the lieutenant to see a doctor about those scratches in his back.

"You can't wait outside with the other spectators?" Hugh snapped.

"Nope," the man said calmly. "Last week we waited outside for a whore, and she scrambled out the window and ran down the street naked as a blue jay."

The likelihood of Millie doing such a thing almost made Hugh smile. "Turn your back at least," he ordered.

The men complied with some reluctance, one of them muttering to the other about their luck in running onto a soiled dove with sensibilities. Hugh placed no confidence in their captors' patience, so he ordered Millie to dry up and hustle into her clothes. She blew her nose on the sheet, glared at him again, and tossed on her apparel even faster than she had removed it.

Hugh scrambled into his own clothes, his mind nearly a blank. Some of his self-possession returned when he buttoned up his uniform blouse with its gold shoulder straps. He did up the back of Millie's shirtwaist and whispered in her ear, "Did you pack our marriage license?"

She shook her head. "I left it home with Mother."

He shouldn't have said anything, because mention of home and mother started the tears again. She leaned against him and cried. Hugh looked at the lawmen. "You're making an awful mistake."

The sheriff turned around. "Prove it, sonny."

Hugh bucked on his sidearm. The sheriff glanced at his Navy Colt, then at Millie, who was cramming pins into her hair while she stared into some grim middle distance. *I don't think she'll wrest the gun from my grasp and shoot you,* Hugh thought. He was hit with a bucketful of remorse then. *I think she's more likely to shoot me.*

"We're ready," he said finally, after Millie found her hat.

The sheriff laughed. "No, we don't want *you!* Just her."

He grabbed Millie by the arm. She squealed and tugged back, and Hugh grabbed the sheriff. The lawman was taller and outweighed him by quite a few pounds, most of which, Hugh reasoned, he had gained by frequenting Cheyenne's bakery. Hugh hadn't spent his last eighteen months at hard labor as a drudge lieutenant for nothing. He stared up at the sheriff and informed him in a quiet voice that Millie would go peacefully, and would the sheriff please take his hands off her?

Clutching each other by the hand, Hugh and Millie walked into the hall. She paled when she saw all the spectators, and Hugh feared that she would faint, but she stiffened her back, raised her chin, released her death's grip on him, and marched down the stairs. She strode across the lobby but stopped with a whimper on the porch outside.

The sheriff must have been making other raids previous to the one currently in progress. Hugh stared in dismay at the wagon in front of them, full to overflowing with whores of all shapes and sizes, in various stages of undress.

Millie turned to her captor. "You expect me to get in there with those. . . those. . . *creatures*?"

The sheriff grinned and made a sweeping bow that set the prostitutes into shrieks of laugher. "Not only do I expect it, madam, I insist upon it." He spoke over his shoulder to Hugh. "Trust you boys in blue, but I don't know where you trolled to find this high-class piece of tail."

From Lyme, Connecticut, you asshole, Hugh thought. *She'll probably head back there on the eastbound train tomorrow.* He sighed. "You wouldn't believe me if I told you." He winced at the look Millie threw at him.

The sheriff held out his arm for her, but Millie ignored him and climbed into the wagon. She sat on the few remaining inches left on one bench, pulled her skirts tight around her and informed the occupants that she was Millie Marsh of Lyme, Connecticut, and her father was the minister of the First Congregational Church.

Hugh winced again as the whores cackled. "At least you know who your father is," one of them declared. Another told her "Not to fret, dearie. We all have pasts to live down."

Millie colored right up to her scalp and set her lips in a tight line. Hugh put his hands on the wagon's tailgate. "Millie, I'll get you out of here. Trust me."

She leaned forward until her face was just inches from his. "You had damned well better, Hugh Marsh! And quick!"

He had never heard her swear before; words failed him. The wagon rumbled down the street. Posture impeccable, head high, her hands folded in her lap, Millie looked like a Royalist from the concluding chapter of *Tale of Two Cities*. Hugh almost waved to her, but he didn't believe she would wave back.

He hurried at a half trot around the corner to the livery but stopped short when he remembered that he had no money to redeem his horse. This meant a three-mile walk to Fort Russell. While he didn't mind the walk, the shadows were already lengthening across the streets. He wondered if he knew any brother officers at Russell well enough to plead for a loan.

The street was calm in the late afternoon sun. Children rolled hoops ahead of him, and he watched them a moment, his hands in his pockets. As he stood there, he heard music coming from what looked like a partly finished church. He looked closer. Someone had leaned a sign against the front step with the words Cheyenne Methodist Church in charcoal.

After removing his hat, he slumped down in the back pew. He counted fifteen people sitting on benches near the packing crate lectern. That surprised him; he wouldn't have thought that there were fifteen Christians in Wyoming Territory.

The singers—his recent humility made him charitable enough to label them so—were going over and over the chorus of a song he remembered from his mother's temperance society days. When he was much younger and more pliable, she had forced him to attend meetings with her in the hope that the improving society would strengthen him against life's blasts. He hummed along.

> *Let the lower lights be burning;*
> *Send a gleam across the wave:*

Some poor fainting, struggling seaman
You may rescue, you may save.

Someone clapped a meaty hand on his shoulder. Startled, he looked around. He was almost eye level with a man who was about as tall as he was round, with a face so fat that Hugh could barely see his eyes. He wore a black suit that seemed to strain in all directions. He had tufts of hair growing out of his ears, and Hugh couldn't think when he had seen an uglier specimen of humanity. He looked closer and could have sighed. The man's little eyes were kind.

"Can I help you?" the man asked.

"You are . . ." Hugh began, starting to squirm under the man's grasp, which was stronger than he would have thought.

"Reverend Charles Wesley McAllister."

Hugh shook his head. "I don't really see how you can help me."

The minister loosened his grip, and Hugh tried to rise. "Son, the Lord loves all kinds of sinners."

"You don't understand," Hugh burst out, then lowered his voice when the choir director looked around and glared at him. "I'm not . . . well, I suppose I am . . . Oh, hell . . . beg your pardon." He stood up then and tried to edge out the door, but the minister reeled him right back and into a room off the chapel.

"Come in my office, lad. Sit down, and we'll talk."

The office turned out to be a cubbyhole that was filled to capacity when the door was closed. The preacher wheezed himself onto the only chair and motioned to a stool. Hugh sat down, knowing he ought to be elsewhere helping Millie, but without a clue what to do.

McAllister looked him over for a few uncomfortable moments. He made a simple gesture with his hand that seemed to cause the words to pour from Hugh. He began at the beginning with the ceremony in Lyme, traced the events of his wedding night, chronicled his eighteen months of deprivation at Fetterman, and honed in on the happenings of that afternoon, leaving out few of the gory details. He couldn't understand what possessed him, normally a reticent man, to tell this stranger the intimate facts of his life.

When he was silent, the minister leaned his chair against the wall. "You have to understand our town, Lieutenant. Cheyenne's been a sewer since the first tent went up two years ago. I've witnessed debauchery here that I doubt you've ever even heard of."

Hugh felt the blush travel up his neck and felt no desire to further expose his naiveté. Hadn't the minister just listened to his entire sexual history?

"The city fathers finally got the gumption to crack down on the local indecency. They drafted a couple of strenuous ordinances and found a sheriff dumb enough to obey them to the letter. There you are, bless your heart." The minister strained to fold his hands over his belly. "Can't believe we voted that nincompoop into office." He chuckled at the memory, then stood up suddenly, or at least as quickly as he could. "But this isn't getting your little wife out of the slammer, is it?"

"Can you *do* that?"

"I am certain I can. Of course, you'll have to marry her."

"I already married her!" Hugh shouted and blushed ferociously when the choir in the other room stopped entirely. "Didn't you hear what I said?" he whispered.

"Patience, lad! Unless you can conjure up the fifty-dollar fine that the sheriff slaps on the whores before he releases them, you'd better make an honest woman of her again." He opened the door. "I only charge two dollars a wedding, which I will waive today as an act of Christian charity."

Hugh was still smiling when they entered the jail. They would have been there sooner, but the Reverend McAllister had to stop every few steps to catch his breath. When they were halfway there, he muttered an expletive that made Hugh blink, and then waddled back to the church for his prayer book.

Millie sat on a cot in the crowded cell. Her hair was neatly arranged and coiled at the back of her neck again, but with a certain elegance that made him wonder who had helped. She was engaged in an animated conversation with one of her cellmates, but she stopped when Hugh and the minister walked in.

She looked so young sitting there, surrounded by those women with their tattered feathers, short skirts, and dirty wraps, that remorse stabbed Hugh again. *Men are heels and cads*, he thought, *and I must be the worst of the lot. What must she think of me? I wonder if we are speaking.*

To his relief, she got up and came over to the bars. Hugh reached through and put his arms around her waist, as best he could. He heard the sheriff slam down his chair on all fours and stalk across the room.

"You again? Hands off the merchandise, sonny boy."

Hugh didn't bother to look around. "She's my wife."

"You still gotta prove it or pay fifty dollars to spring her."

"How about if I marry her right here?"

"What are you saying, Hugh?" Millie whispered. "We're already married!"

"That was my understanding, too, Millie, but I think this will be the one that takes. Just don't tell your father." He looked into her eyes, still puffy from her bout of tears. They were the same big eyes that had caught his attention four years ago at a West Point hop. "You *will* marry me, won't you?"

Her eyes narrowed. She hesitated just long enough to make him silently vow to be the finest husband in all thirty-seven states. Then she nodded.

"All right, you two, join hands," McAllister said. He opened his prayer book, looked around, and cleared his throat.

"You can't do this in my jail!" the sheriff declared.

McAllister looked him up and down then raised one pudgy finger heavenward. "Tell that to the Lord God Almighty, you sorry son of a bitch." In the amazing silence that followed, he cleared his throat again. "Need two witnesses."

"Not him," Millie said firmly, staring at the sheriff until he coughed and looked away. "Or that wretched, brainless deputy." She leaned as close as she could to Hugh. "Do you know what those men *do* when these, uh, ladies are stuck here overnight? Oh, Hugh, the things I've learned this afternoon!"

"I can't imagine what they do," he whispered back.

"Of course you can," she replied, her voice crisp. "You're one of them."

He had the brains not to comment.

The sheriff gestured toward two drunks sleeping in the next cell. He took out his gun and fired a round into the ceiling. The men sat up and blinked. "You're witnesses," the sheriff said. "Damn it, Fahey, scratch some other time!"

The whores in Millie's cell lined up behind her. Hugh had never seen such a collection of bridesmaids before, and he broke into a coughing fit that Millie stopped with a hard pinch. "Behave yourself, Hugh," she threatened.

The Reverend McAllister straightened his collar. "Dearly beloved . . ." he started. Hugh was taxed not to burst into the kind of wild laughter that would require a bucket of water. "We are gathered here in the sight of God and these witnesses." The preacher looked over his book at the drunks and repeated in a louder voice, "these witnesses, to unite this couple in holy matrimony."

Hugh smiled at Millie, who held so tight to his hand that he feared for his circulation. She smiled back and loosened her grip slightly.

"If there be any here who can show just cause why this couple should not be united, let him speak now, or henceforth hold his peace."

McAllister paused. One of the witnesses belched and sagged against the bars. Hugh held his breath when the sheriff opened his mouth, but no one said anything.

"No ties more tender, no vows more sacred . . . ."

Even though he could not fathom a more unholy place, Hugh felt his throat tighten. Captured all over again by the sight of this lovely woman standing beside him through the bars, it dawned on him that he hadn't been paying attention eighteen months earlier when Millie's father read a similar ceremony. He listened this time.

"What's your full name, lad?"

"Hugh Allen Marsh, sir."

"Hugh Allen Marsh, will you have . . . "

McAllister paused again and glanced at Millie, who spoke up in a firm voice. "Millicent Maria Chase."

"Will you have Millicent Maria Chase, to live in holy matrimony with her, to love her, comfort her, and keep her in sickness and health, forsaking all others, as long as you both shall live?"

"I will." Hugh felt his response right down to his socks. He spoke louder than he intended, but no one seemed to notice.

The minister addressed Millie with the same question. She gave the same reply with a firmness that made Hugh tighten his grip on her.

"Who giveth this woman to be married to this man?"

The sheriff shoved himself away from the wall. "Aw, hell, I guess I do, seeing as how she's in my jail."

The deputy's laugh stopped when Millie's bridesmaids turned on him as one with a ferocious stare.

"All right, lad, repeat after me. I, Hugh . . ."

"I, Hugh . . ."

"take thee Millie to be my wife. To have and to hold from this day forward, for better or worse."

Hugh repeated after McAllister. What could be worse than a tour of duty at Fort Fetterman? Who could possibly be poorer than a second lieutenant? Sickness and health? More likely than not, the post surgeon would never be around when Millie needed him. The seriousness of his covenants grabbed hold of Hugh this time as he marveled at his audacity in marrying this woman, this minister's daughter from Connecticut, and hauling her onto the high plains of Wyoming Territory. How did he dare? And now that she had seen the elephant, how did *she* dare?

To love and to cherish until death did them part? It might be fifty years from now; it might be next Tuesday. He could barely continue, but Millie squeezed his hand, smiled at him, and he finished.

The Reverend McAllister asked Millie to repeat after him, and she did in a calm voice, her chin up. Hugh watched her in vast admiration and love. With any luck at all, he would be as strong as she was some day. And if he weren't, she would probably never berate him about it.

There was something about a ring, but Millie glared at the sheriff and declared that she wouldn't take hers off to put it on again. The minister gave a prayer for the marriage, then assured them that they were husband and wife, and those whom God hath joined, no man should put asunder. Hugh had trouble hearing the conclusion because several of Millie's bridesmaids burst into tears.

Hugh kissed his wife through the bars, then turned to the sheriff, who was fumbling for a handkerchief. "Will you open this cell now, sir?"

The sheriff did as he was told. He started to close the door after Hugh pulled Millie out, hesitated, then opened it wider. "All right, all right, the rest of you get the hell out of here. Don't let me catch you floozies working the downtown hotels!"

Hugh shook hands with the Reverend McAllister. "I can send you that two dollars when we get to Fetterman," he apologized.

The minister waved him away. "Tell you what, lad. You bring your little lady back here in fifteen-twenty years. You can look Cheyenne over, and we can look you over. We'll see if either of us has growed up any."

"It's a promise, sir."

The minister beamed at the two of them, then stepped back in surprise when Millie kissed his cheek. He bowed, which made even the whores stare in amazement, said goodnight, and left the jail.

Hugh was escorting Millie to the door when one of the *filles de joie* laid a hand on his arm. "Here, honey, you youngsters take this."

Hugh stared down at a wad of greenbacks in the woman's hand. He opened his mouth to protest, but the whore slapped the money in his hand.

"Lookie here, sonny. Millie told us all about your troubles. Don't you look so mulish! That's honest money. We earned it."

Hugh didn't doubt that for a moment. His fingers closed over the bills. As he pocketed them, he knew he could no more wound their feelings than fly. "Thank you, ladies," he said, and someone giggled. "I will pay this back when we get to Fetterman. To whom should I send the money?"

"Just send it to Big Hole Malloy," she replied without a blink. "Care of the Cat's Cradle. Everyone knows me." She dug him in the ribs. "Even that commanding officer of yours, if you're from Fetterman. I'll see that it gets divvied up." She smiled at Millie, and Hugh was captivated by the tenderness in her eyes. "Honey, don't you forget all that stuff we taught you this afternoon."

"I wouldn't dream of it," his sweet wife replied. "You are certain it works?"

"Trust me," Big Hole said. Hugh knew he would never have the courage to ask.

There wasn't anything more to say. Millie paused in the doorway and blew the whores a kiss. Several of the fillies burst into tears all over again.

The Marshes strolled down the boardwalk hand in hand. Millie stopped and leaned her head against his shoulder. "I love you, Hugh," she said. His uniform blouse muffled her voice, but he heard her clearly enough and was moved. He knew she loved him. He had never been so sure of anything in his life.

"I can't wait to get back to our room," she continued and set them both in motion again.

He grinned. "Something the fillies taught you?"

She smiled at him with a patient look that told him he would forever be putty in her hands. "Actually, I thought we would just do what we did before. I don't think it needed any improvement, do you?"

He was quick to agree.

Millie stopped again. "Now that you mention it, Hugh, one of the fillies showed me a most provocative way to remove my stockings. You might enjoy that."

He did.

Kathleen Flaherty's Long Winter

❦ ❦

In her eight years of marriage to Johnny Flaherty, Kathleen had decided early that the worst part was the waiting. She didn't mind the government food; it was better than anything she had grown up eating. The government housing scarcely troubled her; she had been raised in a slum. Waiting for Johnny to return from a patrol was the worst of all.

She knew he would come back. He told her over and over again he would. She believed him, but there was always that moment when she doubted. It was usually just the moment before he opened the door, held out his arms, and said, "Da-dum!" She would run to him and hug him, then tug off his overcoat and sit him down to some tea sugared the way he liked it and poured into the saucer to cool. She would lean both elbows on the table, chin in her hands, and listen to him run on about the hostiles, or the weather, or what the lieutenant or sergeant did or did not say. That was the best moment of the return and almost worth the waiting—to hear Johnny Flaherty spin his little lies and make her laugh at herself for worrying even a bit.

Kathleen walked back and forth by the window. It was only a window in the summer, when the space was covered with mosquito netting and the shutters flung back. In the winter it was closed, the crossbar thrust through the handles, with rags poked here and there to keep out the cold.

She heard children crying in the quarters next to her own. A pity that they were crammed in so tight there, the Murphys with their five children. The Department of the West had been promising adequate quarters at Camp Halleck since the post was established, but they were off the beaten path, and few congressmen bothered to visit any constituents.

Kathleen sighed. She knew she ought to go next door and offer to help with the younger children so Peg Murphy could get back to her ironing, but she didn't think she could tolerate another evening of jackstraws. Johnny had said it was just as well she couldn't have children. No sense in hauling a baby from post to post, exposing it to all the diseases known to western man. She agreed with her husband in theory, but every month, she cried.

Kathleen went into the lean-to and checked the water simmering in the kettle for Johnny's tea. She had heated water every night for the past week and would do so each night until the men rode in, sitting stiff in their saddles, with icicles on their moustaches and frosty patches on their faces that looked dead white and painful to touch.

Like most women, she couldn't see the need for winter patrols. The Indians, who proved themselves more canny with each passing season, were not about to be caught out in the open, and any road agents extant had probably retired long since to the nearest settlement, now that the stages had stopped running for the season, at least to Camp Halleck, complete in its isolation.

"Why do you have to do it?" she had asked Johnny once.

He rolled his eyes at her. "Oh, Kate," he said, grabbing her around the waist and squeezing her, "Kate, we just do it." It wasn't much of an answer, but maybe he didn't know, either. Maybe the horses needed the exercise.

After a few more minutes of pacing up and down in front of the door and trying to decide if she really wanted to open it for a quick peek and let in all that cold, Kathleen sat down in her rocking chair, which she had pulled as close to the stove as she could. She picked up their one book and opened it. It was *The Talisman*, by Sir Walter Scott, and she was far along the way to having the entire thing memorized.

She fell asleep and was pulled awake by the tinny smell of a kettle boiling dry. Kathleen went into the kitchen and lifted the teakettle off the stove. It was probably too late to refill it, but she did anyway and set it back on the stove.

Before turning back the blankets on her bed, Kathleen threw on her shawl and opened the door a crack. The snow had stopped earlier in the evening, and the moon brightened up the uncluttered land. Snow covered all the sharp angles of the buildings and smoothed out the steep lines of the tents. Kathleen shivered, looking at the tents. The men had sawed and hammered up to the first snowfall, but there hadn't been time to finish the second set of barracks or the rest of the enlisted quarters. No one complained much; there wasn't any point to it. Sometimes Kathleen heard Peg through the wall, threatening her children with the tents. "If you don't behave, the captain will put you in a tent!"

Kathleen glanced over at the stables, peered more closely, and then smiled. The men were back. She could just make them out, leading their animals inside. She closed the door and ran her fingers through her hair, patting the pins in tight. She sat down again to wait for Johnny.

It was taking him longer than usual to come to her. She tapped her foot and drummed her fingers on the arm of the rocker, wondering at his tardiness. She was about to get up again and peek out the door when someone knocked. She jumped up and ran to the door, flinging it open.

Three men stood there, dark shapes against the snowy background. They were bundled up against the weather, but Kathleen recognized the post surgeon, Captain Melbourne, and Sergeant Oleson. She shrieked and slammed the door shut, leaning against it.

They knocked again, and she felt the sound of the wood through her back. Johnny wasn't with them, but there must be some explanation. He would chide her if he knew she had slammed the door on his superiors. She turned and opened the door.

The men still stood there shoulder to shoulder, except that Sergeant Oleson's hand was raised, as if to knock again.

"May we come in, Mrs. Flaherty?" It was Captain Melbourne.

She nodded, and the three men came into the room. She closed the door behind them and leaned against it again, after a quick look outside to see if Johnny was coming behind.

The post surgeon gestured toward the rocking chair. "Perhaps you had better sit down, Mrs. Flaherty," he suggested.

She shook her head. "Maybe you'd just better tell me quick what kind of trouble Johnny has gotten himself into."

The men looked at each other. The post surgeon cleared his throat, but Captain Melbourne took a step toward her. Kathleen would have backed up, but she was already against the door.

"He's dead, Mrs. Flaherty."

She just stared at him. The teakettle in the kitchen started to sing. "But the water's ready for his tea," she said. She wanted to go lift the kettle off the stove, but her legs wouldn't move. Sergeant Oleson went into the lean-to, and the singing stopped.

"I'm sorry, Kate," the doctor said, turning his hat around and around in his hands. "He had the midnight-to-four duty. We figure he just got tired and closed his eyes for a minute. The next watch found him."

Kathleen looked down the floor. The men were thawing out and dripping on the boards. "It wasn't Indians?" she asked.

"No."

"Or road agents?"

"No." The captain shifted his weight from one foot to the other as her voice rose.

"Not even trouble with those Chinamen on the Central Pacific?"

"No."

Kathleen was screaming at them now, but she couldn't help herself. "If there wasn't any trouble, then why did you have to go out in the first place?"

No one answered. Kathleen stumbled away from the door and leaned her forehead against the wall, crying. They stood watching her. The post surgeon came over to her. "Can I get you anything, Mrs. Flaherty?"

Kathleen shook her head. She heard them leave. The door slammed, propelled by the wind. She thought they were gone, but someone put a hand on her shoulder. She jumped, and shook off the hand. It was Sergeant Oleson. Kathleen knew how upset Johnny would be if he knew she were ever rude to his sergeant, so she wiped her nose with the back of her hand and looked at him.

"Kate," he said, "I will bring over Johnny's gear in the morning."

She nodded, fumbling in her pocket for a handkerchief.

"The commanding officer said he wants to talk to you then. I will walk you to headquarters after Guard Mount."

She blew her nose and nodded again. The sergeant left, closing the door quietly behind him. Kathleen blew her nose again, then sat down in the rocking chair. She leaned back and rocked herself slowly, crying. She cried until her head throbbed, then she turned out the lamp and went to bed.

She must have slept through Reveille and Guard Mount, because she woke to the sound of knocking. At first she thought it was her head pounding, and she pressed her hands to her temples. The sound went on, so she sat up in bed. She thought for a moment that it must be Johnny. She must have dreamed the three men in her quarters last night, and now

Johnny was standing outside, pounding on the door. He would probably scold her for bolting it, especially when she knew he was due home.

Kathleen got out of bed and pulled a shawl around her shoulders. She padded across the floor on her bare feet and opened the door. Sergeant Oleson stood there holding a duffel bag and Johnny's boots. Her face crumpled when she saw them, and she started to cry again.

The sergeant stepped inside and shouldered the door shut. He looked at her then set down Johnny's gear.

Kathleen wiped her eyes. "I must have overslept."

"I will come back. Ten minutes."

Kathleen threw on her clothes and made the bed. The sergeant had said something last night about an appointment with the commanding officer. She was embarrassed to keep the sergeant waiting outside in the cold, so she brushed her hair quickly and pinned it up in a knot on top of her head. It would have looked better if she had used a mirror, but Kathleen hadn't the courage to look at herself in the glass.

She pulled on her cloak and opened the door. The sergeant stood there, his back to her, facing the parade ground. He didn't even look cold. Kathleen remembered something Johnny had said to her once about Sergeant Oleson. "I'm thinking the Swede must have ice water in his veins, surely."

"I'm ready, sergeant," she said.

He offered her his arm, but she shook her head and stuffed her hands into the pockets of her dress. The wind billowed under her cloak, and she gritted her teeth and kept her head down. Camp Halleck had seemed such a pleasant spot last summer when Companies D and E rode in. True, the altitude caused headaches, but everyone got accustomed. Who would ever have thought the winters would be so cold?

They were halfway across the parade ground when Kathleen stopped. The sergeant kept on walking, then stopped and looked back at her.

"Where's Johnny?" she asked.

He shook his head and frowned at her. "Well, Kate, he's . . ." He peered at her, "Oh, do you mean . . . he is in one of the quartermaster storerooms."

"Does he have a coffin?"

"Last night, Private Fogarty made it." He spoke slowly, as if the sentence was Swedish in his head and English on his tongue. Johnny told her once what a purgatory it was, waiting for Gunnar Oleson to finish a sentence.

"It's not his language," she had protested. "Besides, not everyone has the gift like you." Johnny liked to hear her talk about his way with words as a gift. He wasn't Irish for nothing.

Kathleen started walking again, her hands deep in her pockets, leaning against the wind. They crossed the parade ground in silence and went into the administration building.

Like everything else at Camp Halleck, the name hardly fit the structure. The building had been knocked together last fall as a temporary measure and would probably be turned into a tack shed at the first opportunity. Johnny called it a brevet building. There was a fine dusting of snow on the wood floor inside, testifying to the skill of Halleck's soldier-carpenters. It was as cold inside as it was outside, so Kathleen shook her head when Oleson offered to take her cloak.

He knocked on the commanding officer's door. The man inside said something, and the sergeant stepped back and motioned Kathleen forward. "I will wait for you."

Kathleen almost asked him to come in with her. She didn't like Captain Melbourne. He had received a wound to his left eye during the late conflict, and his face was screwed in a perpetual wink. He pinched her once, when the regiment was traveling between posts. She told Johnny about it, but he only laughed and told her to stop blathering.

"You do have a handsome backside, Kate," he replied, as if that excused the whole incident. It didn't, but there wasn't any arguing with Johnny when he insisted on making a joke out of something. Of course, there wasn't much he could have done. Kathleen had learned early in life that the Irish were fair game.

Captain Melbourne looked up when she opened the door and closed it behind her. The papers on his desk ruffled up, and he put his hands on them. "Have a chair, Mrs. Flaherty."

She sat down and waited for him to speak. He shuffled through the papers on his desk, found what he was after and looked at her. "According to our records, Corporal John Flaherty still owes the army $16.32 for miscellaneous equipment and an inkwell he broke in 1864." He looked closer at the page. "In a Petersburg trench."

He looked at her with his winking eye, and she stared back at him. Her husband was hardly dead a day, and the captain was dunning her.

"I don't have it."

He sighed. "I didn't imagine you did. I never did know an Irishman ever to hang onto his money."

They looked at each other. Kathleen stared him right in the eye. He gazed back at her. "What're we going to do with you, Kate Flaherty?" he asked softly, thumbing through Johnny's records and debts.

She wished he wouldn't stare at her. It didn't seem right. Even Johnny would have taken exception to the way he was looking at her. "I don't know what you mean, sir," she said, working to keep down her unease.

"The stages have stopped running. You can't leave. You haven't any money to leave with, anyway. Half a dozen families are eyeing your quarters, now that you're no longer associated with the U.S. Army. What do you propose I do with you?"

In the brevity of her widowhood, she hadn't wasted a minute of her grieving on the fact that she was about to be turned out of her quarters.

"You mean I'm to be thrown out, just like that?" She knew better than to get angry with an officer, but she couldn't help the fact that her voice was rising. "Maybe I could move in with the laundresses?" The idea of spending the winter in those tiny quarters with those women brought tears to her eyes. She was afraid of the laundresses, those coarse creatures with a string of fatherless children and mouths full of oaths.

"I thought about that, but they are already crowded four to one room. It would hardly be fair."

They were both silent, looking at each other across the desk. Kathleen rubbed her hands together; they were colder now than when she had entered the office. Melbourne watched her with his winking eye. As she stared at him, he started to smile.

"Now I have an idea, Kate."

She wished he would call her Mrs. Flaherty, as he had done when Johnny was alive. She almost got up and fled the room but feared that would be too impolite.

"You can keep your quarters."

She sighed.

"On one condition."

She tightened her hands, afraid of what he was going to say, and already sensing what his offer would be. She closed her eyes.

"You can go on living there, same as now, except I'll stop in and 'visit' every now and then."

He stood up and walked around the desk, sitting on the edge of it in front of her. His swinging leg touched her dress. She pulled her dress back tighter. Her gesture didn't anger him. If anything, his smile deepened.

"What's it to be, Kate? You don't have much choice. It's either a tent or me. Johnny told me once how prone you are to lung inflammation." He fingered Johnny's file. "And there's that matter of the $16.32."

Kathleen was too frightened to answer. She shook her head and stared down at her lap. The captain leaned forward and rested his hand on her hair. She shuddered and pulled back.

"When spring comes and the stages are running, I'll pay your fare to anywhere you choose." He laughed. "And maybe I'll give you $16.32."

She gasped. The captain went back and sat in his chair again. He appraised her, as though her clothes were transparent. "You're a pretty woman, Kate, for somebody Irish."

She snapped her head up and all but leaped out of her chair. The captain drew back involuntarily. She was at the door in two strides. She paused with her hand on the knob and whirled around to face him. "You're a great, bad man," she hissed. "May you have no place to sleep when you are old." It was one of Johnny's favorite curses, and she couldn't deny how fitting it was. She slammed the door after her and looked around for Sergeant Oleson.

He was outside, talking to one of the men in his company. He couldn't have helped but notice how cold her eyes were and how white she was, but he made no comment.

"Take me to Johnny," she ordered.

"Are you sure?" he asked.

She looked at him. *My goodness it takes him a long time to get out a sentence*, she thought. She had her answer halfway out before he reached the end of his question. "Of course, I'm sure."

He led her behind the commissary storehouse. He stuck his head inside the storehouse and got the key from the sergeant. She followed him to the shed next to D Company's stables. He unlocked the padlock, but the door stuck, and he had to lean into it to get inside. He opened the door wide and propped it with a hardtack box. Kathleen walked past him, blinked in the darkness, and looked around.

There was no mistaking Johnny. His coffin was crowded in between the bacon and hardtack and looked like it was there to stay.

"When will he be buried?"

Sergeant Oleson stood close to her in the small room. "Didn't Captain Melbourne tell you?"

"We didn't get around to that," she snapped. She had no desire to tell anyone what Captain Melbourne had proposed.

"He can't be buried until spring. Ground is too hard."

So here he stays until the thaw. Yesterday that would have sent her into hysterics. "Will you open the coffin for me?"

"If . . . if you want."

Like everything else at Camp Halleck, the coffin had been fashioned out of this and that. The lid was part of the top of a Consolidated Biscuit Company box. 'The Cracker You Love to Serve,' stated the lettering with elaborate curlicues.

Oleson found a crowbar on a nearby shelf and pried off the top. Kathleen leaned over. Johnny's face appeared right above 'The Cracker You Love to Serve,' almost as if he were endorsing the product. *You would have enjoyed that, Johnny darling*, she thought. He looked cold, but that was all. The corners of his mouth turned down, but they did that anyway when he slept. The hair had fallen down over his forehead, and she pushed it up, remembering that he had wanted her to cut it first thing when he got back. She took off her wedding ring and tried to slip it on his little finger, but his hands were frozen across his chest into tight fists.

"Did you check his pockets, Sergeant?"

"Nothing there."

"He owes the army $16.32," she said.

"We can pay that out of company funds," the sergeant said, after thinking about it a while. He put the boards back down over Johnny and tapped the nails in place with the crowbar.

"Sergeant, the captain told me that he would pay the money and let me stay in my quarters if I let him sleep with me. What do you think of that?"

Kathleen stopped short. She hadn't meant to say anything, but the sight of Johnny frozen, dead, and disappearing beneath the boards forced her to realize how alone she was.

The sergeant didn't look at her, and Kathleen was grateful. She looked down at his hands and noticed how tight his knuckles were around the crowbar. "What can I do, Sergeant Oleson?"

He threw the crowbar against the shelf, where it bounced, and then fell to the dirt floor. He sat down on the edge of Johnny's coffin. "Marry me, Kate."

Kathleen didn't say anything. She looked at Sergeant Oleson. He had such broad shoulders.

"I can marry you and pay Melbourne his goddamned $16.32."

"Sergeant, I don't even know you," she said. The room was cold and getting colder, and her lips were stiff. She had the same urge to run as she had had in Melbourne's office, but there was no place to run.

Oleson went on. "We can be married. When the stage is running in the spring, if you do not want to stay, I will give you half my savings."

That was more words at one time than she had ever heard from the sergeant. It must have cost him some effort, because he ran his finger inside his collar, as if he were suffering from the heat. His face was red, and his hair was so light that she could see the blush on top of his head.

"All right, Sergeant, all right," she said, thinking how strange it was to be accepting a proposal of marriage with Johnny lying there in a biscuit coffin. *It's not as though I have a choice, Johnny,* she thought. *Of my two offers, this is the better one.*

The sergeant picked up the crowbar and gave all the nails on the lid another tap, as if to assure himself that Johnny would stay put. "I will go and speak to the captain," he told her.

They went back into the sunlight. The glare on the snow was so blinding that Kathleen put her hands to her eyes. The sergeant said good-bye to her then, and she walked across the parade ground by herself. An hour earlier, she had walked in the other direction, a widow in mourning. Here she was now, facing marriage to another man, one she barely knew, and someone she and Johnny used to chuckle about in private.

Sergeant Oleson stopped by an hour later to drop off his clothes and tell her that they would be married that evening after Retreat. E Company had a Baptist minister serving in the ranks who would perform the ceremony. *Mother of God*, Kathleen said to herself after Gunnar left. *A Baptist minister. What would Mother say if she knew?*

She went through the motions of straightening her quarters. She knew she had to clear out Johnny's things to make room for the sergeant, but she didn't know where to put them. Instead, she looked at the pile Oleson had left near the door. He had books, but they were all in Swedish, except for the dictionary. She opened it and started reading.

It was a thick dictionary, underlined and well-thumbed. If she rationed herself to a few pages a day, it might be almost two months before she had to go back to *The Talisman* again.

She slammed the book shut and got up. Something had to be done about Johnny's clothes. She had a notion that one of his uniforms was fit only for the dustbin, but there were two others that ought to have some life in them yet. "Goodness, what am I thinking?" she whispered.

She would give them to Thomas Riley. He was showing through at the elbows and knees but still sent his pay and uniform allowance home to County Meath. His ankles were showing, too. Only an Irishman would ever grow taller on army grub. Tom Riley would take Johnny's old uniforms and thanks, too.

Kathleen found an empty box and dumped Johnny's clothes in it. She added a couple of handkerchiefs from the ironing basket and put

Johnny's boots in last. She carried the box to the door and pushed it against the wall. She was turning back to the kitchen when Peg Murphy knocked and opened the door. She just stood there, rubbing her hands together, until Kathleen spoke.

"It's all right, Peg. You don't have to say anything."

Peg put her hands on Kathleen's shoulders and gave her a shake. "Kathleen, do you have to be doing this thing?"

Kathleen clutched at Peg's hands that were rough from her eight-hour days of lye soap and scrubbing boards. Johnny never allowed Kathleen to wash and iron for the officers. He said he wanted her hands to be soft. Kathleen smiled as she looked at Peg. How kind Johnny was, but what she wouldn't give now for rough hands and a little money.

"Peg, I don't have a choice. It's either marry the sergeant or . . ." She couldn't bring herself to mention her humiliation with the captain. "Or spend the winter in a tent. I can't do it."

"But, Kate," the other woman pleaded, lowering her voice to a whisper, "he's not one of us, if you know my meaning."

"I know that," Kathleen whispered back, "but he can't be all that bad."

Peg pulled her hands away and took an agitated turn around the room. The smell of lye soap rose from her clothing. She stopped in front of Kathleen. "Kathleen, why not move in with me and mine?"

Kathleen shook her head. "You're a good woman and kind to think of it, but with five children and Peter in two rooms, where would you put me?"

Peg sighed and turned to go. "I suppose you have to do it, Kate, but I wish you had a choice."

There wasn't much time to put her quarters in order, but Kathleen sat down in her rocking chair. "I never have had a choice," she said out loud. "Not ever. I wouldn't know what to do with one."

There had been no reason to marry Johnny, except that she had finished five years of school, and her Da was looking on her either to leave home or start earning some money. Her older sister was out on the streets, and young Padraig already brought home half the winter's coal, pilfered from the train yards. She had looked for work, but nearly every business had a sign by the door, "No Irish Need Apply."

She met Johnny when she slipped on the icy steps in front of St. Ambrose after 6:30 Mass one morning and landed on him. He was short and handsome, with red hair and snapping green eyes. He wore the colors of the Irish Brigade, and after he helped her to her feet, he spent rather more time than necessary brushing the snow off his new uniform.

Kathleen smiled behind her mittens as she watched him. "Are you new to the army then?" she asked.

"Indeed, yes, miss," he answered, in as rich a brogue as she had ever been privileged to hear. Kathleen Fallon was a product of the New World herself, but she knew the ins and outs of the Irish, and she had the soldier placed somewhere near the source of the River Shannon, even before he told her which county.

They were married two weeks later. Kathleen didn't remember that he ever actually proposed, but she found herself kneeling with him in front of the priest and then emptying out her drawer at home. Her mother helped her, crying as she folded her other dress and nightgown and wrapped them in brown paper saved from the butcher's.

Kathleen lived out the war in City Point, Virginia. Johnny's commanding officer had been blistering angry when the two of them arrived. He whipped the private up and down with his tongue and, being Irish, too, made it a memorable event. Kathleen burst into tears when the man stopped to draw a breath. Being Irish, the officer paused and patted her on the shoulder, telling her to "be a good girl now," and find herself "some useful employment." The next morning she found a position with a tailor in City Point.

He set Kathleen to work making buttonholes; new shirts were always in demand. From somewhere, he had acquired bolts and bolts of black-and-white gingham. Kathleen came to hate the checks that looked so unappetizing in the early morning and began to smear in front of her eyes before the shop closed at six in the evening.

The buttonholes were better than her other task. The tailor had made some kind of arrangement with one of the army hospitals in the area, and, once a week, he gathered great bundles of dead men's shirts. It was Kathleen's job to go through the shirts, removing buttons. At first, she could barely bring herself to touch the shirts, so bloody and torn, but gradually, she set her mind to it. *I can always wash my hands*, she told herself again and again until the last shirt of the day was picked over. She remembered the great piles of shirts after Cold Harbor and dreamed she was buried under bloody shirts.

The war came to her in fits and starts. Johnny was with the quartermaster department. He would be gone; then he would return, smiling at her, but staring that long-range stare she recognized in the other soldiers that frequented the tailor's shop. She moved softly about their room, careful not to make any sudden noises.

Her most vivid recollection of the war came during the late winter of 1864, just before the coming of the new year. The weather was colder than anyone could remember. She had been standing first on one foot and then the other waiting for the tailor to arrive and open his shop, when an army ambulance came around the corner. The wagon was piled high with wounded, nothing new in itself, but the blood that must have been washing about inside the wagon had frozen into red icicles that hung down off the tailgate. Kathleen stared at the icicles until the ambulance was out of sight, then turned her face away and sobbed.

She sobbed again, sitting in her rocking chair. It was growing dark, and she knew she should light a lamp, but she didn't want to get up. It did her no good to think about those early years with Johnny, but she couldn't help herself.

After the war ended and Johnny was mustered out, they went back to her parents' flat and slept on the floor in the kitchen while Johnny looked for work. By the end of one week, he reached the conclusion that nobody was hiring the Irish and enlisted in the regular army. Kathleen only nodded and turned away when he told her. She knew it was coming, but there wasn't anything they could do about it.

They spent the next six months in a dugout at Fort Hays, Kansas, and that duty turned out to be their longest stay anywhere until Camp Halleck. Fort Hays was followed by Fort Larned, Fort Riley, Hays again, Fort Lyon, and back to Hays.

It was on the way to Fort Hays that she met Gunnar Oleson. He threw a bucket of water on her when her skirts swept too close to the cooking fire. She thanked him over and over, but he only shrugged and told her to be more careful. Kathleen would have liked to thank him better, but she didn't know how. He was so aloof. He kept to himself on the marches between garrisons, and she rarely saw him on post except during Guard Mount or Retreat.

"Is Sergeant Oleson really as slow as he seems, Johnny?" she asked her husband once.

"That he is not," Johnny answered promptly. "Remember when the captain went on furlough and we had only Lieutenant Mathers, and he fresh from the academy?"

She nodded. Who could forget Lieutenant Mathers at his first post? Or Viola Mathers, his new bride, who always looked like she had just been crying?

"Gunnar acts like he doesn't understand English when Mathers gives one of his blathering commands and then goes ahead and does as he pleases as soon as our lieutenant darling is out of sight."

"Is that wise?" Kathleen wanted to know.

Johnny rolled his eyes and whistled. "We'd all be dead four or five times over, if Sergeant Oleson let our boy wonder really command."

There was the matter of her china. During the rebellion, Kathleen had saved enough of her buttonhole money to buy a set of blue-and-white china that remained forever nestled in straw in a barrel. The china disappeared during a crossing of the Arkansas River one spring when the river was high and the transport wagon flipped over.

Kathleen had already crossed over, and when the wagon capsized, she ran along the bank, following her china as the barrel bobbed and dipped. Johnny had thrown up his hands in disgust and hollered at her to come back. He never could see the sense of hauling around china that was never unpacked.

She ran on down the river, and Sergeant Oleson followed her on horseback. The barrel smashed against an overhanging limb and the china tumbled into the water. Kathleen had her shoes off and, hands gripping the limb, was starting into the water when Gunnar waded his horse into the floodwater and managed to salvage one teacup.

"Sergeant, you shouldn't have gone to the trouble," Johnny insisted when Gunnar handed the cup to Kathleen.

He had said nothing to Johnny but looked at Kathleen. "My mother had a set like that once." That was all he said, even though he was soaking wet, and Johnny told her later that the sergeant couldn't swim. It irritated Johnny, but the first thing she always put in place after a change of quarters was that teacup.

Thinking about the china made Kathleen cry again. Her eyes were beginning to ache from all her tears, and she rubbed them gently with the corner of her apron. "I must do something," she said out loud, as she continued to sit in the rocking chair. She finally got up to heat some water to do the dishes, but the only dishes were the cup and saucer ready since last night for Johnny's tea. She realized as she took the water off the stove that she hadn't eaten anything since last night and then only a piece of bread with the last of the bacon drippings on it.

Why don't I feel hungry? She swished a cloth around the cup and saucer and set them back on the shelf still dripping. She watched them drip onto the floor, too tired to lift a dishtowel. *I just feel numb*, she thought, and sat back down in her chair. She wondered when the feeling would wear off, then wondered if she wanted it to.

She was married in the front room an hour later after Retreat. The E Company private who claimed to be a Baptist preacher performed the ceremony. Kathleen didn't doubt him. She knew at least two lawyers and a schoolteacher serving in the ranks, one driven to enlist by a sharp-tongued wife and another on a drunken dare. To her way of thinking, the ceremony didn't sound legal without any Latin or candles. The witnesses were a sergeant from the quartermaster department, also a Swede, and the fort's ordnance sergeant, a Dane. Oleson had no ring, so she just kept Johnny's on.

The ceremony was mercifully short. She was embarrassed that she had nothing to offer the minister and the witnesses afterward, but the other Swedish sergeant pulled a bottle of something labeled Aquavit out of his overcoat. She went into the kitchen for cups. There weren't enough to go around, so she and Gunnar Oleson shared one. The liquor made her eyes water, so after a sip, she left the rest to her new husband, who downed it in one swallow and held out the cup for more.

It was beyond her how any civilized person could drink that stuff, but, at the same time, she wanted to clear out the room, kick off her shoes and sit down at the table with that bottle. She had never been drunk before in her life, but she wanted to drink until she couldn't remember anything. She wished the men would leave, but then the thought of being alone with Sergeant Oleson made her eyes water again. She sat in her chair and watched the soldiers.

They stood around the table drinking. There was none of the laughter and joking she remembered when Johnny and his cronies sat down with a bottle. These men drank purposefully, almost thoughtfully, with a determination that was not Irish. When they began to speak in Swedish, she closed her eyes. She was alone in a roomful of strangers. She thought about Peg Murphy next door and wished she had moved in there, after all. It was too late now; she had given her word to the Baptist minister that she would love, honor, and obey the stranger who stood up next to her.

When the bottle was empty, the other men left, saying their goodbyes to Gunnar and nodding to her as she sat gently rocking in her chair. A blast of cold air blew in when they opened the door, and Kathleen saw over Gunnar's shoulder that it was snowing again. She sighed, feeling more tired than ever before in her life.

Gunnar closed and bolted the door. He went to the window and stuffed the cracks tighter with the bits of rag. He came closer to her, and she felt herself leaning back in her chair. *I think I'll scream if he touches me,* she thought.

He didn't. He went into the bedroom and lit the lamp. Kathleen heard him putting his gear in the drawer she had emptied that afternoon. She heard him take his boots off, grunting like Johnny as he tugged on them. He came back into the front room with his books and lined them up on the shelf by the potbelly stove. The blue-and-white teacup caught his eye. He picked it up, turning it over in his hands before he set it back on the shelf. He unbuttoned his uniform blouse and stood by the stove, looking at her. She gazed back at him, weary beyond words.

"I paid the captain his $16.32," he said, unbuckling his belt.

"Thank you," she replied, wondering what on earth had possessed her to sell herself for $16.32. She thought about Captain Melbourne then, and her face felt warm.

The sergeant went past her into the bedroom. She heard him rummaging around, hanging up his uniform on the hook that had held Johnny's uniform a couple of hours earlier. The bed creaked.

She sat in the front room until the last bit of warmth was gone from the stove. She shivered and went into the bedroom. Gunnar lay in bed, looking at the ceiling as if there was something written on it. She got her nightgown out from under her pillow, wondering as she did so how Gunnar knew which side of the bed was his. Men must have an instinct, she decided.

Kathleen carried her nightgown into the lean-to and took off her clothes. The wind threw itself against the shutters, and the cold seemed to come driving up out of the floor. She stood on one bare foot and then the other, trying to decide what to do next. It was too cold to be anywhere but in bed. She heard the snow brushing against the walls. She blew on her hands and stuck them under her armpits.

The floor defeated her. She was too cold to stand there any longer, so she went back into the bedroom. She went in slowly, cautiously, hoping that Gunnar might have fallen asleep. He still lay there in the same position, his eyes closed. He opened them when he heard her and flipped back the blankets on her side of the bed.

Kathleen blew out the lamp and sat down on the bed, tucking her nightgown tight around her legs before she lay down. She pulled the blanket up high around her chin and waited.

"I do not know what you are thinking, Kate," Gunnar said. He reached out and touched her hair, winding the curls by her ears around his finger.

She didn't say anything. She felt dizzy and wanted to sit up, but she was afraid to move.

"I . . . I . . . do not know what to say, either," he continued. His fingers left her hair and traced the line of her jaw. "I do not know what else to do, so forgive me."

He reached for her then. She knew that he would, but some part of her brain hoped that he might leave her alone for a few nights or at least until she got used to the idea that Johnny was gone. As Gunnar pressed closer, then jerked up her nightgown, Kathleen remembered that Johnny had joked with her once about women being a commodity on the plains equaled only by fresh vegetables. Gunnar was a man starved, and she was not surprised by the ferocity of his lovemaking. She kept her eyes closed tight and gulped back her tears until she was lightheaded and the room was spinning around. He was heavier than Johnny.

When he finished, Gunnar slept, and she dozed, her slumber disturbed by dreams. She could see her mother rocking back and forth, keening and wailing something about $16.32. Captain Melbourne walked through her dream, his hands in his pockets, winking at her. She dreamed that Johnny was sitting in his chair in the other room, his hands still knotted into cold fists. She sat up in bed, her hand to her mouth.

She looked over at Gunnar. He appeared to be staring at her, even as he snored. She looked closer. His eyes were half open, but he was asleep. "Mother of God!" she whispered, crossing herself. "What a strange man!" She tried not to stare at his half-open eyes, but her own glance kept coming back to his face, serene now in sleep. His skin looked so smooth. She remembered that during the summer, his nose peeled from June to September. The other troopers tanned and blackened in the Nevada sun, but Sergeant Oleson started red and remained that way until the first frost. A curious man.

Kathleen lay back down and pulled herself over to the far side of the bed. She stayed there a few minutes, but the mattress slanted toward the middle, and she slid toward her husband. He moved in his sleep, and she slid closer until she was tucked against his chest, lured there by his warmth, and worn out by her own wakefulness.

He woke her toward morning, but he was gentler this time. When he finished, he kissed her hair, sighed, and returned to sleep. She lay awake until Reveille.

They didn't say much to each other over breakfast. She was too embarrassed, and Gunnar didn't seem inclined to talk. He made a face when she poured him a cup of tea. "Have you no coffee?" he asked, after one sip.

"No. Johnny never . . . I mean . . . we didn't." She stopped in confusion.

"Never mind, Kate," he said at last, pushing away the cup and standing up. "I will get some from supply today." He left then, shrugging into his overcoat and turning the collar up around his ears. He smiled at her, and then was gone in a swirl of snowflakes.

She sat in her rocking chair half the morning, listening to the children in the quarters next door. She got up from her chair to put another chunk of wood in the stove, then made her bed. She found one of Johnny's stray socks under his side of the bed and stuffed it in the crack of the shutters. Kathleen straightened up Gunnar's extra uniform on the hook by the bed, fingering his sergeant's stripes. Johnny made sergeant once during the war but lost his stripes when he went on a three-day spree to celebrate his promotion. She didn't know Gunnar well, but Kathleen knew he would never do anything like that. He was the kind of man who saved his money and probably only drank on special occasions, like weddings. She moved away from the uniform.

"You did say I could leave in the spring, with half your savings," she said out loud. It wouldn't take much to start a dressmaking shop somewhere with half of Gunnar's money. She would need a room, a dressmaker's dummy, and a sewing machine. She already had a wicked pair of shears that she hid from Johnny, so he wouldn't be tempted to use them to cut paper or tin. Maybe in her shop there would be enough work to hire someone to do buttonholes. She knew she didn't want to go back to New York City, but St. Louis would do. As long as people wore clothes, there would be business, and she would get along.

Supper that night was much like breakfast. She stayed in the kitchen as long as she could and boiled the coffee to death that Gunnar brought her. He didn't say anything about the coffee, although he took one sip and eyed the cup thoughtfully as she watched him.

"I'll show you how in the morning, Kate," he said at last, and that was all he said until the bugler blew Extinguish Lights. For the whole evening, except when he went to the barracks for roll call, he sat in the chair reading one of his books. Kathleen thought she would scream from the silence of that evening, remembering Johnny's constant patter of profundities and inanities that were so much fun. She sat in her rocking chair and felt herself covered with wave after wave of shyness. She rocked and watched the sergeant sitting there but still found herself listening for Johnny's footsteps, even though she knew he was lying in a coffin, padlocked in a shed. A great, gasping sob escaped her. She tried to turn it into a cough, but Gunnar closed his book and looked at her.

She wanted to scream, "I just don't know you, sergeant." It was snowing as always, and she had nowhere to go, so she stayed in her chair, silently rocking. Her throat ached with the effort of holding back tears, and her head started to pound.

He made love to her again after the lights were out. In the great depths of her misery, she cooperated with him this time. To her vast embarrassment, she climaxed even before he did. *What must he think of me,* she thought in agony, even as she enjoyed the relief and the good feeling of him, a more substantial man than Johnny.

Breakfast was less of an ordeal. Gunnar made the coffee, measuring it with a precision that was new to her. "You see, it has to be just right," he told her, pouring in a precise amount of water and setting the pot on the stove.

She looked at him dubiously, and he smiled at her. "I have never been able to get good coffee anywhere," he said. "Surely a man is entitled to it in his own home."

She took the cornmeal mush off the stove and carried it to the table. They sat down to eat. "I would like it better with butter on it." It was the first thing Kathleen had said that morning, and she thought it sounded foolish.

To her relief, Gunnar nodded. "And I would like a bit of maple syrup and some milk."

They ate then, the subject exhausted. There would be enough uneaten mush to fry the leftovers for supper. With a little salt, it would be a break from everlasting beans. She had some white flour left. Perhaps she could borrow Mrs. Mathers' recipe for eggless cake. Suddenly it mattered to her that Gunnar should know she could cook. She wanted to ask him if he liked pound cake, but he was putting on his coat and then opening the door.

She made a trip that morning to the commissary storehouse to pick up supplies. The shelves were bare, except for beans, coffee, and hardtack. She leaned on the counter, thinking of whipped cream and omelets and baked apples with brown sugar melted in the cored center and oozing out.

While she stood there as the clerk filled her order, she heard someone whispering behind her back. She turned around. Two of the laundresses stood behind her, talking to each other and glancing her way. They made no effort to lower their voices when they noticed Kathleen watching them. She turned back to the counter when she heard one of them say, "Some people will do anything to hang onto their quarters," and the other one reply, "Yes, and they say the Irish can't live without it."

The troopers lounging against the wall laughed. Kathleen felt her legs turn to jelly, and she wanted to sink through the floor. She quickly stuffed beans and coffee in her basket, trying to ignore the laughter around her. When she turned to face the others again, the room seemed full of people, all of them staring at her. An officer's wife actually pulled her skirts back when Kathleen passed her.

I must not cry, she told herself. Her eyes were wet, and she could barely see the doorknob. She fumbled with it, tugging on the handle, until one of the privates opened it for her. "What'll you give me for that?" he whispered, his lips close to her ear. She gasped and fled the building to the sound of laughter.

She nearly bumped into Captain Melbourne, standing on the edge of the parade ground. His hands were shoved deep in his pockets as he watched D Company slip and slide through dismount drill in the snow. He tipped his hat to her. It was such an unnecessary, mocking gesture that the tears in her eyes spilled over, and she stood there in front of him, clutching her basket and crying.

"Come now, Mrs. . . . Oleson," he said, putting his hat back on. "Stay a bit and watch D Company. Take a good look. If something ever happens to Gunnar, there is one more sergeant and another corporal."

She ran across the parade ground. She knew she was making a spectacle of herself, her skirts flapping in the wind, her ankles showing, but all she could think of was to reach her quarters and slam the door on everyone at Camp Halleck. She ran inside and leaned against the door. The tears were frozen on her face, and all she felt now was terrible rage at Johnny. "How could you do this to me?" she said out loud.

There was no answer. She ran into her bedroom and knelt by the bed, sobbing. She finally looked up at Gunnar's uniform. "There is no power on earth that can keep me here after the stages are running, Sergeant Oleson," she vowed to the uniform. She lay down on the bed and cried herself to sleep.

The room was dark when Gunnar came in. Still foggy with sleep, she called out, "Johnny?" and sat up and brushed the hair from her eyes. Gunnar came into the bedroom, and she pulled her dress down around her ankles.

"I'm sorry, Kate. I did not mean to wake you."

"It's all right. I need to get supper anyway." She got up and tried to brush past him, but he took hold of her shoulder. His eyes were troubled, and she couldn't bear to look at him.

"I heard about what happened, Kate." The pressure of his hand on her shoulder was uncomfortable. "I talked to the troopers. Nothing like that will happen again. I cannot do anything about Captain Melbourne." His voice trailed away, and he went into the other room and sat down in Johnny's chair.

She went to the lean-to and stood in the doorway. "Don't worry about it, Gunnar," she said. "It'll only be until spring, anyway." Her words sounded so hateful that she almost choked. It was one thing to talk to Gunnar's uniform like that but quite another to say the words out loud. Gunnar was silent, with no change of expression beyond a slight frown. He picked up his pipe and stuck it in his mouth. Camp Halleck was out of tobacco, but he sat there with the pipe in his mouth until she said that supper was ready.

Gunnar avoided her eyes during dinner, and Kathleen knew she had to do something to help clear the air. "Tell me," she began, then stopped as he looked at her eagerly. She felt suddenly shy, but he was looking at her with such expectation that she went on. "Tell me something about yourself, sergeant . . . Gunnar."

He pushed back his plate. "I was born near Goteborg. My father was a tenant farmer." He smiled and leaned back in his chair. "He farmed down to the edge of the sea."

"Is he still alive?"

"Oh, no. He died when I was a child."

"Your mother?"

"She died a couple of years later. My two sisters went to live with an uncle. I was hired out to a farmer."

"How old were you?" she asked, leaning her elbows on the table.

"Eleven or twelve."

"That must have been difficult."

"It was," he agreed, fiddling with his fork. "I cried myself to sleep every night."

She cleared the table and started to lift the hot water off the stove. Gunnar got up quickly and took the kettle out of her hands, pouring the water into the basin. He sat down again. "After six years or so, I was due to be conscripted into the army. I did not want to go. No one lived very long in the army. I wrote an uncle in New York, and he sent me passage money here." Gunnar laughed as he got up and pulled the dishtowel off the rack. "I was so seasick. I am not a Viking, Kate."

"What did you do when you got here?"

He took a plate from her and dried it. "My uncle was out of work. He told me I ought to join the army. Said a man could learn English that way and maybe get out West some day. So, I joined the army." He set down the plate and picked up the other one. "I went a thousand miles to get out of joining the army, and that was the first thing I did when I got here. Strange, no?"

"When was this?" she asked. Gunnar did speak slowly, but there was a precision about him that she found appealing.

"During the war. I got as far west as Vicksburg." He perched on the edge of the table, still rubbing the plate. "I thought we were hungry in Sweden, Kate. When we lifted the siege at Vicksburg, those people were eating rats."

Kate took the plate out of his hands. He grinned at her. "Dry enough?" She smiled back and handed him the forks.

"After I learned English, I made sergeant; then the war ended, and we were transferred to Fort Hays. Was that when we met?"

She nodded, reminding herself that their acquaintance at least went back several years. She was through with the dishes, but she kept her hands in the water, enjoying the warmth. Gunnar hung up the dishtowel. He squeezed past her, putting his hands on her waist as he did so.

"Tell me about yourself, Kate," he asked, standing in the doorway.

"Not much to tell. I was raised in Five Points. Da is a hod carrier. I think they are still alive, although I have not heard from them in years." She took her hands out of the water and dried them, while Gunnar opened the back door and threw out the dishwater. "I am almost twenty-four, and I can't really think of anything else."

That wasn't true. There was much more, but it all involved Johnny, and she had hurt Gunnar's feelings enough for one evening. They both sat down in the front room, Gunnar with one of his Swedish books and Kathleen with *The Talisman*. Neither of them said anything, but it was a different kind of silence this time. Kathleen went to bed without a headache.

The winter was unlike anything Kathleen had ever known before. Snow fell almost every day, and the wind whipped it into fantastic shapes and surprises. One morning, they woke to find snow drifted over both company stables. Everyone, even women and children, turned out to dig through to the horses. Another morning, the ordnance storehouse was buried under the work of one night by the wind. The few families remaining in the tents were moved into the commissary storehouse. Kathleen didn't see them there, because Gunnar went for supplies when they ran short. She couldn't bring herself to face the people of Camp Halleck.

She turned to *The Talisman* more and more often as the cold roared down from the North. On days when it was too much to bear, Kathleen opened up the book and read over and over the chapters describing the heat of the desert that the Crusaders faced. She didn't feel any warmer as she followed along with each word, her lips moving, but only a reassurance that somewhere it was warm and it would be here again, too.

She was reading a chapter one morning when someone knocked. She opened the door on Captain Melbourne, who stepped in quickly and shut the door behind him. Kathleen was too surprised to do anything but stand there with the book in her hand. She tightened her grip on it.

"How kind of you to let me in," he said. His eye winked at her, and she drew in a deep breath.

"What can I help you with, sir?" she asked, hating herself because her voice trembled. She hoped he wouldn't notice.

"I'm going to all the quarters telling everyone to ration the fuel. You won't be issued any more until next month, so make do."

"Next month?" she repeated, thinking about the dwindling pile by the back door.

"That's it." He took off his gloves and slapped the snow out of them. "Don't look so chagrined, Mrs. Flaherty. Or is it Oleson now? Pardon me if I have trouble keeping track." He tipped his hat to her and left. Kathleen bolted the door after him, and, as she slammed the bolt in place, she hoped he heard it.

Gunnar greeted her news that evening with a nod. "I knew it was coming. We'll just have to manage," was all he said.

"But doesn't it make you mad?" she burst out. It amazed her that he could just sit there with a book in his hand and that unlit pipe in his mouth and not say anything more than, "We'll just have to manage."

He took the pipe out of his mouth. "What is the point? Can I change it by getting angry? Sometimes I wonder about the Irish." He put the pipe back in his mouth and opened his book again.

Kathleen wore both her dresses and two shawls from then on. Her fingers and toes burned and itched from chilblains, and her head ached from the cold. She found it harder and harder to sit still at night in their cold front room. She unraveled an old sweater of Johnny's, but her fingers were too stiff and painful to knit anything else.

She spent most of one evening in front of the potbellied stove, warming herself until her hands ached. The stove gave off a feeble heat. She probably could have sat on it, and the warmth wouldn't have penetrated her skirts.

She ran her hands along Gunnar's books on the shelf by the stove, then pulled out one book and opened it. The book was illustrated with woodcuts of demons and strange-looking little men with large heads and beards. She turned the pages slowly, running her fingers over the illustrations. Kathleen looked hard at the words with their strange dots and slashes through some of the letters, as if by staring at them she could transform them into English.

"What is this?" she asked her husband. The room was so cold that her breath came out in puffs.

He came over to her, taking the book from her hands. "*Eventyr*," he said, "a translation from the Danish."

"But what about it?" she persisted.

"Fairytales," he answered, handing the book back. "Hans Christian Andersen," he said, as if that explained everything.

She ran her fingers over the woodcuts again. She noticed his eyes on her chilblains, and she quickly put her hands under the book.

He took her hand and turned it over. "You really cannot take the cold."

She shook her head. "Johnny said I never was much of a soldier's wife." She didn't know why she said that; it had nothing to do with chilblains. Gunnar would think her cruel to bring up Johnny for no reason. She tried to pull her hand away, but he covered it with both of his, as if to warm her fingers.

"I cannot see that it is right for anyone to have to live this way," he said finally. She didn't know what to say, so she was silent. "I think this must be the worst garrison in all the territories," he went on.

"You're probably right. I think I should be grateful that I cannot have children," she said. "It would be a hard thing."

He held onto her hand. "I do not think any woman would be grateful for that. Are you so sure?"

She blushed. "Well, Johnny always insisted it was my fault."

"How would he know?"

She laughed. "You know Johnny. He can . . . he could . . . be so Irish sure of a thing!"

He laughed, too, and took the book out of her hand. He sat down with it, crossed his legs, and started reading, forgetting her. She sat down again in her rocking chair. It felt good to talk about Johnny a little. She hoped Gunnar didn't mind. She wanted to keep talking, but he was absorbed in *Eventyr*, turning the pages slowly and then turning back to re-read something. Kathleen dozed in her chair, thinking of spring and her dress shop. The thoughts went hand in hand with each other now. It would have to be a warm place where snow never fell, and the wind never blew. Her fingers itched and burned, and she scratched them until they were raw.

The weather worsened as January came to an end. Gunnar spent more and more of his time in the barracks. He took several of his books with him, and Kathleen could picture him sitting there reading all day while she froze in their quarters. He would come back for dinner, sit a minute, then head for the barracks again.

She felt shy about asking him anything, but as she washed dishes one evening, he came into the kitchen and leaned against the doorsill, his hands in his pockets. "Do you have to go to the barracks tonight?" she asked, putting the plates on the shelf.

"I am sorry, but yes. I sit there and keep them from fighting. They will fight now over the smallest things." He paused. "I am tired of it, Kate."

"Well, spring is coming," she replied as she hung up the dishtowel.

He stood up straight and took his hands out of his pockets. "I meant what I said about the spring, Kate," he said quietly, then went into the front room, put on his overcoat, and left without another word.

Kathleen looked down at her hands. She hadn't meant to remind him of his promise. It was just that he looked so lonely standing there, and she thought spring might cheer him up. Tears came into her eyes, and for the first time in many weeks, they weren't for Johnny, but Gunnar.

She was finishing the breakfast dishes next morning, scraping the burned mush from the pot, when Mrs. Mathers stopped in for a moment. "Kate, I found some wool in the bottom of my trunk," she said and shook her head when Kathleen offered to take her snowy cloak. "No, no, I couldn't stay. I just came over to ask if you could drop by this afternoon and help me figure out what to do with it." She hurried out the door again after a quick look around and a flutter of her hand.

"It's like this, Kate," she confided as the two women stood together in the officer's cold quarters that afternoon. "If I don't do something different . . . if something doesn't happen . . . I think I'll go crazy."

The woman laughed as she said it, a tinkling ripple that sounded so out of place in a room with snow seeping in the cracks. Viola Mathers belonged in a warm, brightly lit ballroom, laughing and flirting as much as her husband would allow and wearing her shoes out dancing. But here she was, same as Kathleen, cold and getting colder every day.

The woman fingered the fabric, a tired-looking hunk of dark wool. "It's nothing I would ever dream of wearing back in Newport, and the pattern is outmoded." She sighed and handed the material to Kathleen, who smoothed it and folded it over her arm. "I have to have something. You understand, don't you? There has to be something."

Kathleen understood. As she listened to Mrs. Mathers and thought of her darling china on the bottom of the Arkansas River, she helped Viola Mathers cut out the fabric, her knees cold on the floor. They spent the afternoon pinning the cloth and basting it. Kathleen's chilblains throbbed so much that she could hardly hold a needle, but Mrs. Mathers' chatter and the chance to be doing something besides rocking in her chair and dreaming about a dress shop diverted her.

She walked back to her quarters as the shadows lengthened over the camp. She sniffed the air for some sign of warmth, some indication that February would yield to March, but the cold roared down from those regions inhabited by the trolls and goblins of Gunnar's fairytale book. She put her hands to her face, trying to keep the snow from biting into her cheeks. The buildings were barely distinguishable in the white drifts, until she couldn't even see the storeroom that held her husband in his cracker-box coffin. They were all gripped and held by the same cold that embraced Johnny. She stood still. He hadn't been dead much more than six weeks, and she was having trouble remembering just what he looked like.

She glanced back at Mrs. Mathers' quarters. Wouldn't Viola Mathers be shocked to hear that? The woman had chattered on half the afternoon about her lieutenant, how the sun rose and set in his eyes. "I could never love another," she had declared to her as Kathleen knelt on the floor over the material, pins in her mouth. She had stopped and put her hand to her face, her eyes wide. "Oh, I'm so sorry, Kate. I didn't think."

Kathleen had taken the pins from her mouth. "Don't worry. I can't pretend that I love Gunnar Oleson."

Mrs. Mathers twisted a button on her dress, the gesture almost child-like. "Oh, you do understand, don't you, Kate? Johnny will always be first in your thoughts, won't he?" It seemed a heartless question, but Mrs. Mathers appeared so intent upon agreement that Kathleen could only nod.

I wonder if that is really so, she asked herself as she walked home. She remembered the young widows who came to the hospitals around City Point to claim the bodies of their husbands, women younger than herself already garbed in black, their faces white and shining, as if martyrdom was its own fulfillment. She thought again of those shirts she worked over in the tailor shop, a dead man for every shirt. A wife or mother for every dead man, women who for years and years would sigh and pine over loved ones. They would become old women, mourning men who were young men still. Life would pass them by as surely as if they were doing penance for having loved at all. Kathleen could not think it was fair.

When Gunnar came home, she wanted to run to him and tell him about those bloody shirts at City Point and about the young widows and about Mrs. Mathers and her only love. The thoughts were all jumbled in her head. She was afraid she wouldn't be able to say what she wanted, so he could understand her; so she said nothing.

Gunnar ate quickly while she toyed with her beans. "I want an egg," she declared suddenly.

Gunnar smiled and put another pinch of salt on his beans. "And I would like an apple, one of those small ones with the snappy taste. The kind that makes your throat hurt a little."

"Macintosh," she said automatically. "I would take out the egg before it was quite boiled, sprinkle a bit of salt on it, and maybe some butter, if there were any to be had."

"Eat your beans, Kate."

While she was finishing dinner, he put on his overcoat and rubbed his hands, murmuring something about monthly reports due soon. Kathleen dumped out the rest of her beans and wondered about the wisdom of an army that insisted on reports when nothing could get through to regimental headquarters, written with ink frozen in the bottle. Johnny always used to laugh at army regulations, while Gunnar took them so seriously.

After Gunnar left, Kathleen got into her nightgown and went to bed, pulling the covers up high and knotting herself into a ball. Sitting in the front room only wasted fuel, and this way she might be able to dream about her dress shop in Florida, or maybe Alabama, where it never snowed, and the sun shone all year around. She listened as the wind wailed and keened overhead, like a banshee warning of death. She thought of the coffin in the storeroom and shut her eyes tight.

The wind picked up as it pried into all the little cracks and holes on the roof, seeking a way inside. She sat up in bed and listened; it wasn't her imagination—the roof was coming off. Kathleen scrambled over the end of the bed, bumping into the bureau as she ran from the room. She stood in the doorway between the front room and the lean-to, her hands over her ears, as the wind lifted the roof off the whole row of quarters. She stood there as the beams fell through the ceiling, one crashing through the rocking chair where she usually sat each evening. The wind and cold rushed in, and she started to shake.

Above the wind she could hear Peg Murphy's children screaming in the other quarters. The sound forced her into motion. She picked her way back through the debris to her bedroom, where she jerked Gunnar's uniforms off the hooks and rolled them into a ball. Uniforms were hard to come by and couldn't be left there to the snow. She threw on both dresses over her nightgown, stuffed her feet into her shoes, and picked up the uniform bundle. She paused long enough to rescue her teacup, miraculously untouched, and add Gunnar's books to the bundle. The back door was stuck as usual, so she negotiated her way through the rubble and ran out the front, after carefully closing the door behind her.

The Murphy children wandered about crying. Two of the older children had scratches and bumps rising, and the two toddlers were howling until Kathleen thought her head would burst. The baby still sat in his highchair, a finger in his mouth, regarding all of them with wide eyes.

Someone in the quarters beyond the Murphys' must have gone for help, because the rooms were soon full of soldiers, everyone talking at once. Captain Melbourne stood there swearing. Kathleen clapped her hands over the nearest Murphy child's ears and looked around for Gunnar. When the captain was silent, she took her hands off the child and went back to her own quarters. The door was open, so she went inside.

Gunnar stood with his back to her in the front room. He must have just got there, because he was jerking boards and pieces of ceiling away from the area where she usually sat, and calling her name in a voice she was unfamiliar with.

"I'm here, Gunnar," she called. He couldn't hear her over the wind, so she shouted it again. He turned around and stumbled over to her, grabbing her shoulders, and then pulling her close to him. "I saved your uniforms," she said, "and your books. They're at the Murphys." Still he clung to her.

He loosened his grip enough to pull away and look at her. "You are all right? Nothing broken?" he managed to say.

She shook her head. "I heard it coming, so I ran out."

He put his arm around her, and they walked next door. She picked up his uniforms, and he carried two of the smaller Murphy children to the barracks. Peg Murphy cried and carried on because one of the beams had smashed her laundry tub. She mourned as for a dead one, carrying the baby on her hip. Kathleen finally took the baby from her, tucked him into Gunnar's uniform bundle, and followed her husband to the barracks.

They spent the night there, crowded into one bunk, listening to Peg Murphy wail over her washtub. When Peg moaned for the hundredth time, "Mother of God, me washtub," Gunnar started to shake.

Kathleen poked him. "Don't you dare laugh," she warned him, then covered her mouth with the blanket and laughed under the covers. She has almost recovered when Gunnar started up again, and she giggled along with him.

"Kate, promise me you will never carry on over so small a thing."

"I promise," she answered, drowsy and almost asleep. Gunnar ran his hand over her hip as she lay sandwiched against him, and the feeling was agreeable. She slept.

All the men who were not on sick list were detailed in the morning to find the roof. It had blown over against E Company's stables and reposed there, upside down, in hunks and handfuls. The men worked all morning, hauling the boards back to the row of quarters, and then came back to the barracks at noon, rubbing their hands and stomping the snow off their boots.

"Nothing in our quarters will blow away," Gunnar declared to Kathleen, who sat holding Peg's two-year-old.

"And why?"

"The rooms are full of snow. I dug around until I found that book you like so much. Sorry to say it is wet and torn."

"No matter. I was tired of it anyway."

He took the sleeping child and laid her down on the bunk next to theirs. She stirred in her sleep and shivered, so Gunnar covered her with one of his extra uniforms. He turned around to Kathleen. "What are you thinking, Kate?" he asked.

"Just that I wish spring would come."

He was silent. He pulled on his gloves again and shrugged into his overcoat. Kathleen watched him. His ears were red, and she wished he didn't have to go out again.

"It will come. It will come," he said. He looked around the cold, crowded room, smelly with wet wool and dirty diapers, noisy with children and babies. "I do not think there is much here for you."

He left then. Kathleen sat down on the bunk and rested her head in her hands. She had done it again. She hadn't meant to hurt Gunnar by reminding him of spring and his promise over a dead man, but so far, it had been such a terrible winter. She longed for spring, yearned for the time when she could fling open the window and see the ground again, smell the grass, watch the birds build nests in the overhang of the roof. Yes, the stage would be running, and she could leave, but that hadn't been her first thought.

And because it wasn't, she wanted to cry. She wanted to find a quiet corner, sit there by herself, and think. She looked around, but the spaces were all filled with dispossessed families and fretful children. The soldiers on sick list sat together playing cards, the children ran around bumping into things and getting sworn at, and the women had their heads together. She was by herself, not part of any group.

Gunnar looked so cold and tired that evening. He moved slowly and made a face when he took off his coat. Kathleen wanted to help him with his boots, but Peg Murphy needed her with the children. By the time she was free of them, Gunnar was already asleep.

The snow never let up all week, but by the end of it, the roof was back in place, patched in spots with boards from hardtack boxes and anchored this time with poles scrounged from somewhere. Kathleen stood outside the door to their quarters, looked at the roof, and then at Gunnar. "Maybe we need a bottle of champagne to christen the place. Or would it sink?" she asked. She didn't expect Gunnar to laugh like Johnny would have, but she was pleased to see him smile.

To her amazement, he picked her up and carried her into their quarters. He set her down inside on a mound of snow, kissed her for the first time, and handed her a shovel. "Welcome home," he said.

They spent all day shoveling out their rooms. *The Talisman* was excavated, mourned over briefly, and tossed aside, along with the remains of her rocking chair, the splintered bureau, and the table and stools.

All that remained were Johnny's chair and the bed. Gunnar scavenged some empty hardtack boxes from supply for their clothes, and Kathleen begged the loan of Mrs. Mathers' china barrel. She covered it with her only other tablecloth, the one that hadn't been torn by the falling timber. The checked cloth looked foolish on the china barrel, but she had nothing else. She was afraid to put her teacup in the front room again, so she cleared a spot for it on the shelf in the kitchen.

"We're down to scratch," she told Gunnar, as he sat in their remaining chair. It mystified her how he could be so calm about the whole turn of events. Johnny would have been raving and cursing the very roof. Gunnar just sat there reading a scrap of old newspaper he had pulled from Mrs. Mathers' china barrel.

He looked up from his piece of paper. "Did you know, Kate, that Lee surrendered to Grant at Appomattox Courthouse?"

She entered into the fun of it, leaning over his shoulder and reading the scrap in his hand. "And only last week," she teased. She wanted to put her hand on his shoulder, but she went back to the kitchen and finished dinner while Gunnar read the other side of the scrap out loud, and then pulled up two hardtack boxes to sit on.

"The only thing we need now is a cholera epidemic," her husband said before he blew out the candle in their bedroom that night. They lay close together for warmth, listening to the Murphys' quarreling and the wind circling the quarters. "I do not think I could have . . . what is the word . . . tolerated . . . Peg Murphy one more night in the barracks," Gunnar murmured as he rubbed Kathleen's back.

"She's only Irish," Kathleen said. Johnny had never rubbed her back. When Gunnar finally stopped and turned her over, she was smiling in the dark.

Gunnar was up and out before she woke up the next morning. She wanted to stay in bed and read, but *The Talisman* was gone, and she was weary of Gunnar's dictionary. She rolled over to go back to sleep, then remembered she had promised Mrs. Mathers that she would get back to the dress. Viola Mathers had come over to the barracks several times while they were crowded in there, urging Kathleen to come and sew on the dress.

"It will give you a chance to think about something besides Johnny," Mrs. Mathers had encouraged, looking around her at the crowded barracks with disbelief in her eyes that anyone could live like that. Of course, Kathleen hadn't thought much about Johnny until Mrs. Mathers mentioned him. She had been too busy trying to keep the children out of the soldiers' way and worrying about Gunnar getting frostbite to think about Johnny.

She thought about him now, in his jerry-built casket in the storeroom. She still found that she listened for his footsteps and waited for his laugh, always appealing to her. It was a habit of eight years not easily broken, even by death. But there was Gunnar now, sitting in Johnny's chair, sleeping in his bed. *It's almost as though the whole thing is temporary still, and I will wake up some morning and Johnny will be here*, she thought as she smoothed the blanket over her legs. *But what about Gunnar then?*

I don't have time to worry about it now, she thought. She made the bed, got dressed, and swept out the kitchen. The wind wasn't blowing yet, so she swept the dirt that had come in with the snow to the back door and tried to open it. She tugged on the handle. Nothing happened, so she braced her foot against the stove and pulled again. The door banged open and a body crashed onto her kitchen floor.

She screamed, leaped back, and ran into the front room, then peered around the corner into the lean-to again. The man was lying face down on her kitchen floor. She crept closer. He was a small man, stiff and covered with frost, with one long pigtail down his back.

Kathleen knelt on the floor by the body. Last August, she and Johnny had ridden the fifteen or so miles north to the Central Pacific construction site and spent the day watching the Chinese crews digging the grade and hauling dirt. So many of the little men had pigtails like this one. She wondered what he was doing so far from the railroad camp.

She hesitated a moment, then turned the body over. She screamed again, jumped up, and ran out the front door, not even bothering with a shawl. She didn't know where Gunnar was, so she ran to the admin building and burst into Captain Melbourne's office. He sat there with the other officers, tipped back in his chair and laughing about something when she threw open the door.

"Captain Melbourne," she gasped, leaning against the door. "There's a dead man in my kitchen . . . right on the floor . . . smallpox."

She stood there gasping for breath and shivering as the men looked at each other and back at her. Melbourne's chair hit the floor with a bang. "Come again?" he asked.

"I tried to open my back door . . . it always sticks . . . he fell in . . . it's one of those Chinamen, I just know it. He's all covered with red marks."

Still the men just sat there. "Won't you do something?" she pleaded.

Melbourne told her to sit down, and he and the post surgeon bundled up and went to her quarters. He came back a few minutes later. Still wearing his overcoat, Captain Melbourne sat down heavily in his chair again.

"You know something, Kate?" he said, his eye winking at her. "You've got a dead Chink on your kitchen floor." He must have thought it funny, because he started to laugh. Then he stopped as suddenly as he started. "Oh, Lord, what'll we do?"

Kathleen didn't say anything. Melbourne's office was as cold as her room, and her teeth chattered. Melbourne looked at her, then took off his overcoat and put it around her shoulders. He sat on the edge of his desk but made no move to touch her.

"You've been vaccinated, Kate?" he asked.

"Last fall, when everyone else was."

"Well, good. The doctor said something about pouring carbolic acid all over the floor and sprinkling lime around. I expect you'll be all right. What about Gunnar?"

There was no mocking tone in his voice; he seemed genuinely concerned. Kathleen noticed that the lines around his eyes were deeper than she remembered and that there was gray hair at his temples that hadn't been there last fall.

She shook her head. "I don't know about Gunnar. I suppose he was vaccinated."

"Let's ask him." He hollered for his adjutant to fetch Sergeant Oleson. The two of them sat there in the office until Gunnar came in and saluted. "You hear what happened, sergeant?" the captain asked.

"Something about smallpox, sir." Gunnar leaned over Kathleen. "Are you all right?"

She nodded. She felt strange sitting there with the captain's coat around her, but she was too cold to take it off.

"Were you vaccinated last fall, sergeant?"

"No, I wasn't, sir. I had a cold then, and the surgeon told me to wait. We must have both forgotten."

Kathleen covered her face with her hands and burst into tears.

"Hush, Kate. You sound like Peg Murphy," Gunnar said to her. "What do we do now, captain?"

"Looks like you'd better get vaccinated right away, sergeant. I suggest that you spend the next couple of weeks in the barracks so we can be sure there's no contagion in your quarters."

Kathleen sniffed. Gunnar gave her his handkerchief, and she blew her nose. No one said anything until the post surgeon came back.

"I can't imagine how that man ended up here, unless someone from the Central Pacific dumped him nearby," the surgeon said, taking off his spectacles and wiping them. "Maybe his own people did it."

"We can take that up with the Central Pacific when the weather clears," Melbourne said. "Just write a detailed report."

The surgeon nodded and looked at Kathleen. "There's lime all over your kitchen floor now. Just leave it for the rest of the week, then sweep it up. Sergeant Oleson, you had better come with me."

They left. Kathleen stood up and took off Captain Melbourne's coat. She handed it to him. He tried to hand it back, but she shook her head.

"I can come by for it later," he insisted. "I hate the thought of you walking anywhere without a coat."

"You needn't worry. I'll be fine," she said hastily.

Captain Melbourne smiled at her. There was no unkindness in his face, and for first time in several years of knowing him, Kathleen smiled back.

He held the door open for her. "Just be sure to keep your doors bolted," he said and winked at her. "Can't trust a Chinaman."

She did laugh then and thanked him. She hurried across the parade ground, but she was reluctant to enter her quarters again. "Hasn't enough happened?" she asked out loud as she stood outside the front door, unwilling to go inside but too cold to stand there long.

At least the body was gone. Someone had bolted the back door, wet the kitchen down with carbolic acid, and sprinkled lime on the floor. The room smelled like all the hospitals at City Point rolled into one. Kathleen went into her bedroom and flopped down on the bed. "Johnny, what am I doing here?" she asked the ceiling.

The two weeks crawled by. Kathleen worked on Mrs. Mathers' dress and came to dread the woman's chatter. It seemed to Kathleen that Mrs. Mathers was determined that she think about Johnny.

"It's so sad that you don't have a picture of Johnny," she commented one day as she stood on a stool while Kathleen pinned the hem. She patted her locket. "I have a picture of my husband and a lock of his hair."

Kathleen wanted to say, "Yes, and your husband is so bald that you probably had to hunt all over his head to find it." Instead, she said, "Well, I don't think Gunnar would really enjoy that, do you?"

"Oh, Kate," Mrs. Mathers chided in that voice she probably reserved for her servants back home and other people's children. "Sergeant Oleson can't expect you to feel about him the way you feel about Johnny." She paused when Kathleen looked up at her and then turned around slowly. "I mean, everyone knows that a woman can only love once."

Kathleen jabbed a couple more pins in the hem of the skirt. She wanted to say something in defense of Gunnar, but Mrs. Mathers grabbed hold of her conversational peg and hung onto it, gently reminding Kathleen about her loyalty to Johnny's memory. True love, devotion, and duty rolled off Mrs. Mathers' tongue until Kathleen wanted to wrap her tape measure around the woman's throat.

Mrs. Mathers was almost through. As Kathleen helped her down from the stool, Viola Mathers delivered her final shot. Smoothing down her skirts, she fiddled with a loose thread and then looked at Kathleen. "After all, Kate, men are such beasts," she said, dismissing the whole sex and obviously relegating her lieutenant darling somewhere in that pile. "Especially those foreign ones! Sometimes I can't imagine what the country is coming to, letting them in. At least everyone knows that you didn't have a choice," she said. "Everyone knows it was either that or starve." She spoke slowly, as if relishing the idea.

"I really have to hurry off, Mrs. Mathers," Kathleen said as the woman opened her mouth to continue. "Let me take the dress and finish it later this evening." The hem might not be as even as she liked, but she didn't think she could endure one more minute listening to Mrs. Mathers carry on about her duty to Johnny.

Kathleen walked home quickly, determined to shut the door and have a good weep, but when she got there, she found that she couldn't cry. She couldn't decide if she wanted to cry for Johnny or Gunnar or for herself, so she tossed the unfinished dress in a corner, swept the lime out of her kitchen, and scrubbed everything until her fingers throbbed and her back ached.

She was sick of it all: Camp Halleck, winter, beans day after day, Gunnar sitting in the barracks, the coffin in the storeroom, Peg Murphy scolding through the wall, the children next door arguing and shrieking, the cold, her splintered furniture, her uncertain future. "Johnny, we could have gone on for years and years yet," she whispered to herself as she paced back and forth in front of the boarded window.

She didn't want to sleep that night, either, because when she slept lately, she dreamed. It was the same dream over and over. She would open the back door and Johnny would fall in, all covered with smallpox, even on his clothes. He would chase her around the room until Gunnar threw him out, and then he would circle their quarters, pounding on the doors and windows, calling her name.

She sat up in bed. She didn't remember going to sleep, and she was still in her dress, but it felt like morning. Someone was pounding on the door and calling her name. She went to the door. "Who's there?" she asked, half afraid of the answer, after her dream.

"Tom. Tom Riley."

She smoothed her hair down and opened the door. The morning sun on the snow made her squint. Tom stood there, holding a handful of paper. He came inside and closed the door behind him.

"And what do you have there, Tom?" she asked, craning her neck to look at the papers.

He handed them to her. "I'll not be knowing what it is, Kate, but Sergeant Oleson told me to give it to you."

She took the papers. They were covered with Gunnar's small, careful handwriting. *Eventyr* was written at the top of the first sheet, but everything else was in English, page after page. She sat down in Johnny's chair. Gunnar must have stayed up late night after night translating the book. No one had even done anything like that for her before. She held on tight to the paper.

"If that's all, I have to go," Tom said, touching his cap. He left then, and Kathleen scarcely realized it.

She got back into bed and spent the morning there, propped up on one elbow, reading the book her husband had translated for her. In the back of her orderly mind, she knew she should be rationing out each story, each page, as she had eked out everything else all winter, but she read all day. When darkness came, she threw caution to the winds and lit two candles. She fixed herself some leftover beans and cornbread, propped the pages in front of her on the china barrel, and started over again.

She went to sleep late again that night, tucking Gunnar's pillow against her back. The room was cold as usual, and the wind was blowing again, but it sounded different this time, as if coming from another direction.

The wind was still blowing when she woke up. She lay there in the dark, listening to it. The sound almost lulled her to sleep again, and then she heard an unfamiliar noise, one almost alien until she recognized dripping water. She listened to the drops falling off the roof, a smile on her face. Spring was coming.

Two days later, Gunnar was back. She was sweeping dirt out of the front door, and she saw him picking his way across the mud of the parade ground. She waved to him, and he waved back.

She made him take off his boots by the door, and then she retreated to the far side of the room, shy again. He came toward her in his stocking feet. "Well, what do you think, Kate?"

She put down her broom and kissed him, and he picked her up and sat her on his lap in Johnny's chair. She leaned against him.

Gunnar cleared her throat. "I hate to tell you this," he began.

"Tell me what?"

"The ground is soft."

"And?" She sat up suddenly. "Mother of God."

"They're burying him tomorrow."

She got up off his lap and went into the kitchen. Dinner was a silent affair, and they passed the evening on opposite sides of the room. When she finally went into the bedroom hours after Gunnar, his back was to her. She didn't think he was asleep, but he didn't say anything, so she was quiet on her side of the bed. He finally slept, but Kathleen lay awake all night, listening to the sentries call the hours all around the post.

She must have slept, because Gunnar was already gone in the morning. She dressed quickly, wishing she had something new to wear, something different from the two dresses she had worn, one on top of the other, all winter. Johnny deserved better than he was getting. She paused . . . or what he got. Her eyes filled with tears.

Gunnar came back for her at ten o'clock, and they walked to the cemetery. The ground was spongy and heavy with mud. She must have lost weight during the winter, because her dress dragged on the ground. The black dirt seeped up the material, and she felt heavier with each step.

Both companies were assembled for Johnny's burial, including everyone from the commanding officer to the laundresses. They were gathered together for the first time in months of snowy isolation, and they chatted and laughed, standing in little groups.

Peg Murphy and her husband were there with their five children, all of them still for once and quiet. Peg looked at her, then looked away. Mrs. Mathers leaned on her lieutenant's arm. She wore the new dress Kathleen had made for her. The black wool and her white face made Viola Mathers look like the woman in mourning.

Tom Riley stood by the grave holding a shovel and watching Kathleen, sympathy on his face. And there was Captain Melbourne, winking as always. He nodded to her and folded his arms across his chest, as if wanting to get this duty done as soon as decently possible.

Kathleen knew everyone was looking at her. Her face flamed, and she drew back, unwilling to go farther. *Whatever are they thinking,* she asked herself as she looked down at the cracker-box coffin strapped and ready to lower into the mud hole underneath.

The captain nodded to the adjutant, who told two of the troopers standing near to lower to coffin. Other soldiers tugged out the crosspieces holding up the casket, while the troopers pulled back on the straps. They started lowering the box.

Nothing happened. "Jesus, Mary, and Joseph," Kathleen whispered, clutching Gunnar. "Won't he be buried?"

The men put the boards back under the coffin. The adjutant leaned over the hole. "Well, hell's bells," he muttered, "Hole's not long enough, Captain."

Captain Melbourne sighed and shifted his weight. "Then dig away boys," he snapped. "Corporal Flaherty's waited long enough!"

Kathleen hung onto Gunnar's arm as the soldiers pried away at the mud, which came away with a sucking noise that made her jump. The men tried again. When the coffin was halfway down into the grave, the man at the head of the coffin dropped the ropes and the coffin tipped forward. Everyone could hear the corpse bashing against the flimsy boards. Mrs. Mathers shrieked. Kathleen wanted to sit down somewhere, but the ground was too muddy.

Tom jumped into the grave and shoveled away as the earth under it gave way under his and Johnny's weight. The coffin splashed to the bottom. Tom Riley climbed out of the grave, wiped off the shovel, and held it out to Kathleen. She backed away.

"The first shovel, Kate," he said.

"Oh, no, no," she pleaded, and then burst into tears. Tom turned away, but Gunnar took the shovel from him and started filling the grave. As the mud dropped on the coffin, Kathleen sobbed. She thought of her husband lying dead, and her tears were as fresh as if it had only been the night before that the three men had come to her door to tell her the news. She cried for all the things that were and all the things that weren't. When she could not cry any more, she fainted.

୧

When she woke up, it was dark, and she was lying in her own bed. Peg Murphy sat on the edge of the bed. When she saw that Kathleen was awake, she went to the door of the bedroom. Kathleen heard her whispering, and then the front door opened and closed. Gunnar came in and sat down on the bed.

"I'm sorry, Gunnar," she whispered.

He leaned forward to hear what she said, and even in the dim light, she saw how puffy his face was, if he had been crying, too. "No, I'm sorry, Kate," he told her. He took her hand and held it. "Captain Melbourne told me to tell you how sorry he is, too."

She tried to draw her hand away, but he wouldn't let go. "No, listen to me, Kate. We were all too hard on you." He stopped. Kathleen knew him well enough to know he would go on. She waited. "You're surrounded by lonely men, Kate. Captain Melbourne wanted you. I wanted you." He paused again. Kathleen could tell he was crying now, but she was too tired to comfort him. "We did not give you time."

He was silent then. He let go of her hand and went to the door, but he did not leave. "I should tell you one thing more."

Suddenly, she knew what it was, and she wished, for his sake, that she were strong enough to appreciate it. *I know what you are going to say*, she thought. *Oh, you are a dear man. How strange life is.*

"Kate, I must confess. I have been in love with you since I followed you along the river and saved that one teacup. God help me. Was this wrong?"

"No," she said.

He shook his head. "No, you're right, I shouldn't have said that. Forgive me, Kate."

But you don't understand, she thought, and tried to put her response into words. Exhaustion claimed her instead. She woke up several times during the night. She could see him sitting in Johnny's chair, his head propped up by his hand. She dreamed she went to him and told him not to cry, but slept again, serene in the knowledge that she could tell him in the morning what she meant.

Peg Murphy was back in the morning. Kathleen smelled tea brewing in the kitchen. She tried to sit up, but her head throbbed, and she felt sick to her stomach. Peg came into the bedroom.

"Are you feeling more yourself, then, Katie?" she asked. She straightened Kathleen's pillow and smoothed the hair back from her forehead. "I have a nice pot of tea for you, dearie."

"Gunnar doesn't like tea."

"My dear, he's gone."

"Gone."

"You didn't know? E Company left this morning to take those two soldiers who went mad this winter to asylum at Fort Leavenworth. They were short a sergeant, so Sergeant Oleson volunteered."

Kathleen turned her face to the wall.

Captain Melbourne visited her the next morning. She dragged a brush through her hair before she would let Peg show him in. Rather than sit on the bed, the captain pulled up a hardtack box. "You could use some furniture, Kate," he commented. "Maybe this'll help." He held out a wad of greenbacks.

Kathleen wouldn't take it. "What's that for?" she asked.

"Gunnar told me you were to have half his savings. He figures you'll be long gone before he gets back from Kansas. There's a stage due through here any time now. It's a pretty hefty wad, Kate." He looked down at the money in his hand. "You can leave, Kate, and I can't say I don't envy you. Wish I could leave here, too. It's been one hell of a winter."

When she refused to touch the money, he put it on the bed and left. Kathleen sipped the tea Peg brought in. She listened to the rain falling and hoped that Gunnar had remembered his slicker. She looked at the money on the bed. There was surely enough there and then some to start over again. She had dreamed of this all winter. Gunnar had left, Johnny was buried, and there was nothing to keep her at this most miserable of posts.

"Why don't I feel better?" she complained to Peg.

"You will, dearie, you will."

But she didn't. The next morning she felt worse. "Peg, I just know I'm going to throw up." She sat on the edge of the bed, her feet on the floor. "I'm so tired! All I've done lately, even before Johnny's burial, is sleep! Why should I be so tired?"

Peg laughed. "Meself, why, I've felt that way on five occasions." She straightened up the sheets, and then stared at Kathleen. " You don't suppose . . ."

"Suppose what?" Kathleen snapped, amazingly out of sorts. "All I know is that I feel dreadful, one of my husbands is dead, and the other one left me in a rare good humor—oh, what he said, Peg—and I really need a basin."

Peg continued to stare at her. Kathleen raised her head and frowned at her friend. "Whatever is possessing you, Peg Murphy?"

Peg asked her a couple of pertinent questions, and Kathleen tried to think back. "Well, I haven't ever really had to keep track now, have I? Oh, Peg, do you think?"

"Why not?" Peg answered. "I know Johnny always swore it was your fault, but what if he was wrong?"

Kathleen hurried from the bedroom, and just made it to the back door, which she flung open—thank goodness Gunnar had fixed the tightness of it—just in time to toss up her tea and toast. She didn't feel any better when she was done, but she sat on the kitchen floor and started to laugh. When she finally stopped, she leaned against the washstand and looked up at Peg, who was standing in the doorway, her hand on her hip.

"Peg, don't you see how funny this is?" she asked, wiping her mouth. "I finally have a choice, and then I'm back to no choice. I couldn't possibly leave now, could I?"

"Would you want to?" Peg asked, her voice quiet.

"No," she answered, just as softly.

Captain Melbourne was delighted when she told him. "If it's a boy, you'd better name him after me," he told her. No one else would have said such a thing, but the captain went on, his smile broad. "After all, if it hadn't been for me, you never would have married Sergeant Oleson, would you?"

Viola Mathers was disappointed. "Kate, I thought your heart was in the grave with Johnny," she scolded, her hands fluttering to her locket with her husband's sparse hair in it.

"Well, no, I suppose it isn't," Kathleen told her. "I learned something this winter. You're wrong about never loving again. I imagine even you could, Mrs. Mathers."

Viola Mathers sniffed.

Spring came like the resurrection to Camp Halleck. The cottonwood trees were bare one day and then covered with a cloud of little lime-colored leaves that deepened and spread out each day. The stream near the enlisted quarters broke free of its ice and sputtered and chuckled like eggs in a frying pan. Unaware, apparently, what a miserable garrison Halleck was, the birds returned. Kathleen woke each morning to the sound of meadowlarks flirting with each other.

The post surgeon told her that regular exercise would be a good thing, so Kathleen walked all over Camp Halleck, usually with one or two of Peg Murphy's brood tagging after. No matter where she walked, she always ended up by Johnny's grave. Someday, other companies would garrison Camp Halleck, and people would wonder who Corporal John Flaherty was. No matter. He was no one important in the vast scheme of things, but Kathleen Fallon had loved him for a time and would always remember him.

The first stage to St. Louis left one morning as she was coming back from a walk. Kathleen watched as the driver bucked the trunks to the top and strapped them down. Several of the officers' wives were leaving, Mrs. Mathers among them. Kathleen looked at her. *You've had a hard winter, Viola Mathers*, she thought to herself. *It was cold, the snow never stopped, the food was dull, there was a smallpox scare, some roofs caved in, some of the men died, others ran mad, no mail came through, you missed your family, and your complexion got pasty. When you get home to Newport, your mother will coddle you and your friends will tell you what a brave thing you are to follow your lieutenant to the ends of the earth.*

She smiled. Mrs. Mathers stood by the stage with the other wives who were leaving. It looked to Kathleen like the goodbyes had already been said. She knew how uncomfortable it could be between husband and wife when the goodbyes were over. The women stood close to each other, their shoulders touching, as if a glass wall had already dropped between them and their husbands.

That afternoon she took Gunnar's money back to the adjutant to put in the post safe. Peg Murphy had stuck the greenbacks Kathleen wouldn't touch in the blue-and-white teacup, and there the money had stayed for a month and more, poking over the rim of the cup like an evil presence. She wanted nothing to do with it.

Spring cleaning was accomplished in a couple of hours. She opened the shutters, washed the curtains, swept the floors and scrubbed them, and blacked the stove. Mrs. Mathers had reclaimed her china barrel before she left, so there was only Gunnar's chair and the hardtack boxes. Tom Riley made her a little table, after he promised her it would not be out of cracker boxes. Kathleen found the sweater she had unraveled and knit a seat and back for Gunnar's chair. That occupied an evening or two, and then she spent her time waiting.

And reading. Captain Melbourne received a whole set of the works of Dickens from his parents in Rhode Island, and Kathleen read each volume when he finished it. She sat in the chair and read until the nights were half over, reading with intensity, but always with an ear listening for the men to return.

E Company rode in the afternoon after she finished *Great Expectations*. Kathleen watched the men from her front window as they walked their mounts to the stable. The troopers were dirty and bearded, with a sameness about them in their shabby clothes and long hair.

Kathleen heated some water on the stove before she remembered that Gunnar had taken the last of the coffee with him when he left. *Well, it would be tea or nothing tonight.* When the kettle started to whistle, she took it off the stove and looked out the window for Gunnar. She could see him over by the barracks, but he made no move to look her way. Kathleen endured the rest of the afternoon, forcing herself to sit still. If Gunnar wanted to come, he would come.

Gunnar finally came in when she was fixing dinner. He stood in the doorway of the kitchen, leaning against the doorframe, before she realized he was there. She smelled him before she saw him.

"What took you so long?" she asked. The smell of beef stew mingled with horse, leather, and sweat was making her stomach churn again, just when Peg Murphy had assured her that she was over the worst of it. And here she was, her hair a mess.

He took his time answering. "I thought you would be gone," he said carefully, choosing his words with precision. "I did not want to come over to empty quarters."

She turned back to the stove, holding her nose. "Gunnar, will you please stir this?"

He took the spoon from her as she fled out the back. He followed her outside and watched, his eyes wide, the spoon still in his hand.

When she finished, she wiped her mouth on her apron, and then patted her hair. "Gunnar, Johnny was wrong."

He just stared at her. Then he smiled, his eyes light in his sunburned face. She would have to find some zinc ointment for his nose.

"Oh."

"That's all you can say?"

He handed back the spoon and touched her cheek. "Oh, let me do some ciphering, wife. I have maybe . . . six months to think up something to say. It may almost be enough time for a Swede."

"If it's a boy, he can be a sergeant someday like his father," Kathleen teased.

"Oh, no," Gunnar said firmly. "Not our son. I am in the army, and I am glad of it, but please to God he will have other choices."

She could think of nothing more eloquent to add. Gunnar looked around to make sure no one was watching and patted her apron where it was starting to ride up over her belly. "The stew is burning."

She hurried inside to stir the pot. He went inside to the front room where his saddlebags were lying beside his chair.

"I have something for you." He pulled an egg out of a dirty sock.

Kathleen dropped the spoon in the pot and reached for the egg. Her eyes misted over, and she couldn't trust herself to look at her husband. "Where did you find it?" she asked, her voice hushed as in church.

"I stole it." He laughed as he fished around for the spoon in the pot. "I liberated it from a hen that was living in an old box. No place to bring up children."

She turned the egg over in her hand, overwhelmed by what it really meant. "Gunnar, you didn't know I was going to be here when you returned, and still, you brought me an egg?"

"I guess I am a fool," he said, after careful thought.

Kathleen watched his face, and then looked away when she saw tears in his eyes. "You're no fool," she said quietly. She wiped off the egg and set it in the teacup on the shelf above the washstand. "I think I'll boil it."

"And then eat a little bit every day until it is gone?" he teased.

"Not this time. All at once. With a little salt. I'll share, too."

He shook his head. "I can wait."

"You've waited a long time, Gunnar."

He frowned, his face serious now. "You are not offended by what I told you before I left?"

She put her arms around his waist and pulled him close to her. "How could I ever be offended? How comforting to know that someone was always watching out for me."

He sighed and kissed her forehead with a loud smack. She let him go and turned back to the stew, pleased with herself. Gunnar went into the front room and pulled a newspaper from his saddlebag. "Here I have a newspaper. It is only one month old, so, tonight, we shall not read of Appomattox."

Kathleen grinned over the stew. She reached up and ran her finger over the egg, feeling the little bumps on the surface and savoring the homely brown of it.

"And Kate," he called from his chair, "we have orders to Fort Bowie."

"When do we leave?"

"Friday."

"What's it like there?"

"Probably worse than here."

She nodded and took the stew off the stove. "I suppose you and the post surgeon will be out chasing heathens when the baby comes."

"I imagine."

"There's no coffee, Gunnar."

"Today I drink tea, Kate, but only because I love you." He rustled the newspaper and settled deeper in his chair.

Kathleen came into the front room and wiped her hands on her apron. "I can't really say that I love you yet, Gunnar," she said slowly, "but I feel confident that I will." She smiled. "Maybe even in a week or less."

He grinned. "That will do for now, Kate."

"I wish you would call me Kathleen instead of Kate. I like it better."

"I will, then. While we are on that, my name is Gunnar, not gunner."

"Gunnar," she repeated, coming up behind him in his chair and leaning over it. He smiled back at her.

"Look, Kathleen, they say the Central Pacific and the Union Pacific will come together this spring. I think it happened last week. This is what I believe Captain Melbourne would call the hot poop, no?"

She laughed. "Yes, the rascal!" she said and leaned her arms on his shoulders. She kissed the top of his head, and together, they read the paper.

The Gift

❧ ❧

*I*t was really his lieutenant's fault that Captain Starbuck was feeling so out-to-pasture. He could tell that something was bothering Norton, and Starbuck hoped that when his lieutenant finally spilled the beans, he wouldn't have to launch into some kind of counseling he wasn't equipped for.

Norton finally came out with it after Guard Mount when the two of them were walking toward the post adjutant's office. The lieutenant pulled up sharp and turned a little, and Captain Starbuck was hard put not to trip over him. He lost his balance and nearly fell, but Norton reached out and grabbed him by the shoulders.

"God, I'm sorry, Captain."

Starbuck straightened up and hoped no one was watching. "It's all right, Lieutenant. It's nothing."

Norton rearranged some gravel with the toe of his boot and looked up at him. "Sir, my wife and I . . . we . . . well, we . . ."

Jerusalem Crickets, the captain thought. It had better not be marriage problems. If anyone was less able to render advice, he couldn't imagine who it would be. "Yes, Mr. Norton?" he prompted, wanting to get out of the cold and off his feet.

"Well, sir, we . . . wanted to ask you over for dinner tomorrow night," said the lieutenant in a burst of words.

Was that all? Norton has probably been giving himself piles over that all week, Starbuck thought as he grinned at the man. He wished Norton wouldn't be so nervous around him, and, at the same time, he wondered if he presented such a forbidding aspect that the man had no choice. *I was a second lieutenant once,* he thought. *God Almighty.* "I'd like that, Lieutenant. Tell Mrs. Norton I accept with pleasure."

He got his hair cut for the occasion. Winter was coming pretty fast at Fort Laramie, and he liked the warmth of the hair that was beginning to curl around the back of his neck, but he didn't think Mollie Norton would approve. He got O'Reilly to cut it for him that evening after the private had finished cleaning up in the company mess.

After retreat the next day, he hurried over to the post trader's store just as the man was starting to sweep out. He knew he ought to take along a present when he came to dinner, but he wasn't quite sure what to get. He watched the clerk dust the canned goods on the shelf behind the chewing tobacco, and then pointed to the last two cans of peaches. At $2.50 a can, he figured peaches would be a real treat in a second lieutenant's household that got by on $125 a month before expenses.

He arrived at seven o'clock and knocked on the door. Norton opened it. He was carrying his little son, and the baby's head was nestled down on his shoulder, his eyes closed. "Come in, Captain," the lieutenant whispered. "Please go in and have a seat while I put Jimmy down."

"Fine," Starbuck said softly. He looked around the parlor. There was a lady-sized rocker pulled up near the potbellied stove, a straight-backed chair, and a packing crate settee in one corner. The cushion was a bed sack covered with gingham, and the straw in it rustled as he sat down.

Mrs. Norton must have heard the crackle of the straw as he sat down because she came out of the lean-to kitchen, fluffing up her hair with one hand and removing her apron with the other.

He stood up and handed her the peaches. "The confectioner's was closed, and roses are out of season," he mumbled. It was probably the silliest thing he had ever said, but Mrs. Norton laughed and twinkled her eyes at him as she took the cans.

"Thank you, Captain. What a kind gesture."

He couldn't think of anything to say, so he just stood there smiling at her until his lieutenant came back into the room. Mollie Norton hurried into the kitchen again, murmuring something about potatoes in the oven.

Dinner was beans, same as he got nearly every night, but Mrs. Norton had added molasses and mustard to them, and they tasted like the beans he used to get at home on Orange Street before the war.

Baked potatoes and canned corn finished the dinner, and Mrs. Norton served raisin pie and coffee after she cleared off the table. The quartermaster had received an enormous shipment of raisins at the end of summer, and the fort was just starting to get out from under them. Starbuck had eaten raisins in every imaginable form and wasn't sure he was up to Mollie Norton's offering, but there she was, handing him a heaping slice and looking so proud about it. *I'm damned if I'll turn it down,* he thought, even though his stomach gasped and protested as he pushed down the pie.

They sat in the front room and talked about this and that. The Nortons had just returned from a trip to Salt Lake City, so they spent a pleasant evening making fun of the Mormons. Norton was just about to start on the latest rumor about Brigham Young when the clock on the whatnot shelf wheezed, then coughed out nine little chimes.

"I'd better be going." Starbuck shook Mrs. Norton's hand. She had a firm grip, and he looked down at her hand in his. It had been ages since he had seen a hand without calluses.

He said thank you and goodnight and started walking kitty-corner across the parade ground to his room in Old Bedlam. Halfway across, he turned around and looked at Norton's quarters, watching until the lights were out except in what must be the bedroom. He turned around again and kept walking. His foot was paining him something fierce, and he knew it would snow billy-be-damned pretty soon—maybe by morning.

So it was really Norton's fault that he was out of sorts. He lay awake a long time that night, staring up at the ceiling and listening to the officer in the other cot snore. He usually had the room to himself, but what with increased activity this winter to the north, any officers casually at post were usually bunked with him. He didn't mind, except when they snored. He was a light sleeper.

He finally sat up in bed around two o'clock and looked out at the parade ground through the wavy glass. It was snowing, sure enough, and as he watched the flakes drift down at first and then fall with increasing purpose, the raisins clogging up his stomach surged and rumbled. "Jerusalem Crickets," he said softly but with enough force that the window fogged. "I am a lonely little petunia."

Guard Mount the following morning was an unqualified success. In spite of the snow, or perhaps because of it, they had a record turnout among the civilian inmates of the post. The first snow of the season was still white on the ground. It hid the dirt and scars of the old fort and made the ugly buildings appear less daunting. Hoarfrost filigreed the cotton-woods by the river, and the branches sparkled like lace against the sky.

The usual onlookers were there, plus a few more—the post children, not yet confined to school, the sutler and his family, officers casually at post, scouts, some of the officers' wives, Mrs. Norton pushing Jimmy back and forth in his pram, and Laurie Moorcroft.

He knew her full name was Annie Laurie Moorcroft, and her father had named her that because he liked the song. Lieutenant Jensen told him a little about her once while they were idling away a few hours on patrol. Jensen had courted her steadily for going on six months, along with all the other unattached male bipeds on the post, so Starbuck learned quite a bit without ever having said much to her.

She wasn't beautiful. She wore gold-rimmed glasses that perched halfway down her longish nose. She had a funny habit of looking over the top of her glasses that Starbuck found pleasing in some whimsical way. The most important thing about her was that she was female and single, and, as the commanding officer observed more than once, the sap rises even on treeless plains.

Miss Moorcroft was on the short side. He had stood next to her at a hop once for half an hour without summoning the courage to say anything. He had noted that she came up to his shoulder, her eyes were blue, and she had a dimple in her right cheek. She flashed the dimple pretty regularly at Lieutenant Jensen, who was standing on her other side (when they weren't dancing) and not letting any grass grow under his feet.

Her figure was unremarkable, except that it was a woman's shape, and that fact alone made any other endorsement unnecessary. Starbuck decided that she was the kind of woman who would probably grow prettier and prettier the older she got and the more children she had. Some women were like that. On the other hand, Mollie Norton, the post beauty, had probably already peaked and was headed for decline any day now. Or so Starbuck reasoned.

Miss Moorcroft had come West about a year ago when her sister, who was married to Captain Bridges, had given birth to twins. As it had been impossible to procure a nanny or even a hired girl, Mrs. Bridges had turned to her younger sister.

Starbuck had seen other younger sisters on the plains. Even the homely ones were married off inside of a month or two, so he couldn't figure out Laurie Moorcroft. She danced from early evening to early morning at the hops and germans, she went riding and picnicking regularly, and Lieutenant Jensen even took her fishing. In fact, he said afterward that she was the first woman he had ever met who wasn't afraid to put a bug on a hook. She had escorts aplenty for every function, and Starbuck had it on good authority that, with a couple exceptions, all the single men in Companies D and F of the Fifth Infantry and E and F of his own Third Cavalry had proposed, and she had turned them all down.

And then there was Lieutenant Jensen. He had come aboard Company F of the Fifth six months ago and had pursued Laurie ever since. He hadn't proposed yet, but he confided to Starbuck one night that he was saving up the big moment for a really special occasion.

There was another side to Annie Laurie Moorcroft. A few weeks ago he had walked up to the post hospital to check on one of his men who had gone for a midnight lark in the Laramie and had nearly drowned. Laurie was sitting by the bed of one of the patients, taking down a letter he was dictating to her. She looked up when she heard his footsteps and smiled at him and then went on with her writing.

He made a remark to the post surgeon about her, and the doctor shook his head. "I'm of the opinion that most females are too delicate for nursing, but Miss Moorcroft is a hell of a useful lady." Starbuck was kind enough to overlook the wistful tone in the man's voice and keep to himself any comment that the surgeon's wife had chosen never to come West.

Captain Starbuck gave himself up for a hopeless case and resolved to attempt a little wooing. His first stab ever at courtship ended in such a disaster that he never tried again.

He was standing next to her at a hop not long after his hospital visit. He had done that on countless occasions, but this time he was determined to strike up a conversation. At least she would know that although he didn't dance, he did talk. He cleared his throat and opened his mouth to ask her something about the twins, when she turned to him and smiled.

"Captain Starbuck," she began, looking as if she wanted to make conversation too, "is it true that you saw action at Gettysburg?"

It was the wrong question. His mouth worked a couple times until he felt like a mullet, and he felt the sweat pop onto his forehead. He looked at her and was aghast at himself when he turned on his heel and walked away. He set his glass down by the punchbowl with such force that the contents sloshed all over his white gloves. The door was miles and miles away, but he kept walking until he got there and disappeared into the dark outside.

He had the dream again that night, where he was sitting up in the primary aid station behind Cemetery Hill, listening to the rebel bombardment. When the rounds started to drop among the wounded and dying, he leaped up and tried to drag a screaming soldier away from the makeshift hospital that was on fire now and turning into a bloody cesspool. The officer rooming with him shook him awake before he got to the worst part of the dream.

So much for his wooing. All this went through his mind as he stood by his company on the parade ground and watched Laurie Moorcroft out of the corner of his eye. After his company was dismissed, he started for the guardhouse to look in on one of his troopers when Lieutenant Jensen called to him. The officer was standing next to Miss Moorcroft, and Starbuck tried not to limp as he walked toward them.

"Captain Starbuck," the lieutenant began after saluting, "isn't part of the Third garrisoned in Louisiana?"

"Baton Rouge." *What the hell did Jensen care?*

"Sir, do you think you could get one of your friends there to send us some mistletoe?"

"Mistletoe?" He grinned in spite of himself and then colored up when he noticed that Miss Moorcroft was flashing her dimple at him.

"We thought we'd do the Christmas ball really proper this time, sir, with plum pudding, holly, a Yule log, and mistletoe."

He laughed out loud. "You have a holly source, Mr. Jensen?"

"My mother, sir. She said she'd send us a bunch when it starts looking shiny."

Mistletoe. He'd been posted in Louisiana himself on Reconstruction duty and remembered the great clumps of the stuff that grew as fungus in the live oak. He shifted his weight onto his good foot and glanced down at Miss Moorcroft. "I'll send off a telegram this afternoon. Allowing as it's only October, I can't imagine why it wouldn't get here in time."

"Thank you, captain," Laurie Moorcroft said. Her voice was soft and low, and Starbuck knew he could lie with his head in her lap and listen to her read the *Manual of Arms* and feel no pain. He recalled his only attempt at conversation with her, nodded to her, and continued to the guardhouse.

He got a reply a week later from Baton Rouge to the effect that the mistletoe was boxed and on its way to Dakota Territory. He didn't know where he got the courage, but he took the telegram over to the Bridges' quarters.

Miss Moorcroft answered the door. She was holding one of the twins, the baby turning in her arms to grab at her spectacles. Without thinking, Starbuck took her glasses off and held them out of the baby's reach.

She smiled at him, then handed him the baby as the child turned his attention to the hairpins holding her snood in place. The baby was easily distracted by his gilt uniform buttons, so he handed back her spectacles and watched her as she put them on, then patted the hairpins back in place. They stood there a moment looking at each other until Starbuck remembered why he had come. He gave her the telegram.

"It's a silly notion, Captain," she said after she read the telegram. "I expect you think we're foolish."

"Oh, no. No." Starbuck searched for something gallant to say, acutely aware that four years of rebellion had not included gallant school. He fingered the yellow curls of the twin he held. "It always seemed to me, Miss Moorcroft, that I'd rather kiss a girl for a good sandwich than a bunch of berries." He was amazed at his audacity, and for the first time, painfully aware how New England-twangy his voice was.

To his vast relief, she didn't seem surprised. She tilted her head to one side. "You sound a good deal like my father."

He couldn't think of a comment, so he took back the telegram, handed over the twin, and said good day. As he walked across the parade ground, he thought of a hundred interesting comments to make, a hundred witty comebacks. He figured he could out-Jensen Jensen, if he had enough time to ponder. But it didn't really matter. He had cooked his goose with Laurie Moorcroft that awful night she had asked him about Gettysburg.

He slowed his steps and asked himself for the millionth time why he couldn't get over the whole thing; other men did. *Hell, everyone did*, but here he was, still dreaming, still remembering, still hurting, still shivering himself awake on the hottest night. He knew it wasn't just his foot. He had adjusted pretty well to having no toes on his right foot. He only limped when he had to walk a long time or when he feared someone was watching him. The regimental ordnance sergeant had lost an arm at Iuka, and the man didn't let it slow him down. "Why can't I let it go?" he asked out loud.

He knew he was afraid to talk. His experience at Gettysburg wasn't that stuff that got tossed around during bull sessions, and he had a lingering fear he wouldn't be understood. The idea of baring his soul in mixed company was even more unthinkable. He could just see himself waltzing up to Major Denham's wife, or the commanding officer's lady and saying, "Wouldn't you like to hear a really horrible war story?"

You just didn't tell ladies things like that. Every man knew that they had more refined natures and needed to be sheltered from the realities of life. And so he suffered through the tales of the little drummer boy snatching up the battle flag and the brave boys in blue swarming over the barricades with no thought to their own safety. He wanted to shout, "If you men would admit what it was really like, we'd certainly live in a more honest world!" But real war was obviously a well-kept secret.

November came and went, and still no package arrived from Baton Rouge. Starbuck pestered the mail clerk in the post trader's store until the man threw up his hands whenever he saw him coming. He had occasion to be in Cheyenne for testimony in a court-martial at Fort Russell, and while he was there, he haunted the post office and train station, hoping for some word of the mistletoe. The agent at the depot even let him paw through a pile of packages where the parcels were torn or the address illegible, but there was nothing from Louisiana.

He wandered by a jewelry store across from the depot and spent an unreasonable amount of time admiring the rings and brooches. There was one pin, opals set with diamonds, that caught his fancy. He almost bought it, but he didn't have anyone to give it to.

When he got back to Fort Laramie, Christmas was only two weeks away. As soon as he tossed his saddlebags on his cot, the adjutant poked his head in the doorway and said that the commanding officer wanted to see him quick. Starbuck knew what was coming. It happened every year.

"Got some settlers crying about Lo up around Chalk Buttes. Mount up about half of your single men and take a look, Starbuck."

He was the only unmarried company commander, so every year he got stuck with the Christmas duty. In each of the six years since Appomattox, he had been out on the trail nosing around while the rest of the garrison celebrated the season with family. He'd gotten used to it, but this time he was irritated. Jensen had confided to him that Miss Moorcroft was going back to the States on the day after Christmas, and Starbuck had planned to attend the big shindig on Christmas Eve for a last glimpse.

Of course, Jensen also told him that he was going all out on this celebration and planned to pop the question on Christmas Eve during some lull in the festivities. The gleam in the lieutenant's eye told Starbuck the probable outcome.

He mounted up ten men, and they rode out of the fort going northeast, while the enlisted men's glee club practiced "Angels We Have Heard on High." They didn't spot a single Indian, which surprised none of them. The homesteaders, a stark-looking bunch, had been happy to see the troopers. They didn't hand out any open-arms welcome, but at least the company wasn't greeted with the usual suspicious looks. Funny thing about settlers: they would practically lock up their wives and daughters if you rode up with the troopers and wanted a little water. It was a different story when Lo the Red Man was in the vicinity. One settler's wife even went so far as to break out a fruitcake from home and give each of them a sliver. It tasted a little like Massachusetts.

They started back for the post at a smart pace. The wind was blowing at their backs, and Starbuck didn't feel adequate to first-aid any frostbite. Besides, if they hurried, they might get back in time for the party Christmas Eve.

December twenty-third found them about twenty miles from the fort. The wind had picked up some more, and snow was spitting around, so Captain Starbuck called a halt, and they bedded down in a ravine out of the breeze. He had the dream again that night.

It was the second day at Gettysburg, and it was hot on Culp's Hill. The Rebs had failed in their early morning attempt to gain the hill, and things were quieting down some when a gray artilleryman lobbed a cannonball his way. He watched it come, saw it arc in the sky, then roll down the offside of the hill, gathering speed as it came toward him.

He must have been awfully tired, because he stuck out his foot to keep the ball from rolling past him and into the head of a dead man lying behind him. The ball slammed into his foot and stopped. He didn't feel anything until later that night when he sat down and then couldn't get up again. One of his men helped him to the aid station near Meade's headquarters.

It was a pretty picayune wound, compared to what he saw littering the ground all around the surgeons. It was as if everyone in the world was bleeding at the same time, but eerily quiet, all the while. He tried to get up to return to his unit, but he fainted before he took two steps.

When he came to, he was lying on a cot. The steward asked him to please lie still, when he tried to get up again. He told the man to put somebody else on this thing who really needed to be there, but the man told him it was an officer's cot, so he'd better stay where he was. None of it made any sense, but he hadn't the energy to argue and lay back down. The cot was stiff with blood and scratchy and smelled like an officer with his bowels shot away had been its most recent occupant.

He dozed off and on all night, drifting to sleep and then jerking awake. The night was muggy, and the barn serving as a hospital glowed with lamplight. In his dream, the surgeons that walked up and down the rows of wounded men grew taller and taller and cast enormous shadows.

About morning, a surgeon finally took a look at his wound. The doctor was swaying on his feet, and his eyes were so bloodshot that Starbuck couldn't see any white to them. The man poked at Starbuck's mangled toes with crusty fingers, then nodded to a steward, who brought over a little saw. Before Starbuck even had time to brace himself, the surgeon lopped off his toes in an even row, tied a few knots, slapped on a tight bandage, and moved on to the next man.

He did say something to Starbuck over his shoulder. "You're a lucky son of a bitch, Major."

Starbuck was propped up on one elbow looking around for a water bucket when the artillery barrage began. The roar of more than one hundred field pieces going off at the same time blew out the few remaining windows in the farmhouse next to the barn and set the air humming. Starbuck thought they were safe enough behind the lines, but he sat up and swung his feet over the side of the cot. No sense in taking any chances.

The guns blasted again and again, and the balls started dropping like rain in the aid station. The Rebs had over-elevated their pieces and the projectiles sailed over the heads of the men fighting on the ridge and landed in the hospital.

The barn was on fire now and full of smoke, and men who shouldn't have been moving at all were running to escape. Starbuck got to his feet. He nearly tripped over a corporal from the Iron Brigade lying next to his cot on the ground. The man held up his hands to him, and Starbuck grabbed hold and started to drag him out of the barn.

He only managed a few feet when the guns went off again, and a Parrot shell landed right in the corporal's lap. This was the worst part of the dream and seemed to drag on for hours in slow motion. He kept tugging at the man's arms and listening to the sound of the body separating. Blood shot up in a cascade and covered him. As he staggered backward, still hanging on, he pulled the dripping half-man on top of him. That was where the dream always ended. Starbuck sat up in his bedroll and sobbed out loud.

His first sergeant stuck his head inside the tent. The man's eyes were bugging out and he crossed himself. "Jesus, Mary, and Joseph, Captain! Are you all right, sir?"

"Sure, Sergeant. Just a dream. Go back to sleep."

Starbuck wrapped his greatcoat around his shoulders and sat cross-legged on the bedroll. It was getting close to sunup, and he couldn't see much point in trying to get back to sleep.

He was invalided home after Gettysburg and spent the next month on Nantucket Island. He dreamed the dream every night and came to dread the sight of his mother standing by his bed, lamp in hand. He couldn't bring himself to tell her about the moment in the aid station. When he didn't say anything, she patted his arm and went back to bed.

He acquired quite a following of local young ladies that month at home. Someone was forever banging out "Just before the Battle, Mother" or "The Vacant Chair" on the pianoforte in the parlor. Gifts of calves-foot jelly and Victoria sauce lined up in ranks on the kitchen shelves.

The young boys wanted him to tell about the battle. They sat at his feet on the front porch and looked up at him with reverence in their eyes. He knew they wanted to hear more of the same gallant bullshit he'd handed out during his furlough last winter, but he couldn't do it. They finally went away, leaving him alone to contemplate the salt grass and listen to the ocean.

His doctor advised re-amputating his foot a little higher up, which scared him so badly that he fled one night and rejoined his unit at City Point. After the war, he realized that he was best at soldiering, and that it was a thing he did well. He took a rank reduction like everyone else and accepted an assignment in a cavalry regiment on Reconstruction duty in Texas. It wasn't much of a life for humans and college graduates, but he figured it didn't amount to a hill of beans, anyway.

By pushing the horses harder than they should have, D Company arrived at Fort Laramie just as the sun was setting. After seeing to his remount, Starbuck was walking back to his quarters when he noticed a clump of rabbit brush near a water trough. He went over to it and squatted on his haunches. It didn't look much like mistletoe, but maybe if one of the ladies tied a red bow around it and hung it high enough, no one would really notice. He sawed off a handful with his pocketknife and carried it to his room.

He settled as much of himself as he could in to the tin hip bath and just sat there, listening to Lieutenant Jensen getting ready in the next room. Jensen was whistling "Hark, the Herald Angels Sing." He kept at it until Starbuck leaned out of his tub, picked up a boot, and threw it at the door separating their rooms.

He had just finished buttoning himself into full dress and was thinking about checking the kitchen to see if there was anything left from dinner when someone knocked at his door. He opened it to see Mollie Norton, already dressed for the dance. Her hair was piled up in little ringlets, and she had woven strands of gold-colored thread through the curls until her whole head shimmered in the lamplight.

"What . . . can I do for you, Mrs. Norton?" He knew better than to ask her into his room, and he wondered why she had come.

She looked at his dress uniform, with all the knots and medals. "Were you planning to go to the party, Captain?"

"Well, yes. I thought I'd at least look in on it. Is something wrong?"

"Oh, everything!" she burst out. "Jim and I are supposed to sing and perform in the tableaux, and little Jimmy just broke out with measles. I can't get anyone to stay with him tonight, and I was wondering if you might . . . ."

He just looked at her. She sniffed a bit until a few tears gleamed on her eyelashes. "Since you don't always go to these things, and figuring you'd be too tired after that patrol, we thought you might sit with Jimmy. He's already asleep. He won't be any trouble."

Well, Merry damned Christmas, Starbuck thought to himself. *Couldn't she figure out he'd crowded sail on those nags all day just so he could get here in time for the party?* He looked at her again. She was dressed so nicely, smelled so sweet, and had probably been planning this night for months. Jensen had switched to "Adeste Fidelis" in the next room, and he decided there wasn't any point in going to the party. It was going to be Jensen's evening.

"Sure I'll do it, Mrs. Norton. When do you want me over there?"

She sighed and closed her eyes for a second. "Thank you, captain. You're a dear," she murmured. In a whirl of skirts, she turned for the outside door then glanced back. "Please come as soon as you can." She left in a rustle of taffeta.

Starbuck changed uniforms, pulled on his boots, and tucked his moccasins in his overcoat pocket. No sense in being uncomfortable; it would probably be a long evening. He paused long enough to smile in his shaving mirror. "You're a chump, Captain Starbuck," he told his reflection. He picked up the bunch of rabbit brush and blew out the lamp. Mrs. Norton could give the weeds to Laurie Moorcroft with his compliments, or apologies, or whatever she cared to say.

When he got to the Nortons' quarters, Mollie almost pulled him inside, and Jim relieved him of his greatcoat, stammering his thanks and his regrets at the same time. Mrs. Norton chattered a string of breathless instructions at him, and then the two of them darted away.

He sat down on the settee, took off his boots, and slipped on his moccasins. He knew Jim Norton had a copy of *Oliver Twist* somewhere, and he planned to while away the evening re-reading it. He found the book, but before he made himself comfortable, he tiptoed into the Nortons' bedroom for a look at Jimmy.

The baby was sleeping on his back with his arms thrown wide. His mother had daubed calamine lotion on his measles, and he looked polka-dotted. Starbuck hesitated, then touched the child's forehead with the back of his hand. He was warm but not burning up. *People are strange,* Starbuck thought. *If Jimmy were mine, no power on earth could drag me away from my quarters.*

Several hours went by; he was just starting chapter nineteen, "How Oliver passed his time in the improving society of his reputable friends," when he heard someone on the porch stamping snow off. Guessing it was one of the Nortons, he marked the page with his finger but didn't rise from where he reclined. To his surprise, someone knocked, so he got up and opened the door.

Laurie Moorcroft stood there. She stepped inside, and immediately, her spectacles steamed up. Starbuck put down the book and dug out a handkerchief. She took it from him and made a few swipes at the glass with one hand.

"Did the Nortons send you?" he asked.

"No. Well, not really. When Mollie said you were tending Jimmy and that he had the measles, I thought I'd bring you some plum pudding." She handed him a glass dish. "I'm sorry it's so cold. I couldn't think of any way to keep it warm between the mess hall and here."

He set the dessert dish on the whatnot shelf. He couldn't stand plum pudding, but she had been kind to think of him. As usual, he didn't know what to say, but it didn't matter because Laurie was taking off her cloak and talking. "Since I'm here, I'd just as well look in on Jimmy."

Her dress was a deep green velvet with full bishop's sleeves and cut so low across the front that he hoped she wouldn't catch her death on the way back to the ball. She slipped off her dancing shoes and tiptoed in for a peek at the baby. He followed her. She leaned over the crib and put her hand on Jimmy's forehead the same as he had done.

"Poor little fellow," she whispered, and pulled the quilt up higher around his neck. Then she sat down on the end of the Nortons' bed, tucked her feet up under her, and wrapped an arm around the bedpost, to his mind resisting any efforts to dislodge her. She looked a bit like a figurehead sitting there, and Starbuck wondered what she was doing. He sat down in the rocking chair facing her, not sure where this was leading.

She cleared her throat, then glanced at the crib. "I've really come to apologize," she said.

"What on earth for?" he asked, whispering.

"Well, for asking you about Gettysburg that time. It's been bothering me, and I just . . . wanted to tell you I was sorry." Her fingers were busy twisting the yarn ties on the Nortons' bedspread.

"You were just trying to make conversation." Starbuck leaned back in the rocker, noting how pretty she was, perched on the bed with moonlight all around her lovely shoulders.

She looked at him, a frown on her face. "No, I wasn't, not really. You see, my brother died at Gettysburg, and you remind me of him. But . . . it isn't that you look like him. Well, maybe it is." She made a face. "You must think I'm awfully gauche. Look, can I be honest with you, Captain?"

That was probably his cue to get up and leave the room, but wild horses and Sioux couldn't have dragged him out of the rocking chair. He made a motion with his hand, and she continued.

"Gerald was my twin—I guess it runs in the family. We were quite close. Right after Fredericksburg, he came home on furlough, and he had that same look in his eyes as you did that night I opened my big mouth." She stopped, then leaned forward and touched him on the knee. The gesture brought tears to his eyes, and he was glad the room was dark.

"I could tell something was wrong, really wrong," she continued, "but when I asked him to tell me what was the matter, he wouldn't." She touched him again. "He just sat there and looked at me, same as you're doing right now. Then he went back to his regiment, and I never saw him again."

She rested her head against the bedpost and took a deep breath. "Mama got a letter that August from his commanding officer. Something about how he died instantly and felt no pain."

"I used to write those letters, too," he murmured. "Something about dying bravely for a just cause and not suffering on the field of battle."

She smiled at him out of one side of her mouth. "I thought it was a sham. Mama carried that letter around for months and wept over it, but all I had to remember of Gerald was that look in his eyes."

"I hated to write those letters," Starbuck whispered, leaning forward. "And I hated myself, but I didn't know what else to say."

"You could have told the truth!" she burst out, then inched closer as Jimmy stirred in his sleep. "Do you realize there is a whole generation of ladies growing old that has been lied to? I used to ask the men coming back what it was really like, and no one would tell me! I got the jokes about weevils in the bread and singing songs across the lines on Christmas Eve, but those stories don't explain the look in Gerald's eyes. Or yours."

Her voice trailed off. She stood up quickly, pulled the quilt up around Jimmy again, and went into the other room. Starbuck sat in the dark, leaning back in the rocker and staring at the ceiling until he heard the front door open. He leaped out of the chair and ran into the other room.

"Wait! Don't go," he pleaded with her. He took her cloak off and set her down on the settee, then drew up the bench until they were sitting almost knee to knee. "I'll tell you how it was, Annie Laurie."

He told her his whole story, leaving nothing out, and then the stories he heard about the anxiety of Little Round Top and the way the two lines hit with an audible smack at Pickett's charge. There were tears on her face and his too by the time he finished. At some point during his brutal narrative, she had grabbed his hands, gripping them hard, until he winced. She loosened her grip finally but did not release him. He would have cried harder, if she had.

"You're a strange man, Captain Starbuck," she said, when she could talk. "You've spent the last six years wondering what was wrong with you, when you should have been wondering what was wrong with everyone else."

They were sitting there like that, holding hands, when the Nortons came in. Mollie stared at them. "Laurie, you're supposed to be at the party!" she exclaimed. "Lieutenant Jensen has organized the whole glee club to serenade you, and everyone chipped in to give you a going away present!"

Laurie let go of his hands, and stood up only to sit down again much closer to him on the bench. "That's awfully sweet of the lieutenant, but I'm not leaving after all."

Considering that he broke out with measles on the night of his wedding, Starbuck called his Fort Laramie honeymoon a complete success. His throat had felt a bit scratchy before the ceremony. He was hot, and his head ached, but he put it down to excitement and forgot about it until he was peeling down his long johns and planning ahead that night.

Laurie was already sitting in bed and looking slightly like a deer in the crosshairs, when she glanced up at his bare chest. She let out a whoop and laughed until she flopped over on her side. By morning, his face was all spotted, and he could barely open his eyes.

He was content to let the post surgeon—who almost choked on a laughing jag—quarantine them. Laurie patted calamine lotion on him in such a lingering fashion that he didn't regret a minute of his confinement. He had the dream one night when he was almost over the itching stage. Laurie held him tight, and he wrapped his arms around her. She murmured to him, and they rocked back and forth on the bed until he fell asleep. He never had the dream again.

They were garrisoned at Fort Davis a summer later when the mail clerk handed him a package. He could just make out the words Baton Rouge in the return address. He brought the box home unopened and dropped it in his wife's lap. She finished buttoning her shirtwaist and put Eliza to her shoulder for a burp. "Something for you, dear," he said.

She handed the baby to him, and her fingers were busy on the string. "Whatever it is, you probably shouldn't have, Dave," she admonished. "You know how poor we are."

She pried open the lid with his pocketknife and lifted it off. Inside was a pile of gray dust, a piece of twig and a few desiccated berries. She held out the twig to him with thumb and forefinger. "What on earth?"

He took it from her, held it over her head, and kissed her.

"Merry Christmas, Annie Laurie."

Casually at Post

❧ ❧

The first steamboat of the season to tie up at Fort Buford's landing usually meant general rejoicing in the Fred Pierce household but not this evening. That morning, when his orderly had trundled what seemed like a bushel basket onto his desk in the post hospital, his anticipation of a pleasant hour or two reading old newspapers had been considerably dampened by the arrival of a letter.

Not just any letter but a letter from David Lodge. Curse it all, the damned document was addressed to his wife, Lorna. A lesser man would have steamed open the envelope, and the thought did cross Pierce's mind. He rejected it, knowing that generations of his Yankee antecedents would have scowled and pointed bony fingers at him for such unrighteous behavior. Nah. Better to let Lorna open the nasty thing.

Still, the letter ruined what had begun as a promising day of reading last winter's medical journals, *Boston Globes*, and letters the U.S. Army had not deemed sufficiently important to send overland with the courier, after the Missouri froze. He hadn't even enjoyed setting Wilkie Barstow's leg halfway through the day. Wilkie, the son of the quarter-master sergeant, was the garrison's cross to bear. Bent, apparently, on some nefarious errand, he had slipped in the blood piped from the slaughterhouse onto the ground and somehow managed to earn himself a greenstick break of the right fibula.

Although Pierce knew he would have to remind the butchers of the necessity of placing a barrel to catch the blood (why, oh why, couldn't they remember?), there ought to be some way to congratulate them for slowing down Wilkie for perhaps the better part of the summer. Without a qualm, he had done his part by insisting to Mrs. Barstow that Wilkie not place any weight on that leg for at least six weeks, whereupon he would make another examination and pronounce Wilkie's fate for the remainder of the summer.

Forgive me, Hippocrates, he had thought to himself as he gave Mrs. Barstow the bad news. *Hippocrates, if you had Wilkie Barstow in garrison, you would resort to stratagem and downright lie, too. There is nothing to keep that scamp from bounding about after only four weeks, but he will not hear it from me.*

Still, the Barstow matter would have given him the pleasure rightfully his, if only that letter had not arrived to foul his mood. Why on earth did David Damn Him Lodge feel the need to write to Lorna Pierce, Pierce's helpmeet, bed partner, and general all-around excellent woman? Surely Lodge couldn't still be piqued about coming in second place in the matrimonial horse race four years ago. As irritated as he was with the letter, Fred knew that there was no way to pry Lorna from his side. He believed her when she said she loved him, and she had said so only last night, during a particularly heated romp when the babies were asleep. *Still.*

To make matters worse, Lorna seemed not to comprehend the importance of the letter when he presented it to her before dinner, along with other correspondence. Granted, she was nursing The Little Fellow and had that contented, dreamy look on her face that the tugs and pulls of motherhood seemed to bring out in her. She merely looked at the address, set down the envelope, and turned her attention back to the baby, curling his black hair around her finger.

"Do you want me to open it for you?" he asked helpfully.

"Oh, no. I'll get to it," she replied with that maddening calm that he generally considered one of her more attractive features, right up there with blue eyes and a magnificent figure. Right now, her attitude only seemed obtuse to him. *Don't you care that I almost quiver to know what Lodge said?* Fred asked himself. *Unfeeling woman.*

He suffered through dinner, feeling less and less charitable with Lorna, his beloved. If she could sit there at the table and eat and nurse Abigail now at the same time, why couldn't such a talented female open that letter and read it?

Finally, she looked at him. "Fred, what are you stewing about?"

My God, she knows me so well, he thought and felt instantly ashamed. Is there some gear in modern man that still causes him to revert to the caveman level when another male sniffs around? "I'm not stewing," he insisted.

She smiled at him. "You are, too." With that prescience that would ever keep the female of the species far more in tune with reality than the male, she glanced at the letter that lay on the table like an excised tumor. "You want to know what's in that letter, don't you?"

"I surely do," he said. He could deny it; he could bluster and rave, but there was no reason, when he had been found out so easily. He had the good grace to grin at her. "Dash it, Lorna, I wish even the sight of his name didn't still make me jealous and on my guard."

It was the right thing to say. She pinked up and looked at him from under her improbably long eyelashes. The matter must have communicated itself to their daughter, who turned to look at him too, her chin milky and her dimple just as pronounced. *My Lord, I am blessed with beautiful women in this household,* he thought.

"Fred, I turned him down twice. Even beyond the obligatory first time, so maybe that makes three times." She coaxed Abigail back to the nipple and picked up her fork again.

She had never told him that. "You never turned me down at all," he said, startled, "not even obligatorily."

She laughed, which made her daughter smile around the nipple. "I was terrified you would propose to some other woman, and not whisk me out here to God-help-us Dakota. I didn't dare turn you down. You might not have asked again. You're such a frugal Yankee."

He joined in her laughter, appreciating her sense of humor in this place that, while not the end of the earth, couldn't have been far away from it. The both knew officers' ladies who chose to live in the East rather than subject themselves to eternal wind, endless snow, endless heat, and endless mosquitoes, depending on the turn of the calendar. Lorna Pierce was no descendant of Boston Puritans, but when she made a vow, she meant it. He could only be grateful.

"Open the letter, my dear," she said. Deftly, she put Abigail to her shoulder for a burp and pulled her shirtwaist across her breasts. She cocked her head to one side. "Perhaps you had better get The Little Fellow first. I think I hear him tuning up." She looked down at her half-eaten dinner. "I do believe I am a human cow."

He left the table and went into their bedroom at the back of the house, thinking to himself that her quiet words were the closest she had come to a protest—if that's what it was—in the last three months. The Little Fellow was in the baby basket, waving his arms about and screwing up his face. "Well, now, sir," Fred said, as he picked up the baby. "Weren't you attached to my sweet wife when I came home? Can we not give her a moment's peace?"

His answer was a vigorous cry that made tears come to Fred's eyes, despite his medical professionalism. Always the assessor, he held out the infant and then cuddled him close, rubbing his cheek against the dark head; he felt only gratitude. He put the baby on their bed and changed him, admiring the rolls of flesh on his arms and legs now. He hoped that someday enough time would have passed and his mind's eye would not flash back to that first view of him, naked, thin, and only hours old, lying next to his dead mother on the floor of the hospital entryway. The blood frozen on her chin and the ragged shape of the umbilical cord told him the whole story.

He blinked away the picture; some things weren't worth dwelling on. "Well, lad, dinner awaits."

He went to the window instead, pleased to look out on something besides snow now that the ground was warming. By habit, he faced east toward the Indian prisoner-of-war camp, his other hospital these days. Since '78 or so, according to the records of the previous post surgeon, the Sioux had been drifting back across the line from the Grandmother's Land. This winter saw more and more of them come, and in worse condition. He sighed and rested his chin on the baby's head.

By the time he returned to the dining room, Lorna had deposited their daughter in a nest of blankets by his chair and managed to finish most of her dinner. She held out her arms for the younger baby and opened her shirtwaist again, the soul of generosity. He sat down in his chair to watch them both, the boy so earnestly engaged and his wife relaxing again into that pleasant somnolence that nursing brought out in her.

Considering that three months had passed, he should have been long over his wonder at the sight of the two of them, his red-haired, blue-eyed woman and the Indian baby. And there it was again, the image of him kneeling by the dead woman, peeling back her blanket to uncover the newborn just this side of death. His hospital steward had told him later that he had never heard him so ferocious as he ordered him to send for Mrs. Pierce.

She must have come on the run, because she was still breathing hard when she came into the hospital and stopped, eyes wide, hand to her mouth, to stare at the dead woman before her and then at his own desperate expression. The steward had obviously communicated the urgency of the situation. Despite the cold, she had only thrown a robe over her nightdress, and her glorious red hair shone around her face like a nimbus. In a moment, she was on her knees beside him.

"Feed this baby, Lorna," he had ordered. It hadn't been a suggestion, or a request, but a demand. He had thrust the naked, barely moving newborn into her hands.

She could have done anything, but as he watched her now in the low light of the dining room, he knew she had done the right thing that awful night. Standing there in the hallway, with orderlies, soldiers, and Indians around, she had whipped open her nightgown and held the baby to her bare breast, her whole mind and heart on the child in her arms.

Pierce never took a poll of the other men in that hallway, but he remained convinced that it was the finest moment of a dreadful day. The hospital steward and orderlies gaped for a small moment—no matter, he knew how magnificent his wife looked—then turned back to their own saving work with renewed intensity.

He led her into the empty ward on the other side of the hall, set her down on one of the beds, and said he would return in a few minutes. Mercifully, when he came into the hall again, his orderlies were carrying the Indian mother to the dead house. He stopped them long enough to wipe off the waxy umbilical blood from her chin.

It was more than two hours later, after amputating one frozen leg and tending the worst frostbite and deep malnutrition cases, that he found the time to return to the empty ward. What he saw made him smile and then stare hard at the ceiling and grit his teeth so he would not cry. Lorna had curled herself around the infant in a manner remarkably like the posture of its own dead mother. They both slept, but as he crept closer, the baby's lips began to move again, as though deep in what could only be the best dream of its short life so far.

He touched Lorna's shoulder gently so as not to startle her. She lay quietly watching him while he trimmed the baby's umbilical cord down to the length he preferred and tied it off with twine. The newborn had soiled himself, so he carefully cleaned him, knotted on a diaper made from a triangular bandage, and wrapped him in a towel. The baby opened his eyes and watched him in that solemn manner of his elders. "Well, Little Fellow, these are strange doings, eh?" he asked.

What now? he remembered thinking as he stood over the Indian baby and his own dear wife. When he tried to pick up The Little Fellow, Lorna's arms tightened around him. "No," she said. "He goes home with me."

The sun was coming up over the quartermaster warehouses when he escorted her across the parade ground to their quarters. Suzie, their maid, met them at the door carrying Abigail, who was demanding breakfast in no uncertain terms. Only then did Lorna hand him the baby and take her own from Suzie. "Put him in her crib, Fred," she said as she sat down and unbuttoned her nightgown again. "We'll sort that out later." She had paused long enough to grin at him. "I think I'm going to be busy for a few months."

"Just a few weeks," he assured her. "I'm certain I can find another woman among the Indians to do your duty."

She looked at him, and he felt the tiniest unease. "Just a few weeks? We'll see."

Nope, David Lodge, you have no idea, he thought. He picked up the letter.

"Oh, go on, and open it!" she said, a smile in her eyes. "You know you want to." She settled herself more comfortably and touched the baby's head. "If he wants me to desert you and flee with him to Florence or Paris, you can give him my regrets, but he'll have to wait until the babies are older."

He laughed and spread out the letter on his knee. "Oh, this is good, Lorna," he said, after reading it. "He wants you to remind me about the class reunion in August and to encourage me to write a little description of my activities of the last ten years, if I can't attend."

"You could, you know," she reminded him. "You're long overdue for a furlough."

That was true enough, but he couldn't quite imagine it, not even in the peace and quiet of his dining room. "I can see it now, Lorna," he replied, folding the letter. "One shabby post surgeon in a roomful of physicians who specialize in diseases of the rich."

She smiled at him, touched his knee, and then returned to her drowsy contemplation of the baby at her breast. He watched her, never tiring of her beautiful face. Her whole body relaxed; then she sat upright when the steamboat blew its whistle at the landing. To his surprise, she began to frown. When she looked at him, she was squinting in that way of hers when she was upset.

"It's going upriver now?" she asked.

"Aye-ah," he replied, over-pronouncing his Yankee speech, which usually made her laugh. "To Fort Benton and then back."

"I suppose some of the Indians here will go downriver when it returns?"

Her voice was too casual now, and he knew what she really meant. "Some of them," he said carefully. "We have more than three hundred in camp now, and I know they cannot all go at once. I've certified some fit for travel, but not all."

"But other steamers will come, won't they?"

"I'm afraid so, honey," he told her, wincing a bit inside when she tightened her arm around the boy she nursed. She was quieter than usual that night when they undressed for bed. When he held her in his arms before they both drifted off to sleep, she had nothing to say. *Damn it, David Lodge,* he thought, as he breathed deep of her fragrant hair, *I'll wager you never had a challenge like this with your Boston practice.*

About a week later, God came to his attention. He had just finished debriding a burn—his least favorite task—when he heard the front door open and close. His hospital steward was on detached duty at Camp Poplar, so he went to the door of the ward, wiping his hands on his surgeon's apron.

Captain Clark, officer of the day, stood there with another man. More properly, Clark was attempting to make a little space between him and the man, and the reason became quickly obvious. *Dear me, when did he last bathe?* Pierce asked himself. His work accustomed him to frequent unpleasant exudations, but this passed even his customary threshold.

"Tom?" he asked, not brave enough to come a step closer.

Clark walked toward him and so did the other man. The officer turned around and held up his hand. "Wait here and don't move," he ordered, then indicated Pierce's office with his head. They went inside, and he shut the door.

"Where'd you find him?" Pierce asked, seating himself on the edge of his desk.

"One of the sentries told the corporal of the guard about a wild man down in the steamer landing," he said. Clark went to the window, flung it open, and stuck out his head, even though the morning was cool.

Pierce grinned, enjoying the moment. Clark was usually such a tight-ass that it was almost a pleasure to see him ruffled. "And you figured I needed him?"

After a moment, the officer gathered his dignity around him. "Fred, I didn't know where else to take him, and the commanding officer recommended you," he said. "He says he's God."

The post surgeon laughed. "Who'd have though the Buford steamboat landing would be the place of the Second Coming?"

"Oh, don't," Clark replied. "If I get one more remark . . . . He's obviously insane, so I brought him to you."

Pierce sighed. "You don't think he's violent?"

Clark shrugged and opened the door into the hallway. "I certainly made every effort not to get close enough to find out! Captain Pierce, he's all yours. The commanding officer wants you to find out if he's sane or not." He smiled his gallows smile that made him the terror of his company. "I wish you joy."

The man had not moved from his first position in the hallway. He was of medium height, thin nearly to cadaverous proportions, bearded, and wearing several layers of clothing that had probably kept him warm all winter. Pierce felt his eyes begin to water from the stench. The man reminded Pierce of a dog that had once owned him: friendly, with a benign expression, but with the regrettable propensity to roll in the most ill-mannered refuse that could be found in a good neighborhood in Boston.

"You are to remain here with the post surgeon," Clark ordered as he backed toward the door.

"Do introduce us, sir," the man said. His voice was quite the nicest part of him. Pierce couldn't place his accent.

The officer glared at him. The man merely cocked his head and raised his eyebrows, a slight smile on his face. "Oh, very well!" In spite of his own discomfort, Pierce enjoyed watching the flush spread up from Clark's neck. "This is . . . God."

"Augustus Gustavus God," the man added helpfully. He stepped forward and held out a hand that may or may not have been white at one time. "And you are . . ."

"Captain Fred Pierce, post surgeon," he said. He hesitated a slight moment, then extended his own hand.

Puzzled, the man frowned. "Pay-ass? What an unusual name."

God is obviously not from Boston, Pierce thought as they shook hands. "P-i-e-r-c-e," he spelled.

"Oh. Pierce," God said. "Pleased to meet you, my son. I trust you are having a good morning?"

For some unaccountable reason, Pierce felt the urge to unburden himself and describe the recent debriding, expressing how it hurt him to the quick to cause so much pain in a patient, even though it was part of the healing process. *Silly,* he thought. "It's been tolerable."

From the way God leaned closer and squinted, Pierce realized there was a language barrier. The officer of the day did laugh this time. "I'll spell it for him, Pay-ass," he said, before he beat a hasty retreat. "T-o-l-e-r-a-b-l-e." Pierce heard him laughing on the porch.

Then he stood alone in the hall with God, whom he deemed in serious need of soap and water. "Come with me, sir," he said. "You are going to have a bath."

An hour later, the man was still soaking. The orderly that Pierce had summoned from upstairs where he was inventorying supplies only lasted a few minutes before he fled the building, retching. Pierce collared him out by the privy and gave him a good shake, which he regretted immediately, softhearted man that he was. "Get the fire going, and at least fill the tub, Private," he ordered, deeply conscious of the bare pleading in the orderly's eyes. "Then find something from the clothing locker for him to wear." The private looked at him with gratitude, and Pierce sighed inwardly. "Leave it outside the washroom door, and go back upstairs, Private."

When the water was hot enough, he took a deep breath, opened the door to the washroom, and ordered God inside. "You are to strip, get in the tub, and wash everything," he commanded. "Use the pine tar soap on your body and your beard and hair."

"Certainly, Captain," God said pleasantly.

When he came in the washroom later, God was leaning back in the hip tub, a beatific expression his face. Pierce came closer and tipped a bucket of warmer water in the tub. "Better now?" he asked, pleased when God nodded.

He glanced over at the pile of clothing on the floor and sucked in his breath, unable to help himself. At first he thought the shirt and pants were moving, then realized that veritable armies of lice swarmed over the fabric, as if searching for the warmth that God must have been providing all winter. *My Lord,* he thought, *it's a miracle God didn't die of typhus.* He hurried into the hall, calling for his orderly again.

The private came downstairs slowly, reluctance evident in every step on the treads. *There are times when rank has its privileges,* Pierce thought. "Private, I have a proposition for you," he said. "Neither task is palatable, but I will do one, and you the other."

"Sir?"

"The, uh, gentleman in there has spent the winter entertaining lice." He paused. "You may either get his clothes to the burn pit, then see that the washroom is thoroughly disinfected, or you may cut his hair and beard."

He had no doubt which the orderly would choose. The man muttered something about a manure fork and left again. Pierce rolled down his sleeves and found the adhesive tape, which he bound around his cuffs and wrists, leaving no openings. He did the same with his pant legs, then rinsed his hands in a five-percent solution of carbolic acid. The bracing smell of it snapped him to attention. He bound a triangular bandage over his hair.

God had left the tub. Smelling of creosote from the pine tar soap, he had wrapped the towel around his skinny middle. His hair and beard were a sodden mass: gooey, almost gelatinous, a dare for anyone with a comb to come close. *No thank you*, Pierce thought grimly. He found his favorite shears and set the other man on a stool. Working at arm's length, he cut off God's beard and hair, feeling for all the world like an explorer hacking through the jungles of Venezuela.

Through it all, God made no protest beyond flinching a little when Pierce came close to his ear. "Careful, my son," he murmured. "You'll recall my advice about an eye for an eye and a tooth for a tooth. I believe it also applies to ears."

Pierce laughed in spite of himself. "I'm certainly relieved to know that God has a sense of humor."

His expression difficult to read, God turned his head to look at Pierce. "The whole human race is here! What more evidence could you possibly need?"

With the thickest layer of hair gone, deposited in the receptacle used for contaminated bandages, Pierce permitted himself to relax. Keeping his voice casual, he continued clipping as he quizzed God regarding the president of the United States. "Hayes, but it should have been Tilden," God said, confirming his Democratic outlook, which scarcely surprised Pierce. He nearly asked God who was vice president but changed his mind, because he could not remember himself.

God agreed that the year was 1879, "The Year of Our Lord," he added as a reminder. He knew all the states, but added Alaska, which Pierce thought perfectly ridiculous and told him so. "Well, then, I will not tell you about the Sandwich Islands, if you won't believe me," God told him. "You appear to be a man of little faith."

"I am a scientist." I am also a barber, he thought, clipping God's hair close to his head. I doubt that David Lodge does this too often in his practice. If medicine gets slack in Boston, David has no other skills, whereas I can cut hair. The thought of Lodge barbering made him smile, and he finished his task more agreeably than he began it.

The orderly came into the room and tossed a kerosene-soaked burlap bag next to the still-writhing mound of clothes. Using the long-handled manure fork, he gingerly lifted the discarded rags onto the bag. He shrieked and leaped back when the lice tried to flee the kerosene, then crept closer when Pierce, out of patience, growled at him. Moving fast, the orderly tied a string around the bundle, hooked it on the end of the manure fork, and walked it at arm's length into the yard behind the hospital. Pierce stopped clipping to listen for the whoosh and the roar, as the orderly set fire to the bundle. "Trust the nincompoop to burn down the privy," he muttered.

"Now, now," God said.

God had no objection to the noon meal, even though it was a low diet of gruel and toast. He also made no objection when Pierce gently put a hand on his forehead, then helped him into the bed next to the corporal with the burned arm. He closed his eyes and soon was breathing regularly. Pierce stood by the bed a moment more, then bent over to pull the blanket higher on his chest. As he did so, God grasped his hand and squeezed it. "Bless you, my son," he whispered, then closed his eyes again.

Pierce spent a surprisingly cheerful afternoon in his office, filling out reports and starting a file on Augustus Gustavus God. In it, he described God's physical attributes, which were far from celestial. In his professional opinion, God appeared to be quite normal, if on the small side and somewhat undernourished. As to his mental state, who knew?

When he was assigned to Fort Russell four years ago, he had been called on to diagnose insanity in a homesteader's wife who had stabbed her own child with a butcher knife, stripped off her clothes and fled naked across the prairie. Indians had found her, sunburned and tormented by mosquitoes, and brought her to Russell. He shook his head against that memory; he doubted he had ever made an easier diagnosis.

But God? He wandered back into the ward. Both men were asleep, the corporal resting peacefully, his burned arm stretched out now and not held protectively close to his body. *Maybe I will not have to debride his arm again,* Pierce thought hopefully. That would be a blessing. He glanced at God, who was snoring, and went back to his office.

When the evening orderly came on duty at four o'clock, Pierce took him into his office and explained the situation. He handed a note addressed to Lorna to the orderly going off duty and asked him to deliver it to her. He looked at the note again: "My dear, I am bringing God home for dinner at six o'clock. We will let him ask grace. Your loving and totally rational husband, Fred Pay-ass."

He paid a visit next to the post adjutant, that man of sorrows and acquainted with grief who lived perpetually on the edge of one garrison crisis or another. "I really don't see the necessity of packing Augustus Gustavus God off to the guardhouse tonight," he told the lieutenant.

"He's not insane?" the adjutant asked. "You could have fooled me. God isn't often casually at post at Buford."

"He's as loony as they come, but he's not dangerous," Pierce said. "What I would like to do is request another orderly for a few days of extra duty. I want God watched, but I don't want him confined."

"I wish you wouldn't call him God!" the adjutant exclaimed.

Pierce laughed. "Should I call him Gus? Seems a bit informal for the master of the universe."

He left the office in good humor, convinced that the adjutant would tell anyone who would listen that the post surgeon had just gone around the bend and wasn't it a pity? When he got back to the hospital, he glanced in the ward to see God and the corporal engaged in earnest conversation. Content that all was well, he made his rounds in Suds Row, looking in on a laundress whose newborn was slightly jaundiced, and then removing sutures from the forehead of a teamster who had come out on the poor end of an altercation in the post trader's pool hall.

When he returned to the hospital, he invited God home to dinner. God accepted with alacrity and excused himself for a visit to the privy. Pierce sat down next to the corporal, pleased to see that his arm was no longer angry looking. He nodded, satisfied with his morning's distasteful work in debriding it. He got up, and the corporal cleared his throat.

"Yes?" Pierce asked.

"Sir, do you know that man is God?" His voice was quiet, full of awe.

Pierce gave an indulgent laugh. "So he claims, Corporal. I wouldn't put too much dependence on it."

"He is," the soldier whispered after a look around. "He touched my arm and told me it would be better, and you know, it is! I think this is a miracle, sir."

Hell's bells, Pierce thought in disgust. *Your arm is better because I debrided it this morning.* He opened his mouth to speak, then closed it and reconsidered. The corporal had suffered through a trying winter. His wife, one of the company laundresses, had run off with a passing teamster, and their small son had sickened and died almost before his eyes of something Pierce could not diagnose. And now this arm. It would take a more arrogant man than he to dash someone's struggling faith.

"You could be right, Corporal," he said. "Your arm certainly didn't look this good this morning, did it?"

"No, sir, begging your pardon." The corporal sighed and closed his eyes. "I think I'm going to be all right."

Pierce smiled. "I believe you are, too."

Dinner was an unmitigated delight. If Lorna seemed suspicious at first, the moment quickly passed. By the time they finished the soup course, she was telling their visitor about her girlhood in Philadelphia, where her Unionist father had fled after his Columbia, South Carolina, store was burned down around his ears by secessionists. When Lorna brought in the raisin pie, God was cuddling Abigail on his lap. This amazed Pierce. Of late, Abigail had become decidedly picky about who held her and why. Only last week, the commanding officer had turned into a shaken man after Guard Mount when a mere smile at Pierce's little darling in her pram brought on screams of terror generally associated with an attack by hostiles.

When Lorna brought out The Little Fellow, bright-eyed and ready for his turn at the spigot, she told God about his acquisition. "I'm not so certain that many ladies would be as generous as you have been," he told her before she retreated to the bedroom with the infant.

She looked at God in surprise. "I cannot imagine any woman not doing this." She kissed the baby on top of his head and made her apologies.

God looked after her. "A rare lady" he said, and gently ran his thumb over Abigail's little hand in his. "I trust you realize how fortunate you are, my son."

"Only every day of every year," Pierce replied. Again there was that moment when he wanted to say much more, to tell this lunatic how he met her, how he knew, just *knew*, that no other woman would do for him, and wasn't it all such a mystery? Although he knew his face was red, he kept his own Yankee counsel. Nearly. "My father told me when I married, that I would be a happy man if I would always do what she wants."

God laughed, a rich, rumbling sound that came from somewhere in his scrawny body. "He was right, wasn't he?"

Pierce nodded and leaned forward to touch his daughter's head. "I intend to pass on such information some day." He stood up. "You know, this calls for a drink. I believe I have a bottle of wine."

He ducked down the hall and into their bedroom. "Lorna, where do you keep the wine?"

"We drank the last of it in December when Abigail was born," she told him. "Besides that, we can't have you getting the Almighty juiced." She made a face at him when he laughed. "*If* we have any—and I know we don't—it would be in the back of the cabinet next to the woodbox."

He looked anyway, and there was a bottle tucked behind the water biscuits, cornstarch, salt, and mineral oil. He took it out, wiped off the dust, and snagged the two remaining wine glasses that had survived the general mayhem when Lorna's china barrel had tumbled from the wagon during a crossing of the Platte not long after their wedding.

Abigail was sound asleep in the crook of God's arm, her thumbs tucked tight under her other fingers, the picture of contentment. Pierce popped the cork and poured a few inches for each of them. "Here's to the ladies," he toasted, and they drank together. He poured two more fingers of wine and nodded to God, who raised his glass. "Peace on earth, goodwill to men," the man said.

Pierce drank to that, thinking to himself that it should seem absurd but relieved that it did not. *I pray that my service in the U.S. Army Medical Corps will not make me cynical,* he thought silently.

God looked at him. "It won't," he said in a low voice, leaving Pierce to wonder if he had said anything at all.

In silence, he walked his dinner guest back to the hospital and saw him to bed. The corporal slept peacefully, his face relaxed, with none of the pinched anxiety and pain of earlier days. Pierce stood over him a few moments, enjoying the sight, even if he knew that the corporal had given him none of the credit.

"You will be all right here tonight?" he asked God, who nodded.

Pierce smiled at the orderly, who sat reading in a rocking chair at the end of the ward. "One thing more, my son," God said, before he left the room.

"Yes?"

"You and your wife should name The Little Fellow."

Pierce nodded. "I . . . I've been calling him David but not where Lorna could hear."

When he got back to the house, the babies were slumbering in crib and basket. Lorna sat cross-legged in her nightgown on their bed, brushing out her hair. He flopped down on the bed beside her, and she curled up next to him.

"Lovely wine, Fred. I poured myself a glass; well, maybe two. Where did it come from?" she asked. She began to unbutton his uniform blouse.

"It was right where you said," he replied. He gathered her close, pressed her down to the mattress, and kissed her.

"I know there wasn't any wine," she insisted. She started on his pants buttons.

He helped her. "Then thank goodness I brought home a guest who knows how to turn water to wine, my love."

Later, when her leg was still thrown over him and she hadn't stirred herself yet to search for her nightgown, he told her that he had been calling the Indian baby David. She rubbed her cheek against his chest. "I've been calling him Sam."

They laughed together. "Which is it to be?" he asked, "Samuel David, or David Samuel?"

"Samuel David," she said.

"Excellent."

They had staked their claim, he knew, and he thought about it in the next week as he went about his usual rounds and duties. He chose to leave God pretty much to his own devices. The man tagged along when he made some of his house calls and seemed to have a way with the children of the garrison. He spent some time in the regimental library, where his reading taste ran to the national news in month-old papers and the more current authors, like Mark Twain and Thomas Hardy.

The corporal had been discharged from the hospital to return to his company. The soldier must have spared nothing in telling his friends that God had healed him, because Pierce noticed many furtive looks (and some smirks) in their direction when God tagged along on medical errands of mercy. Mostly, God was no trouble.

More Sioux slipped across the border and were escorted to Fort Buford by the troops patrolling the boundary line. Only because his conscience pricked him, Pierce made discreet inquiries, through an interpreter, about a young woman who would have given birth in February. He learned nothing, which relieved him, even as it told him volumes about the chaotic condition among the Sioux exiles. As he thumped backs, listened to lungs, and signed certificates of health for the Indians, he knew he would have to send the baby downriver to Standing Rock where he belonged. He knew he should hurry the matter to prevent Lorna from becoming even more attached than she already was, but he never got around to it.

At first, his only dread had been how Lorna would take separation from Sam. It warmed his soul that she loved the two children equally, the one flesh of their flesh and the other found naked on a cold floor. As the days passed, it dawned on him that he felt the same way.

Sam had wind on his stomach one night. After administering an appropriate amount of paregoric, Pierce had walked him up and down in the sitting room and then outside in the cooler night air. Sam found that comfortable place between Pierces' neck and shoulder, passed the gas that troubled him, and soon slumbered, but still Pierce walked until he stood on the edge of the parade ground, looking toward the prisoner-of-war camp.

A steamer coming downriver from Benton had docked at the landing. That morning Pierce had certified thirty more of the winter Indians fit for travel, and he knew in the morning they would head downriver to Standing Rock Reservation. He had been there once; at the thought of it, he tightened his grip on Sam until the baby stirred, made a mewing sound, then flopped his head back into his favorite position.

"God help me, I can't do it," Pierce said out loud. *And if you can't,* he told himself, *imagine Lorna.* He was a long time getting to sleep that night.

Call him callous, but Fred Pierce was always able to bury himself in work. Even the most obnoxious job seemed less onerous, because the busier he was, the less time he had to think about the inevitable day when he would have to send Sam downriver to Standing Rock Reservation. He reasoned he could put off the event for a few weeks. There were Indians slipping back across the boundary line now and then. Before the summer ended, he would find a woman who would agree to take care of Sam on the steamboat journey.

Or so he reasoned and explained to Lorna, even if he could not look her in the face when he told her. "What will happen to him then?" Lorna had whispered one night after they had been standing over the babies' cribs.

Why do you have to be so logical, wife? he asked himself in irritation. *Why can't you be simple-minded, like too many ladies I know, and ask no questions?* He took her hand and pulled her from the room. "Surely one of the Indian women will take care of him, Lorna." He tried to sound reasonable and confident. Drat his wife for seeing right through him.

"You don't know that, Fred," she said, her voice flat. "When no one has time for Sam, because God knows they will be busy just trying to keep their own children alive at that wretched place, where will he go then? To an orphanage?"

"I suppose," he muttered, the words wrung out of him.

She was relentless. "Someone will feed him and maybe change him now and then when he starts to stink, but he will just lie there, won't he?

No one will care because he is an Indian." She tried to stop the sob in her throat. "Fred, he will die, and you know it!"

She tried to wrench away from him, but he would not turn loose of her. He pulled her close, utterly miserable, not even enjoying the normally pleasant feeling of her breasts against his chest. *Here is this generous woman, giving her body to two babies,* he thought, *and I am sentencing one to death.* "Lorna, I don't know what to do," he murmured into her hair.

She clung to him. "Yes, you do, Fred. Don't tell me about regulations! I have—we have to keep him."

"I don't know, Lorna," he said. "He is a Sioux, and he should be with his people. That's what we do in the Medical Corps. It's for the best," he concluded, amazed at how limp his argument sounded.

He put off the inevitable day and busied himself even with the t asks that he hated: reminding the butchers to funnel the blood into a vat outside and not allow it to drip on the ground; conducting weekly inspections of the company sinks; certifying rotten food for the burn pit or the river. The garrison was remarkably free of disease and injury, and this should have delighted him. Instead, he dreaded each day, knowing that he had to send Sam downriver.

The nights weren't much better. Lorna was lying awake now, staring at the ceiling, when ordinarily she would have been curled up close to him in sleep. It had been at least a week since she had awakened him late at night, offering herself to him in her generous way, and that was not like Lorna.

He nearly said something to God about it one morning as the two of them started for Suds Row and a visit to Willie Barstow, he of the broken leg. He nearly asked God what he should do about Lorna, who was drooping and suffering before his eyes. *I must be crazy,* he thought, when he stopped himself just in time. As it was, God looked at him, a quizzical expression on his face, as though anticipating his question. *This is absurd,* he told himself, *absurd.*

"Do you have a question, my son?" God asked, his eyes kind.

"Oh! No, nothing," he said, wishing he did not sound so brisk. "And I wish you would not call me 'my son.'" God only smiled at him, to his increasing irritation.

Willie Barstow's mother had propped her son on the settee in their small sitting room, his splinted leg padded underneath by a quilt. "I have been doing exactly as you said, Captain," she told him. "I have kept him off that leg." She beamed at God, who smiled back. "Captain Pierce told me I had to be so careful, because this was a bad fracture."

Pierce winced, owning to a twinge of conscience, then justified himself. *We have enjoyed a full month of peace and calm at Fort Buford, since Willie the Horrible has been confined to quarters. I hope I am justified in calling a greenstick break a bad fracture.*

But there he was, even looking pitiable, a rare expression for Willie Barstow. "How are you doing, Willie?" he asked.

"I wish I could be outside, sir," the boy replied. Pierce felt another twinge at his wistful tone, but it soon passed.

God sat down beside the boy, and touched his leg. "Did you break your leg, my son?" he asked.

Mrs. Barstow bustled in with a reply. "Oh, 'twas a fearful bad fracture, according to our post surgeon here. Fearful bad." She looked at Pierce. "He'll be off his leg all summer, I fear. Seems a shame."

Not to most of the garrison, Pierce thought. "These things happen," he said and felt no pain at his deception.

God ran his hand along the splinted leg. "It should be better soon."

Lord, I hope not, Pierce thought. "Mrs. Barstow, just continue to keep him resting quietly for another month. I'll be back in a week to check on him."

God surprised him then; perhaps astounded would be the better word, because he had been lulled in the last few weeks into thinking that the man was really sane, even though he had not admitted as much to his commanding officer. As he watched, open-mouthed, God stood up and extended his arms in front of him. He stared down at Willie and commanded in a loud voice, "Rise, my son, and walk!"

Pierce should have said something, but he was too amazed. With determination on his face, Willie Barstow edged himself off the quilt and set both feet on the floor. He moved gingerly at first. The splint that Pierce had applied so extensively and firmly a month ago hampered his motion, as Pierce well nigh intended. The boy wobbled a moment; then, tightening his lips, he placed his weight on the greenstick fracture, which had—Pierce knew—completely knit. He breathed deep and then smiled at God and his mother. "Mama, He healed me!"

Mrs. Barstow burst into tears. "It's a miracle!" she sobbed.

As Pierce stared, Willie sat down and tore at the bandages hampering him. His mother produced a pair of scissors, and in a matter of moments, Fort Buford's most naughty child had been liberated to continue his career of shenanigans in the garrison. Delight on his face, Willie hopped on one foot and then the other and then hugged God around the waist.

Mrs. Barstow was on her knees by now, staring up at God with so much devotion that Pierce had to look away. "I thank thee, O Lord," she said, her voice no more than a whisper. "The captain said it would be weeks and weeks yet, and Thou hast healed my son."

Pierce writhed inside, quite unable to admit his own deception. *Of course the little imp is healed,* he thought sourly; *he was barely injured in the first place!* He thought of David Lodge back in his medical practice in Boston, who did not ever have to contend with a sergeant's urchin in a broken-down garrison or a skinny, lice-ridden fleabag of a lunatic pretending to be God. He thought of Lorna, growing more remote and turning inward as she feared to lose their son. *Oh, God,* he thought, and felt his face grow red. *I am thinking of him as my son, too.* The pain of it all struck him with such force that it was all he could do to keep from tears. He picked up his medical satchel and left the house.

He hoped no one would speak to him as he crossed the parade ground. Head down, he hurried toward the security of his office, where he could shut the door and ask himself just when it was he had come to love Samuel David like his own blue-eyed daughter. Was it the nights of holding him with colic or watching Lorna's growing devotion? Was it changing the nappies or feeding him his first solid food or lying on the settee with his knees up and both babies resting on them and staring at him with the trust of the very young? When did it happen? When did every lesson about professional reserve go flying out the window? When did he cease being a physician and become a father to an Indian baby? He had to stop and just stand there, because the pain was so great.

When he started to move again, he felt older than Methuselah. The post adjutant caught up with him as he passed the telegraph office and waved a piece of paper at him. "Captain Pierce, you'll want to see this."

With a great effort, Pierce gathered together whatever scraps of civility remained and forced a smile. "Good news?"

"I would think so, sir," the adjutant said. "It seems that Fort Keogh is missing a lunatic." He laughed. "It's a teamster in the quartermaster department, one Jake Schmidt. A few months ago, he started telling everyone who would listen that he was Abraham Lincoln." He looked down at the telegram. "They restrained him finally when he went to the guardhouse and tried to let out the prisoners, saying that he was freeing the slaves." He laughed again and held out the telegram. "It seems to me, sir, that President Lincoln gave himself a promotion when he came to Buford. Should I wire Keogh and tell them that we have their lunatic?"

"By all means, Lieutenant," Pierce said. "I'll see that Augustus Gustavus God is in the guardhouse by Retreat. We'll send him downriver with the next steamer." *With the remaining Indian prisoners*, he thought, *and my boy. I suppose Sam will have to learn to tolerate canned milk. I wonder if there is a woman who will take him.*

After some inanity that he couldn't remember the moment he uttered it, Pierce turned away from the adjutant and hurried to the hospital, where he slammed the door and sank down in his swivel chair, his head in his hands. With the perfect clarity that intense agitation sometimes brings, he remembered a spring day in his childhood. There had been a driving rain in their Beacon Hill neighborhood and then fierce wind that shook a bird's nest from a tree. He had been hurrying home from school and nearly stepped on the nest.

Instead, he knelt and turned it over to see three baby birds. One was obviously dead from the fall, but the other two, sensing rescue perhaps, began to peep. Carefully he scooped up the babies in his hand and ran home the rest of the way, shielding them from the cold rain.

His mother was out, but he would not have stopped to ask for her help anyway. Breathless now, he ran into the kitchen and put the two birds on the table in the servants' hall. Cook, his dear Cook, had come immediately, wiping her floury hands on her apron. When he could speak, he told her where he had found the birds, their nest tumbled out of the elm and onto the sidewalk, and asked what he should do.

Without a word, she picked up the little morsels gently, holding them close to her face and listening to their pleading. She took them to the hearth and set them down on the stones, then whistled for the cats. As he watched, horrified and unable to move, the two cats, tails twitching, leaped up from their corner of the hearth. In a moment, the birds were dead and dangling from claw and mouth.

He burst into tears but was too much in need of comfort to back away from the monster disguised as Cook who had sent the birds to their deaths. He let her pick him up and sit down with him in her rocking chair by the fire, where she rocked and told him that little birds without nests are bound to die. "And there isn't a thing in nature we can do about it, Master Freddy," she had told him. It was weeks before he could bring himself to go into the kitchen again.

As he sat at his desk in the post hospital at Fort Buford, the scientific part of his brain smugly reminded him that when he found the dying baby with its dead mother on the floor of his hospital, he could have done nothing; death was no more than an hour or two away. No post surgeon would probably have faulted him. Here was an Indian orphan child, with no real hope of home, or succor, or understanding in a white world devoted to survival of the fittest. He had saved it and now must send it to an orphanage or a reservation, one as bleak as the other. It was scarcely any different from birds on a hearth and probably less humane.

"God help me," he whispered out loud, rested his head on his desk, and closed his eyes.

He opened them when he heard a chair creak, looked up, and narrowed his eyes. "Get out of here," he said to God, who was regarding him with a benign expression.

"My son, I only came because you called me," the man said.

Pierce leaped to his feet and then banged on his desk. "I swear you are a worse cross to bear than . . . than Willie Barstow!"

"Young Willie has promised me that he will be exemplary in his behavior, from now on," God said. "I think the garrison will see a changed boy."

"Balls!" Pierce shouted, quite beside himself. "You are a God-damned teamster from Fort Keogh who thinks he's Abraham Lincoln! Stop this! I do not have time for lunatics!"

God only smiled. "I know you don't. Why on earth would I want to be Abraham Lincoln?"

"Stop it!" Pierce shouted. "You haven't healed a single person! The corporal's arm improved because I debrided it! Willie Barstow walked because his fracture was almost inconsequential!" He was silent then, embarrassed at how puny and spiteful he sounded. "I have bigger problems!" he concluded.

"I know." It was the stillest, smallest voice.

Pierce sat down again, weary right to his toenails. *I am the lunatic,* he told himself. *Anyone coming in here right now hearing me shout would think that I should be committed. I thought I could save a child, but for what? Am I playing God, too?* He stared at the man seated across the desk from him and spoke before he thought. "What am I to do?"

He expected no reply from the insane man, and for a moment there was none. God seemed content to lean back a little in his chair and look around the room, from the crisp curtains Lorna had hung when she was only a month from her confinement last fall, and gloriously rotund, to the geranium flourishing in the window, to the diploma from Harvard College School of Medicine. God smiled again.

"My son, I know he was an old pagan, but what did Hippocrates write in that oath that you recited at the culmination of your graduation?"

I never met a balmier or more worthy candidate for a lunatic asylum, Pierce thought in disbelief. Harsh words rose in his throat, but he found himself quite unable to force them past his teeth. Instead, he leaned back in his chair and grew calm.

"In the whole oath, what is the most important vow you made, my dear son?"

Pierce spoke with no hesitation. "That I would do no harm."

"Would it be harmful to take Samuel David from your wife and send him downriver?"

"The worst harm I can think of." He sighed, chilled to the bone. "I would be harming Lorna, too, and I would rather die than do that."

"What about you?"

He thought about himself. "If I send that baby downriver, I will cease to be human and will not be worthy to be called a physician." There. He had said it, the thing he feared the most, except losing Lorna. Oh, Lorna. He knew he would lose her if Sam went downriver. Perhaps not physically, but he doubted she would ever look upon him the same way again, and that was too awful to contemplate.

He leaned back further still and stared at the ceiling, as the realization of his own smallness encompassed him. In that moment he was not doctor, but patient. He forced himself to consider the matter in the light of his own insignificance, and it suddenly held no terrors. None of it did. He felt a serenity he had never known before cover him. "I might have to resign my commission over this, when I tell the commanding officer what I am going to do," he said, barely recognizing his own voice, so calm he felt. He knew he would never go East again. When they began their marriage at Fort D.A. Russell, Lorna had remarked then how well she liked Cheyenne. He could always take his wife and children there and set himself up in a private practice.

"Well, then?" God prompted.

Pierce smiled and sat upright again. "I think it is time for me to go home to my family." He got to his feet. "Mr. Schmidt, I told the post adjutant that I would see you to the guardhouse and then downriver in the morning under escort to an asylum in St. Paul."

"I am not Jake Schmidt," God insisted, though not forcefully.

"Well, never mind," Pierce said. "You've created an uproar here."

"I know. Perhaps I should disappear," God said, as though thinking out loud.

"It might be wise. Good day, sir. Close the door behind you when you leave."

He crossed the parade ground in a better frame of mind this time, pausing when the steamboat *Dacotah* came in sight and blew its whistle. All those Indians who had witnessed that terrible scene on the hospital floor had long since been transported south. He had never recorded his son's birth in any post records, simply because in the press of events, he forgot. He thought again about the birds he had rescued so many years ago and unwittingly sent to death. Some things couldn't be helped; probably Cook was right. But other things could.

Lorna waited for him in their sitting room, a mulish look on her face, as though daring him to touch her boy. Abigail nestled against her shoulder, but Samuel was spread out across her lap, her hand protectively covering him. He sat down next to her and put his arms around them all. "Lorna, Lorna, the human spigot," he crooned in her ear. "Thanks for telling David Lodge to take a flying leap four years ago. Do you think you can continue to manage two babies and a foolish husband? I rather like this arrangement of ours."

She kissed his cheek and let out a deep breath that she must have been holding for a month or more. "Won't the commanding officer object?"

"Who cares? I can resign, and we'll move to Cheyenne with Abby and Sam."

In the morning, God was gone, as Pierce knew he would be. He endured a chewing out for not incarcerating God, a.k.a. Jake Schmidt from Keogh, in the guardhouse. He put his remaining Indians on the *Dacotah* and endured another blistering scold for not sending Samuel David Pierce, a.k.a. "that Indian baby you have no business keeping," to Standing Rock. He heard out his commanding officer, then calmly offered to resign his commission. The officer only blinked, told him not to be a complete ass, and refused to accept it.

Two days later, Jake Schmidt, a.k.a. Abraham Lincoln, was found by a woodcutting detail and escorted to Fort Buford, where he was held in the guardhouse, and then sent downriver to St. Paul and an insane asylum. While by no means a perfect residence, it promised to be better than walking around in circles between the Yellowstone and Missouri Rivers until death came. Schmidt seemed grateful for a delousing, a hot bath, and clean clothes. After only a few brief hours in Schmidt's presence, Pierce knew he could sign a certificate of derangement without a qualm or a mistake. Of God, he knew he would never be sure.

God was never seen again at Fort Buford, which did not surprise anyone. For Him even to have been casually at post at that most wretched of garrisons was amazement enough.

Pierce thought about God as autumn came. Willie Barstow had made a remarkable recovery not only in his leg but his character, and some called it a miracle. The corporal with the burned arm made sergeant and attracted the attention of a much worthier woman who worked as the commanding officer's maid. Sam grew and thrived along with Abigail, and Lorna found herself increasing again. (That was no miracle; Pierce stopped short of giving the credit to God. He was, after all, a man of science and knew his biology.)

Mary Murphy

❧ ❧

$\mathcal{I}$ met Mary Murphy on a train heading west to Fort Laramie. But I can't really say that I met her, because no one introduced us then, and no one ever did later, either.

I was just out of the academy. It was August, and after graduation in June, I had rushed through a furlough at Newport Beach with my folks, and then received my orders to Company K, Second Cavalry, garrisoned at Fort Laramie, Wyoming Territory. According to my orders, I was to stop at Omaha Barracks long enough to attach myself to ten new recruits for Company K and escort them West.

I remember even now the feeling I had as I stood in the middle of the parade grounds at Omaha Barracks and watched the heat shimmer off the quarters on Officers Row. I wondered what I was supposed to do. I had been assigned to the cavalry arm of the U.S. Army, and Omaha Barracks was my first look at a cavalry post.

I eventually found my ten recruits. Some of them had served in the recent War of the Rebellion and reenlisted after busting out in civilian life. The others spoke German or Irish-accented English that I could barely understand. Most of them were older than I was. Luckily for all of us, a Sergeant O'Brien from Fort Laramie showed up before we departed. He piloted us West.

Mary's name was on the company roster the sergeant handed me before we pulled out—"Mary Murphy, twenty, white, single, laundress."

The army hired females as laundresses to wash the company clothes. Each company of fifty to eighty men employed two or three laundresses, who received rations like the men and were paid one dollar per month by each soldier for doing his laundry. By 1877, most of the laundresses were replaced by wives of the soldiers, but this was 1875, and Mary was our laundress.

I noticed her when she got on the train, clutching a knotted bundle of clothing, a baby crooked in one arm, and a toddler dragging behind her. She was sweating like the rest of us, with half-moons of perspiration under her arms and a streak of sweat soaking through the back of her shirtwaist. That surprised me. I never really thought about women sweating. My mother never did nor any of the women I had even known.

The baby in her arms wasn't more than a few months old. It had her dark hair and a placid expression that seemed out of place on the hot, crowded train. The toddler had the bored look of a child who has been on the move constantly. He ran ahead of his mother, found an empty seat, and crawled up on it. He smiled when the soldier across the aisle handed him a sugar candy.

Mary came down the aisle, swaying a little to keep her balance as the train started to move. She saw me, paused, and smiled. It wasn't the usual ingratiating smile of an inferior but a relieved, patient kind of smile, as if I could help her.

The train lurched down the track, gathering speed, and the sudden motion threw Mary against the back of the seat in front of me. She stumbled and dropped her bundle but hung onto the baby, who started to cry. The soldier behind her put a hand on her waist for balance, and she blushed as the other men in the car nudged each other and snickered.

She sat down next to her boy, across the aisle from me. To quiet the baby, she opened her shirtwaist and began to nurse. I had never seen anything like that before. Mother had wet nurses for all of us, and the door to the nursery was always closed during feedings. Mary covered herself as best she could with her shirtwaist, and most of us looked away—including me, but not before I had a glimpse of her creamy skin and the large blue veins in her breast.

The men who didn't turn their heads divided their time between staring at Mary, making low comments to their bunkies, and laughing at me. I know that my face was red. I could feel it.

Mary's children were quiet most of that long, hot trip. The older boy (his name was Flynn) whimpered a bit in the heat as we chugged across Nebraska. I have never enjoyed crossing Nebraska, either by train or on horseback. It is either hot and flat or cold and flat. Anyway, Flynn was passed from soldier to soldier, and by the time we reached Cheyenne Depot, he had accumulated two revolvers carved out of soap, a wooden horse, and some jelly beans which melted and got all over my new boots.

It did take time to reach Cheyenne Depot. We were delayed by buffalo on the tracks and more often by hotboxes, when the axle-bearing joints heated up. The train had to stop and cool down before proceeding.

Mary's baby began to fret as we neared Cheyenne. Adele has told me since that Mary's milk was probably drying up, and the baby wasn't getting enough, but I didn't know anything then. Mary spent most of her time walking up and down the aisle, jiggling the baby (I never did learn its name), and making crooning sounds. The baby developed a thin cry, and I noticed that whenever it started to wail, some of the older soldiers would look at each other. Sergeant O'Brien crossed himself a couple of times.

At Cheyenne Depot, the horses were unloaded, and there was a Dougherty wagon from the fort to meet us. It filled up quickly. There were two captains' wives and children from first class to fit in, plus some of their luggage. There wasn't any room for Mary and her children in the wagon, so the tailgate was lowered, and they perched on that.

The other women stayed as far away from Mary as they could, and I heard one of the wives commanding her children not to play with Flynn. I'm sure Mary heard, too, but her face was peaceful, and she hugged her crying baby and sang to it.

The baby cried more and more, with a gasping sound that made me wish the surgeon was along. I found myself riding back by the Dougherty to check on the baby. They were eating dust back there. Flynn choked and sputtered until a private swung him up in his saddle and rode back toward the front of the column.

We camped that night at Lodgepole Creek, and Mary's baby kept me awake. Not because it was crying, because by then, it wasn't crying. It struggled and fought for breath in the heat that refused to leave us, even after the sun went down.

I found myself breathing along with the baby. I heard Mary whispering Hail Mary over and over, and my lips moved along with hers in the dark on the other side of the Dougherty.

I will never forget the second night out when we halted just before dusk at Chug Station. Mary jumped off the wagon before it rolled to a complete stop and hurried to the sergeant. She gestured to the baby, and I couldn't hear what she said, but O'Brien dismounted as if his saddle were on fire and bent over the infant. He called to me.

"Lieutenant, this baby's dead."

Heads poked out of the Dougherty wagon and then were pulled in again.

The baby was dead. It was even getting a little stiff.

"How long, Mary?" the sergeant asked.

"Since before the last rest stop." Mary's voice quavered, and she looked at me. "I just couldn't say anything."

That was the first time I had ever seen anyone dead before. That dead baby touched me more than I care to remember, and I have seen much death here on the plains in the twenty years since. The baby's eyes were closed, and the dark hair was curly and damp from Mary's perspiration. Except for a china-doll appearance that made my knees weak, the baby looked asleep.

The sergeant detailed a couple of privates to dig a little grave under a cottonwood by the river. Mary wrapped her shawl around the body and handed it to me.

"Here, please," she begged. "I can't do it."

I knelt by the hole and put the baby in. Mary covered her face with her hands, and I saw tears running through her fingers. The other women stayed near the wagon. I knew why. They had been taught, same as I, to avoid women like Mary, those bits of flotsam without husbands and with a string of children who followed the army from post to post. Mary needed comfort, but none of us would give her any.

Mary clung to Flynn the rest of the journey, her face wearing a white, transfigured look that I could see even under the road dust that covered all of us. She clutched her little boy to her and hung onto the chains that held the tailgate.

The remainder of the trip is still a painful memory. I was the ranking officer. With the death of that baby, responsibility for the lives of others descended on me and has been a burden ever since. And when Mary looked at me with her patient expression, I knew I was ill equipped.

Once we arrived at Fort Laramie, I forgot about Mary. Well, I did think about her every time my laundry was returned washed, ironed, and folded neatly on top of my campaign trunk. She did a good job with shirts. There were none of the little scorch marks and wrinkles I later came to associate with army life. I almost slipped a note in with my dirty clothes one day to let her know that I appreciated the good job, but I reconsidered. I didn't even know if she could read.

I didn't think much about Mary until a year later. In the early spring of 1876, Mary came to my attention again.

I was officer of the guard. It was around eleven o'clock at night, and I had just stretched out on the officer-of-the-day's cot. I hated sleeping in the guardhouse. It was infested with graybacks, and just the thought of that made me start to itch. Down below me that night in the cells were a private sleeping off a mighty drunk and a German held for garrison court-martial.

It was the night after payday. The army was paid every two months then, and that usually meant pretty intense card playing and drinking until the money was in someone else's pockets.

The sergeant of the guard came puffing up from Suds Row and hollered to me to come quick. A corporal in the band had been drinking and had knifed his wife.

By the time I got there, she was already dead. He had slit her throat from ear to ear, and there was a mild, surprised look in her wide-open eyes that made me turn away. Blood was everywhere—on the ceiling, on the walls, and splattered on the iron stove, where it bubbled and stank.

The corporal was drunk and just beginning to realize what he had done. The sergeant jerked his hands behind his back and bound them tight with a rawhide thong. The two of them lurched across the slippery floor, heading for the guardhouse.

I heard children crying in the kitchen. I went in there to look and to get away from the awful mess in the front room.

Mary Murphy sat there with the children. She was holding two blood-daubed little girls on her lap. She was in her nightgown, which was flecked with blood. Again, she gave me that patient, relieved smile, and, again, I didn't know what to do for her.

"Can you take the children?" I asked her finally, "At least, for a while?"

"Yes, certainly, Lieutenant." Her voice had the Irish lilt so common back then in the Indian-fighting army.

While I supervised the removal of the body from the front room, Mary must have left with the children. When I looked in the kitchen later, they were gone.

The next morning, sometime before First Call, the corporal worked his hands free and looped his belt with his neck in it over the bolt in the wall of his solitary cell. He wasn't in my company, but as I filled out the report, the adjutant assigned me to track down any living relatives to find a home for the orphans. As was the case in too many of these situations, I couldn't find anyone.

Mary kept the girls. I know now what a burden that must have been to her, because when Adele and I had children, we had trouble making ends meet on officer's pay. Mary was doing it on laundress' wages.

A few weeks after the incident, our company was sent north in time to get all hell beat out of us by Crazy Horse on the Rosebud. I took an arrow in the back and was invalided back to Fort Laramie. While I was recovering, I did a lot of walking and often went down to the river. Mary was always there with the other laundresses, dipping water in good and bad weather, and washing down there on the bank when it was hot. She scrubbed, pounded, and beat the clothes on her wash-board, all the time singing and talking to Flynn and the two little girls who clung to her skirts. They played at the river's edge and made mud pies on the ground near her washtub. A month later, I was promoted and transferred to Company B, Second Cav (I knew someone in D.C.), then posted to Fort Bowie, Arizona Territory.

I never saw Mary again. I met Adele in Massachusetts a few years later while on furlough, and we have spent much of our time here in the Southwest. Whenever Adele and I quarrel, which isn't too often, I think of Mary and her patient smile and wonder whatever became of her.

I imagine she raised those children by herself. They are probably married now, with children of their own.

Well, never mind. Mary Murphy. I think of her.

A Season for Heroes

❧❧

*E*zra Freeman died yesterday. I don't usually read the obituaries; at least I didn't until after Pearl Harbor. With four grandsons in the service now and one of them based in the Solomons and missing over a place called Rabaul, or some such thing, I generally turn to the obituaries after the front page and the editorials.

There it was, right at the bottom of the column, in such small print that I had to hold the paper out at arm's length . . . *Ezra Freeman.* There was no date of birth listed, probably because even Ezra hadn't known that, but it did mention there were no surviving relatives and that the deceased had been a veteran of the Indian Wars.

When I thought about Ezra Freeman, I ended up thinking about Mother and Father. Still carrying the newspaper, I went into my bedroom and looked at the picture of Mother and Father and D Company hanging on the wall next to the window. It was taken just before Father was promoted and bumped up to a desk job in San Antonio, so he is still leaning on a cane in the picture. Mother is sitting on a bench holding quite a small baby, and, next to her, his shoulders thrown back and his boots together, is Sergeant Ezra Freeman.

The picture was taken at Fort Bowie, Arizona Territory. I was ten or eleven then, and that memory was one of the first that really stuck in my mind. It was where Father nearly got killed, my little brother was born, and I discovered a few things about love.

My mother was what people call lace-curtain Irish. She was born Kathleen Mary Flynn. Her father owned a successful brewery in upstate New York, and Mother was educated at a convent, where she learned to speak French and make lace. She never owned up to learning anything else there, although she wrote with a fine copperplate hand and did a lot of reading when Father was campaigning. The nuns taught her good manners and how to pour tea the right way. Father could always make her flare up by winking at her and saying in his broadest brogue, "What'll ye hev to dhrink now, Kate Flynn?"

She had beautiful red hair that curled every which way. Little springs of it were forever popping out of the bun she wore low on her neck. She had a sprinkling of light brown freckles that always mystified the Indians. I remember the time an old San Carlos Apache stopped us as we were walking down Tucson's main street. He spoke to Father in Apache. Father answered him, and we could see he was trying to keep a straight face.

We pounced on him after the Indian nodded, gave Mother a searching look, and walked away.

"What did he say, Father, what did he say?"

Father shook his head and herded us around the corner where he leaned against the wall and laughed silently until tears shone on his eyelashes. Mother got exasperated.

"What *did* he say, John?"

"Oh, Kate Flynn," he wheezed and gasped, "he wanted to know . . . Oh, God . . ." He went off in another quiet spasm.

"John!" Mother didn't approve of people taking the Lord's name in vain (which made garrison life a trial for her at times).

"Sorry, Kathleen." Father looked at her and winked. I could feel Mother stiffening up. "He wanted to know if you had those little brown dots all over."

We children screamed with laughter. Mother blushed. A lesser Victorian lady would have swooned, I suppose, but Tucson's streets were dusty then, and Father was laughing too hard to catch her on the way down.

Mother and Father met after Father's third summer at West Point. He had been visiting friends of his family in Buffalo, and Mother had been a guest of one of the daughters. They had spent a week in each other's company; then Mother had gone back to the convent. They corresponded on the sly for several months. Father proposed during Christmas furlough. They were married after graduation in June.

There had been serious objections on both sides of the family. Papa Flynn made Father promise to raise any children as Catholics, and Grandpa Stokes wanted to be reassured that he and Grandma wouldn't be obliged to call on the Flynns too often.

Father agreed to everything, and he would have raised us as Catholics, except that we seldom saw a priest out on the plains. Besides, Mother wasn't a very efficient daughter of the church. I think she figured she'd had enough, what with daily mass at the convent for six years straight. In spite of that, she always kept her little ebony-and-silver rosary in her top drawer under her handkerchiefs, and I only saw her fingering it once.

I don't remember what my father looked like in those early years. I do remember that he wasn't too tall (few of the horse soldiers were), and that the other officers called him Handsome Johnny. Mother generally called him "the Captain" when we were around. "The Captain says you should do this, Janey," or "Take the Captain's paper to him, Gerald." When he was promoted, she called him "the Major," and the last name before he died was "the Colonel." Fifteen years later, just before she died, Mother had started over and was calling him "the Lieutenant" again.

I was born about a year after they were married. Pete came along two years later at Fort Sill, and Gerald was born at Fort Robinson near the Black Hills.

When I was ten, we were assigned to Fort Bowie, Arizona Territory. That was in the fall of 1881, more than sixty years ago. Father commanded D Company of the Tenth Cavalry (the Ninth and Tenth Cavalry were composed entirely of Negro enlisted men, serving under white officers). The Indians called them Buffalo Soldiers, I suppose because their kinky black hair reminded them of the hair of a buffalo. Father always swore they were the best troops in the whole U.S. Army and said he was proud to serve with them, even though some of his brother officers considered such duty a penance.

My favorite memory of D Company was listening to them ride into Fort Bowie after duty in the field. They always came in singing. The only man who couldn't carry a tune was my father. I remember one time right before Christmas when they rode out of Apache Pass singing "Star of the East." Mother came out on the porch to listen, her hand on my shoulder.

D Company had two Negro sergeants. Sergeant Albert Washington was a former slave from Valdosta, Georgia. He was a short, skinny little man who never said very much, maybe because he was married to Clara Washington, who did our washing and sewing and who had the loudest, strongest voice between the Mississippi and the Pacific.

The other sergeant was Ezra Freeman. Ezra wasn't much taller than my father, and he had the biggest hands I ever saw. They fascinated me because he was so black and the palms of his hands were so white.

Ezra had a lovely deep voice that reminded me of chocolate pudding. I loved to hear him call the commands to the troops during Guard Mount, and I loved to watch him sit in his saddle. My father was a good horseman, but he never sat as tall as Ezra Freeman, and Father's shoulders got more and more stooped as the years passed. Not Ezra's.

Last time I saw him sitting in his wheelchair, his posture was as good as ever; I think he would have died before he would have leaned forward.

Once I asked Ezra about his childhood. He said that he had been raised on a plantation in South Carolina. At the age of twelve, he and two sisters and his mother and father had been sold at the Savannah auction to help pay off his master's gambling debts. He never saw any of his family again. A planter from Louisiana bought him, and he stayed a field hand until Admiral Farragut steamed up the Mississippi and ended slavery on the lower river. He sometimes spoke a funny kind of pidgin French that made my mother laugh and shake her head.

But she never got too close to Ezra or to any of Father's other troopers. None of the white women of the regiment did, either. Mother never would actually pull her skirts aside when the colored troopers passed, as some of the ladies did, but she had a formality about her in the presence of the Buffalo Soldiers that we weren't accustomed to. As least, she did until the summer of 1882, when we came to owe Ezra Freeman everything.

That was the summer Ignacio and his Apaches left the San Carlos Agency and raided, looted, burned, and captured women and children to sell in Mexico. The troops garrisoned at Bowie knew that Ignacio's activities would touch them soon, and the early part of the summer was spent in refitting and requisitioning supplies and ordnance in preparation for the orders they knew would come.

Mother wasn't receiving any callers that summer. That was how we put it then. Or we might have said that she was "in delicate health." Now, in 1942, we say, "she is expecting," or, "she is in the family way." Back then, that would have been altogether too vulgar and decidedly low class.

Neither of them told us. I just happened to notice Mother one morning when I burst into her room and caught her in her shift. She bulged a little in the front, and I figured we were going to have another baby brother sometime. They seemed to lose interest in having girls after me. She didn't say anything then, and I didn't, either. Later on in the week, when we were polishing silver, she paused, put her hand on her middle, and stared off in space for a few minutes, a slight smile on her face.

At breakfast a few mornings later, Father came right out and asked Mother if she wanted to go home for the summer to have the baby. The railroad had been completed between Bowie and Tucson, and it would be a much less difficult trip.

"Oh, no, I couldn't, John," she replied.

"Why not? I'll probably be gone all summer anyway, and you know the surgeon travels with us." Father wiped the egg juice off his plate with one swipe of his toast and grinned when Mother frowned at him.

"Oh, I just couldn't, John," she repeated, and that was the end of that.

Two weeks later, three of the cavalry companies and two of the infantry were detached from Bowie to look for Ignacio. Mother said her goodbyes to Father in their bedroom. As I think of it, few of the wives ever saw their husbands off from the porch, except for Lieutenant Grizzard's wife, and everyone said she was a brassy piece anyway.

We kids followed Father out onto the porch. My little brother Pete wore the battered black felt hat Father always took on campaign, and Gerald lugged out the saber, only to be sent back into the house with the useless thing. Father let me carry out his big Colt revolver, and I remember that it took both hands to carry it.

He took the gun from me and pushed it into his holster. He put his hand on my head and shook it back and forth. Then he knelt down and kissed me on both cheeks.

"Keep an eye on Mother for me, Janey," he said.

I nodded, and he stood up and shook my head again. He plucked the black hat off Pete's head and swatted him lightly with it. He knelt down again, and both Pete and Gerald clung to him.

"Now, you two mind Janey. She's sergeant major."

D Company rode out at the head of the column after Guard Mount, and the corporal who taught school for the garrison's children was kind enough to dismiss us for the day.

Summers are always endless to children, but that summer of 1882 seemed to stretch out like cooling taffy. One month dragged by, and then two, and still the men didn't return. In fact, another company was sent out, and Bowie had only the protection of one understrength company of infantry and the invalids in the infirmary.

The trains stopped running between Bowie and Tucson because of Ignacio and his warriors, and I recall how irritated Mother was when the last installment of a serial in Frank Leslie's *Illustrated Weekly* never showed up. The only mail that got through was official business that the couriers brought in.

But Mother was irritated with many things that summer. She usually didn't show much until the eighth month, but this time she had Clara Washington sew her some new Mother Hubbards before her sixth month. Her ankles were swollen, too. I rarely saw Mother's legs, but once I caught her on the back porch one evening with her dress up around her knees.

"Oh, Mama!" was all I said.

It startled her, and she dropped her skirts and tucked her feet under the chair. "Jane, you shouldn't spy on people!" she scolded, and then she smiled when she saw my face. "Oh, I'm sorry, Jane. And don't look so worried. They'll be all right again soon."

Toward the middle of August, we began to hear rumors in the garrison. Ordinarily we just shrugged off rumors, but the men were now quite overdue, and still, Ignacio hadn't been subdued or chased back across the border. One rumor had the troops halfway across Mexico pursuing Apaches, and another rumor had them in San Diego waiting for a troop train back.

On the eighteenth of August (I remember the date because it was Gerald's fifth birthday), the rumor changed. A couple of reservation Apaches slouched in on their hard-ridden ponies to report a skirmish to the south of us, hard by the Mexican border. Captain Donnelly, B Company, Fourth Infantry, was senior officer of the fort then, and he ignored the whole thing. The Indians weren't students of the truth, and they often confused Mexican and U.S. soldiers.

I mentioned the latest rumor to Mother, who smiled at me and gave me a little shake. I went back outside to play, but I noticed a look in her eyes that hadn't been there before.

Two days later, the troops rode in. They were tired, sunburned, and dirty, and their remounts looked mostly starved. Mother came out on the porch. She leaned on the porch railing and stood on one foot and then the other. I saw that she had taken off her wedding ring and Father's West Point ring that she always wore on her first finger. Her hands looked swollen and tight.

The troops assembled on the parade ground and some of the women and children ran out to them. We looked hard for D Company, but it wasn't there. Mother sat down on the bench under the parlor window.

Several of the officers dismounted and stood talking together. One of them gestured our way, and Mother got up quickly. When Major Connors started walking over to our quarters, she backed into the house and jerked me in with her.

"Listen to me, Jane Elizabeth," she hissed, and her fingers dug into my shoulders until I squirmed in her grasp. "You take their message."

"But Mother," I whined, trying to get out of her grip, "why don't you?"

"It's bad luck," she said and turned and went into the parlor, slamming the door behind her.

Major Connors didn't seem too surprised that Mother wouldn't come out to talk to him. I backed away from him myself because he smelled so awful. "Jane, tell your mother than D Company and A are both a bit overdue but not to worry because we expect them any time."

After he left, I told Mother, but she wouldn't come out of the parlor until suppertime.

Several days passed, and then a week, and still no sign of either company. None of the other officers' wives said anything to Mother about the delay, but several of them paid her morning calls and brought along baked goods.

"Why are they doing this, Mama?" I asked her, after Captain O'Neill's wife left an eggless custard.

Mother murmured something about an early wake. I asked her what she meant, but she shook her head. My brothers and I downed all the cakes and pies, but Mother wouldn't eat any of it.

One night when I couldn't sleep because of the heat, I crept downstairs to get a drink of water from the pump. Mother was sitting on the back porch, rocking slowly in the moonlight. She heard me and closed her fist over something in her lap, but not before I'd seen what it was: the little ebony rosary she kept in her drawer. I could tell by the look in her face that she didn't want me to say anything about it. She rocked, and I sat down near her on the porch steps.

"Mama, what happens if he doesn't come back?" I hadn't really meant to say that; it just came out. She stopped rocking. I thought she might be angry with me, but she wasn't.

"Oh, we'll just manage, Jane. It won't be as much fun, but we'll just manage."

"Would . . . would we move back East?"

She must not have thought that far, because she was silent a while. "No, I don't think so," she said finally. "I like it out West. So did . . . does . . . your father."

She rocked on in silence, and I could hear, above the creak of the rocking chair, the click of the little ebony beads. I got up to go, and she took my hand.

"You know, Jane, there's one terrible thing about being a woman."

I looked down at her. Her ankles and hands were swollen, her belly stretched tight against the nightgown that usually hung loose on her, and her face was splotched. "What's that, Mama?"

"The waiting, the waiting."

She didn't say anything else, so I went back upstairs and finally fell asleep after the duty guards had called the time from post to post all around the fort.

Another week passed, and still no sign of the companies. The next week began as all the others had. The blue sky was cloudless, and the sun beat down until the whole fort shimmered. Every glance held a mirage.

It was just after Stable Call that I heard the singing. The sound came up faintly, and for a few moments, I wasn't sure I heard anything except the wind and the stable noises to the south of us. But there it was again, and closer. It sounded like "Dry Bones," and that had always been one of Father's favorite songs.

I turned to call Mother, but she was standing in the doorway, her hand shading her eyes as she squinted toward Apache Pass. People popped out of houses all along Officers Row, and the younger children began pointing and then running west past the administration building and the infirmary.

There they were, two columns of blue filing out of the pass, moving slowly. The singing wasn't very loud, and then it died out as the two companies approached the stables. Mother took her hand away from her eyes. "He's not there, Janey," she whispered.

I looked again. I couldn't see Father anywhere. She stood still on the porch and shaded her eyes again. Then she gave a sob and began running.

So many nights in my dreams I've seen my mother running across the parade ground. She was so large and clumsy then, and, as I recall, she was barefoot, but she ran as lightly as a young child, her arms held out in front of her. In my dreams, she runs and runs until I wake up.

I was too startled to follow her at first, and then I saw her run to the back of the column and drop down on her knees by a travois one of the horses was pulling. The animal reared back and then nearly kicked her, but I don't think she even noticed. Her arms were around a man lying on the travois. As I ran closer, I could see him raise his hand slowly and put it on her hair.

I didn't recognize my father at first. His hair was matted with blood, and I thought half his head had been blown away. There was a bloody, yellowish bandage over one eye, and his face was swollen. He turned his head in my direction, and I think he tried to smile, but he only bared his teeth at me, and I stepped back.

I want to turn and run, and I didn't see how Mother could stand it. But there she was, her head on his chest. She was saying something to him I couldn't hear, and all the while, he was stroking her hair with that filthy, bruised hand.

I backed up some more and bumped into Ezra Freeman. I tried to turn and run, but he held me there. "Go over to him, Janey," he urged and gave me a push. "He wants you."

I couldn't see how Ezra could interpret the slight movement of Father's hand, but he was pushing me toward the travois. "Pa? Pa?" I could feel tears starting behind my eyelids.

He said something that I couldn't understand because it sounded as if his mouth was full of mashed potatoes. I leaned closer. He smelled of blood, sweat, dirt, and wood smoke. As I bent over him, I could see under the bandage on his face and gasped to see teeth and gums where his cheek should have been.

Mother was kneeling by him, her hand on his splinted leg. She took my hand in her other hand and placed it on his chest. He tried to raise his head, and I leaned closer. I could make out the words "Janey" and "home," but what he was saying was unimportant. All of a sudden I didn't care what he looked like. He was my father, and I loved him.

He must have seen my feelings in my eyes because he lay back again and closed his eye. His hand relaxed and let go of mine. I helped Mother to her feet, and we stood back as two orderlies lifted him off the travois and onto a stretcher. He moaned a little, and Mother bit her lip.

They took him to the infirmary, and Ezra Freeman walked alongside the stretcher, steadying it. Mother would have followed him, but the post surgeon took one look at her and told her to go lie down, because he didn't have time to deliver a baby just then. Mother blushed, and the two of us walked back to our quarters hand in hand.

Mother spent an hour that evening in the infirmary with Father. She came home and reported that he looked a lot better and was asleep. We went upstairs then, and while she tucked Gerald and Pete in bed, I sat on the rag rug by Pete's army cot, and she told us what happened.

"The two companies had separated from the main detachment and after a couple days, they found an Apache rancheria. It was at the bottom of a small canyon near Deer Spring. When they tried to surround it before daybreak, they were pinned down by rifle fire from the rim of the canyon." Mother paused, and I noticed that she had twisted her fingers into the afghan at the foot of Pete's bed.

He sat up. "What happened, Ma? What happened?" He pulled on her arm a little, and his eyes were shining. He had been down at the creek that afternoon and hadn't seen Father yet. The whole thing was still just a story to him.

While the candle on the nightstand burned lower and lower, Mother told how Father had been shot while trying to lead the men back to the horses. He had lain on an exposed rock all morning until Ezra Freeman crawled out and pulled him to safety. The two men had stayed in a mesquite thicket, firing at the Apaches until the sun went down. They withdrew in the dark.

Peter fell asleep then, but Mother went on to say that the men had holed up for several days about sixty miles south of us because they were afraid Father would die if they moved him. When it looked like he would make it, they started slowly for the fort.

Gerald fell asleep then, and as Mother pulled the sheet up around him, she said to me, "I can't understand it, Jane. Everyone else thought the Captain was dead. Why did Sergeant Freeman do it?"

She tucked me in my bed, but I couldn't sleep. Every time I closed my eyes, I kept seeing Father on that travois and the look in Mother's eyes as she knelt by him. I got out of bed and started into Mother's room.

She wasn't there; the bed hadn't even been slept in. I tiptoed down the stairs, stepping over the third tread because it always squeaked. As I groped to the bottom in the dark, I saw the front door open and then close quietly.

I waited a few seconds, then opened it and stood on the porch. Mother was dressed and wrapped in a dark shawl, despite the heat, and walking across the parade ground. She wasn't going toward the infirmary, so I trailed her, skirting around the parade ground and keeping in the shadow of the officers' quarters. I didn't know where she was going, but I had a feeling that she would send me back if she knew I was following her.

She passed the quartermaster's building and the stables, pausing to say something to the private on guard, who saluted her and waved her on. I waited until he had turned and walked into the shadows of the blacksmith shop before I continued.

I could see now that she was heading for Suds Row, where the enlisted men with families lived. Halfway down the row of attached quarters she stopped and knocked on one of the doors. I ducked behind the row until I came to the back of the place where she had knocked. There was a washtub in the yard, and I staggered with it to the window, turned it over, and climbed up.

Ezra lived in the barracks with his company, but Mother must have found out he was visiting Sergeant Jackson Walter of A Company and Jackson's wife, Chloe. Mother and Ezra were standing in the middle of the room. She had taken off her shawl. Freeman offered her the chair he had been sitting in, but she shook her head. I could see Chloe knitting in the rocking chair by the kitchen.

Mother was silent a few moments. "I just wanted to say thank you, Sergeant Freeman," she said finally. Her voice sounded high and thin, like it did after Grandpa Flynn's funeral three years before.

"Oh ... well ... I ... Jeez, ma'am, you're welcome," Ezra stammered.

She shrugged her shoulders and held out her hands. "I mean, Sergeant, you didn't even know if he was alive, and you went out there anyway."

He didn't say anything. All I could hear was the click of Chloe's bone needles. I barely heard Mother's next word.

"Why?"

Again that silence. Ezra Freeman turned a little, and I could see his face. His head was down, he had sucked in his lower lip, and he was crying. The light from the kerosene lamp was reflected in his tears, and they shone like diamonds on his black face.

"Well, hell, ma'am . . . he's the only man I ever served of my own free will." He paused. "And I guess I love him."

Mother put her hands to her face, and I could see her shoulders shaking. Then she raised her head, and I don't think she ever looked more beautiful. "I love him, too, Ezra. Maybe for the same reason."

Then she sort of leaned against him, and his arms went around her, and they held onto each other, crying. She was patting him on the back like she did when Father hugged her, and his hand was smoothing down her hair where it curled at the neck.

I am forever grateful that the white ladies and gents of Fort Bowie never saw the two of them together like that, for I am sure they would have been scandalized. As I stood there peeking in the window, I had the most wonderful feeling of being surrounded by love, all kinds of love, and I wanted the moment to last forever.

But the moment soon passed. They both backed away from each other, and Mother took out a handkerchief from the front of her dress and blew her nose. Ezra fished around in his pocket until he found a red bandanna and wiped his eyes. He sniffed and grinned at the same time.

"Lord, Almighty, ma'am. I ain't cried since that Emancipation Proclamation."

She smiled at him and put her hand on his arm but didn't say anything. Then she nodded to Chloe, put her shawl around her head again, and turned to the door. "Goodnight, and thank you again," she said before she went outside.

I jumped off the washtub and ran down the little alley behind the quarters. Staying in the shadows and watching out for the guards, I ran home. I wanted to be home before Mother because I knew she would look in on us before she went to sleep.

She did. She opened the door a crack, and then opened it wider and glided in. I opened my eyes a little and stretched, as if she had just wakened me. She bent down and kissed me, then kissed Gerald and Pete. She closed the door, and soon I heard her getting into bed.

One week later, a couple of troopers from D Company carried Father home on a stretcher. The doctor insisted on putting him in the parlor on the daybed because he didn't want him climbing the stairs.

The post surgeon had done a pretty good job on Father's face. The bandages were off so the air could get at his cheek, which was a crisscross maze of little black sutures. He had lost his left eye and wore a patch over the socket. Later on, he tried to get used to a glass eye but never could get a good fit. He gradually accumulated a cigar box full of glass eyes, and we used them to scare our city cousins and play a kind of lopsided marbles game. His mouth drooped down at one corner and made him look a little sad on one side. None of the other officers called him Handsome Johnny again.

The day after he had been set up in the parlor, Mother went into labor. The post surgeon tried to stop him, but Father climbed the stairs slowly, hand over hand on the railing, and sat by Mother until their third boy was born.

An hour later, the doctor motioned my brothers and me into the room. Mother was lying in the middle of the bed, her red hair spread around the pillow like a fan. Her freckles stood out a little more than usual, but she was smiling. Father sat in an armchair near the bed holding the baby, who had a red face and hair to match.

"What are you going to name him?" I asked, after giving him a good look.

Mother hesitated a moment, then looked over at the baby and Father. "Ezra Freeman Stokes," she replied quietly, her eyes on Father.

He said something to her that I couldn't understand because his face was still swollen. Mother kept her eyes on his and snapped back to him in a low voice that sent shivers down my back. "I don't give a damn what the garrison thinks! He's going to be Ezra Freeman!"

None of us had ever heard Mother swear, and Father nearly dropped the baby. That was how Ez got his name.

A month later, Father was promoted to major. By the end of the year, he was awarded the Medal of Honor for "meritorious gallantry under fire at Deer Spring." I remember how he pushed that medal around in its plush velvet case, and then closed the box with a click. "I'm not the one who should be getting this," he murmured. No one could ever prevail upon him to wear it. Even when he was laid out in his coffin years later, with his full dress uniform and all his medals, I never saw that one.

With his promotion, Father was transferred to the Third Cavalry, a white regiment. We didn't see Ezra Freeman after that and never did correspond with him because he couldn't read or write. Somehow we always heard about him from the other officers and men of D Company, and every year, at Christmas, Mother sent him a dried apple fruitcake and socks she had knitted. We knew when he retired twenty-five years later and learned in 1915 that he had entered the Old Soldiers' Home in Los Angeles.

Before Father's stroke, he paid him one visit there. I remembered that it was 1919, and Father went to tell him that Captain Ezra F. Stokes had died in France of Spanish influenza.

"You know, Janey," he told me after that visit, "Ez may have been my son, but I ended up comforting Sergeant Freeman. I almost wish I hadn't told him."

After Father passed away, Mother paid Ezra a yearly visit. She insisted on going alone on the train up from San Diego, but when her eyesight began to fade, she finally relented and let me come with her once. As it turned out, it was her last trip. I think she knew.

Sergeant Freeman was in a wheelchair by then, and after giving me a nod and telling me to wait there, Mother pushed Ezra down the sidewalk to a little patio under the trees. She sat next to him on the bench, and they talked together. After about half an hour, she took an object out of her purse, leaned toward Ezra, and put something on the front of his robe. I could tell that Ezra was protesting. He tried to push her hands away, but she went ahead and put something on him. It flashed in the sunlight, but I was too far away to make out what it was.

She took a handkerchief out of her pocket and wiped his eyes. She sat down again beside him, and they sat there together until his head nodded forward, and he fell asleep. She wheeled him back to the far entrance of the building, and I never had a chance to say goodbye.

She was silent on the trip home. After we got to the house, she said, "Jane, I feel tired," and went to bed. She drifted in and out of sleep for the next two days, and then she died.

After the funeral, I was going through her things when I came across the plush velvet case containing the Medal of Honor Father had been awarded for Deer Spring. I snapped it open but the medal was gone. I know where it went.

And now Ezra's dead. Well.

I can see I've spent more time on this than I intended. I hear the postman's whistle outside. I hope there's a letter from my daughter, Ann. It's her oldest boy, Steve, that has been missing over Rabaul for more than a month now. I don't suppose I can give her much comfort, but I can tell her something about waiting.

Jesse MacGregor

❧ ❧

*R*ose and I went to the moving pictures last night. The feature was something called *Twelve Brave Men* and was supposed to be (according to a review in the *Carlsbad Current*) a "gripping, suspense-filled saga of the real cavalry in the Old West." Naturally, we went. Toward the end of the picture, there was a scene where the cavalry patrol is pinned down under withering fire by Hollywood Apaches. When it looks like everyone has gone beaver, the whole regiment, guidons flapping, bugles blowing, comes riding over the ridge. They kill ten thousand Indians in five minutes and save the patrol. The piano player down front crashed into the "saving the patrol" music, then began a triumphal march.

I had my hands on the back of the seat in front of me and was starting to rise when Rose laid a hand on my arm and hissed at me, "If you get up and shout anything, I'll pretend I don't know you!"

"But Rose," I whispered back, "it wasn't anything like that!"

"Of course not," she snapped, tugging at my arm, "but sit down, you old fool!"

No, it wasn't anything like that. Now Rose is at her Ladies Aid meeting and is spending the afternoon with an old schoolmate, so I have a chance to set the record straight. No telling if anyone will read it. My kids think my Fort Bowie stories are the foolish wanderings of an old man's mind, so I don't tell them anymore. This'll go in the safe deposit box and maybe someday some grandkid will read it and marvel what fools mortals be.

I'm pretty sure the whole story has never been told before. The other participants had their own reasons for not writing it down. I saw the official report of the incident later, but that cut-and-dried formal document didn't begin to tell what really happened.

When orders came for B Company, Fifth Cavalry, to report to Fort Bowie, Arizona Territory, my wife sighed and murmured, "You promised me." After earning my commission the year before, I had assured Rose we probably wouldn't ever be assigned to Arizona. I still can't believe how green I was.

We arrived at Bowie in the spring of 1880. The ninety miles between Bowie and the railhead at Tucson were the hottest, driest miles I had ever traveled, and I was worried about Rose, who was eight months along then. Every jolt of the wagon made her clutch her belly and grit her teeth, and when she closed her eyes and sighed, I began to wonder why I hadn't gone into law.

The old-timers at Tucson told us this was the hottest spring since Hector was a pup. There hadn't been any winter rains at all, and there was hardly a cactus healthy enough to shade a horny toad. The sun looked like a brass ball, and even the sky was gold instead of blue.

But as I look back on it, I wouldn't have missed what followed for anything. The tour at Bowie decided my future in the U.S. Army and introduced me to a man I have never forgotten.

Captain Jesse MacGregor, post surgeon, was almost the first person to greet B Company as we walked our horses into Fort Bowie that blistering afternoon. He must have been watching us from the infirmary, because as soon as Captain Brownlee called a halt, he banged open the screen door and walked across the porch to the railing. He had on a gray-ish-white surgeon's coat with the sleeves rolled up and some black threads dangling from the breast pocket. His arms were flecked to the elbows with what looked like dried blood.

"Asa Brownlee," he shouted, taking the pipe out of his mouth, then putting it back in again, "didn't think I'd ever see you again this side of Baltimore or hell!"

My wife stuck her head out of the side of the Dougherty wagon, saw the doctor and the blood, and made a face. Mrs. Brownlee was smiling and getting down from the wagon. Brownlee had dismounted and crossed to the porch. He reached up and grabbed the doctor's bloody hand and gripped it hard.

"Lord, Mac, I thought you'd been killed in a fancy house in Baton Rouge!" he glanced back at the women in the wagon. "What're you doing here?"

"Hell, Ace," he laughed, "I guess staff thought I'd stay out of trouble here. And I'm still a captain!"

That was my introduction to Mac. He was of average height, of medium build, with sandy-colored hair he wore rather long on top to hide a bald spot. He wore gold-rimmed glasses and spent an inordinate amount of time pushing them up tighter on the bridge of his nose. I mentioned to him once that his trouble would be over if he would only tighten the little hinges on the frames. He looked at me in amazement and said, "Well, damn me!" I don't recall that he ever did anything about it, though.

His eyes were a bright blue and shone frequently with what the commanding officer called a "damned misguided look." He was a poor poker player because you could always see his hand in his eyes. He had little wrinkles around his mouth that made him look like he was always smiling.

As I came to know Mac better, I observed several abilities that set him apart from the rest of us. He had a good seat. He rode better than any surgeon had a right to, and I have seen him dismount after a day's punishment in the saddle and stride to his quarters without a grimace. A lesser man would have been dubbed Iron Ass, but we just called him Mac. He had surgeon's hands, long and narrow, even ladylike, with tapering fingers and well-trimmed nails. His hands were unusually steady, and Lord, could he put in stitches to stay.

I think the next thing people noticed about Mac was his pipe. He was never without it. I know this for a fact because I was in the room when he delivered John, Jr., and he kept that pipe clenched in his teeth throughout the whole long, hot ordeal.

He smoked a pipe he swore Grant had given him after the siege of Vicksburg. He had a habit of taking it out of his mouth and twisting it between his thumb and forefinger, then putting it back in. He smoked a tobacco called Sailor's Delight, and a tin arrived nearly every month from Boston, depending on how the mails were running. I remarked once that so much smoking couldn't be good for him, but he only laughed, patted me on the shoulder, and said *he* was the doctor.

When I met Mac, he was in his late thirties or early forties. It was hard to tell. The adjutant joked once that if we cut off Mac's head and counted the rings, we could determine his age. Anyway, Mac was at the age when most post surgeons of any skill at all were wearing a major's oak-leaf clusters and were beginning to eye the office of surgeon general as more than an idle dream. Mac was still a captain, the rank with which he had entered the army medical corps. It didn't seem to bother him.

I wondered why he was still a captain. Surely there couldn't be any doubt about his surgical gifts, with which he was richly blessed. Judging from the steady cursing that came from his office at least once a month, I suspected that he kept good records.

I soon learned the reason for Mac's stagnation. A week after our arrival at Bowie, the adjutant sent word that the commanding officer had some paperwork for me to settle and requested my presence at headquarters.

I snapped to my fanciest academy salute in front of the colonel's desk. When he glanced up from the morning reports, his eyes had a pre-occupied look. He pointed one finger toward his eye to acknowledge my salute and looked over my shoulder at the adjutant, who must have been trying to back out of the room.

"Mr. Reynolds," he barked, waving the morning report in his hand. "I see here that before the flag was raised this morning, it was necessary to remove a pair of balbriggans with the lettering 'E.C. Devlin' stenciled on the neck. Apparently they had been waving at half staff throughout most of the night. I questioned the sergeant of the guard about it, but he had no notion as to how this item came to be there. Can you enlighten me, sir?"

I moved out of the way of the colonel's stare. It could have cut through iron.

"Well, sir," the adjutant began, "you see, sir, there was a party last night in Mac's quarters, and . . ."

"Ah, hah!" the commanding officer burst in. He slammed down the morning reports so hard that the spittoon halfway across the room shivered on its base.

"Yes, sir," the adjutant continued, "celebrating Devlin's promotion." He hesitated.

"And?" the commanding officer prompted. He came out of his swivel chair in a half crouch.

"And Devlin's long johns ended up on the flagpole," the adjutant finished in a rush of words.

The commanding officer lowered himself into his chair and began again. "You wouldn't happen to know who had engineered such a stunt, would you?"

"No, sir, not exactly, sir. You see, I wasn't precisely conscious when that particular incident transpired."

The commanding officer raised his eyebrows and then frowned until they came together across his forehead. His shoulders began to sag, and his hands relaxed. I think he knew he wasn't going to get anything more out of Reynolds, but you could say about the man that he didn't give up easily. "Is drunkenness a proper state for my officers?" he growled. His glance included me, too, and my stomach began to hurt.

"Well, no, sir," the adjutant murmured, "but Devlin had been a second looie for ten years, sir."

"How well I know. How well I know," the colonel said. "I trust that Devlin didn't suffer any ill effects from exposure last night." He leaned back in his chair and waved away the adjutant. "That's all, Mr. Reynolds. I don't suppose anyone has any knowledge of how those things wound up on the flagpole." He paused a moment. "Wait a minute, Mr. Reynolds. Tell Mac to come and see me when he has a moment."

And so it went. When the officer of the guard and his cot were quietly moved onto the middle of the parade ground in the dead of night, when the water troughs bubbled soapsuds, when the company gardens sprouted wax fruit, when a copy of the *Police Gazette* turned up in the sewing basket of the commanding officer's wife, when anything happened, the finger of blame always pointed at Jesse MacGregor.

Not that it was easy to catch him at his pranks. It was hard. I was officer of the day the time he painted the commanding officer's chicken coop blue with egg-shaped white dots, and I didn't see a thing.

A few of Mac's activities were blatant. After the commanding officer had commanded all of us to learn a few basic sentences in Apache, Mac was spotted going from privy to privy, tacking up posters with such useful phrases in English-spiked Apache as "Stop, or I'll shoot," and "We will camp here," on the inside doors. You would have been amazed how much Apache the men, women, and children of the garrison picked up in those idle moments of contemplation. Even the colonel had to admit that the desired effect had been achieved.

"But it just isn't . . . well . . . damn it . . . it's just not decent!" he had hollered, but the commanding officer knew he was licked that time.

Mac couldn't be held responsible for all the big and little tricks that went on at the post, but he was. After our company's pet goat was found nibbling the colonel's geraniums down to the roots, the commanding officer could be heard muttering, "I'll have him cashiered," over and over during Guard Mount.

Nothing happened. I asked one of the other officers about it, and he replied, "I suppose the commanding officer could get him cashiered under the 'conduct prejudicial clause,' but, John, even *he* likes Mac."

In addition to that, there was a network of security around Mac that Pinkerton would have envied. Everyone from the pea-greenest recruit to the oldest sergeant would have been buried up to his neck in an anthill before he would have divulged any knowledge of Mac's pranks. Mac gave us something to laugh at.

That was the secret of Mac's survival. His tricks never hurt anyone, and Lord knows anyone garrisoned in Arizona Territory needed something to laugh at. When you exist for months and months in a place where the heat digs in before sunrise and won't let go until long after Extinguish Lights, where the water tastes like urine, where everything that bites is poisonous, you need to laugh. Mac understood that better than any of us; of course, he never got promoted.

Not only did we need to laugh, we needed Mac. I've seen him perform surgery under primitive conditions. He could calm a woman in labor (and her nervous husband) with a few words and a smile, and I don't think any of the garrison children ever bit him. We trusted him.

Mac could be charming. Not long after our arrival at Bowie, we had Mac over for an evening. We filled him full of government beef and mock apple pie, and he entertained us with tales of his exploits in medical school and in the South on Reconstruction duty, where he had spent much of his service time. He had a way of sitting on the edge of his chair and hunching forward that made you want to draw up to him like a conspirator.

He left just before Last Roll Call. I turned from the door to Rose, who was bending over to blow out the lamp. "Why do you suppose he's like that?" I asked her.

She straightened up and looked at me as if my head were on backward. "Why, John, it's so obvious. He's lonely!"

"Lonely?" I echoed. "How could he be lonely? Every time I walk past his quarters, there are always two or three fellows in there. How could he be lonely?"

"Lonely," she repeated, drawing her arm through mine and leading me to bed.

I laughed at her but later on got to thinking that perhaps she was right. Life on the frontier affected all of us differently. Some men took to drinking, some to whoring, others became sloppy in the performance of their duties (they usually didn't live too long), and some withdrew from everyone. I became obsessed with my journal, and Mac played practical jokes.

B Company was involved in pretty steady drilling and training, so I didn't see much of Mac after that evening. By August, we got busy with end-of-the-month reports and the upcoming visit of the inspector general, so Mac got filed somewhere in my mind.

The morning after the inspector general left to terrorize another post, my captain pulled me aside after Guard Mount. "John, we've been assigned to go to Tucson to pick up a shipment of fresh fish."

"Oh, Lord."

"Yeah. Eight new recruits for the company. Hope they're better than the last awkward squad that went to C Company."

"You want me to get up a detail, sir?"

"Yes. Pick ten or so good men. We'll leave tomorrow morning before it gets too hot. Ration them for a week."

In an understrength company of fifty men, it wasn't easy to find ten men able for duty. Eight of them had been put on extra duty repairing roofs, three troopers were still serving time in the mill for disorderly conduct, four more were in the infirmary recovering from one or another of the ailments indigenous to Arizona, and ten others had been detailed to escort the inspector general to Camp Grant. In the end, I found six men and rationed them.

Captain Brownlee looked a little dubious. "I don't know, Lieutenant. You never can tell about Apaches."

"Last I heard, sir, everyone was accounted for at the agencies."

Captain Brownlee slapped his thigh with his hat and shook his head. "Don't see as we have any other choice."

I was walking back to my quarters when I smelled Sailor's Delight. Mac fell into step beside me. He was still wearing his hospital coat, decorated with fresh daubs of blood and mysterious yellow stains. "I wish to God you'd change coats occasionally."

He took his pipe out of his mouth, looked at me, and put it back in. "John, I'm disappointed in you. I put this one on clean this morning. Had to pull a tooth, and I'm not very good at that."

We walked along in silence for a few minutes. "I hear you and Brownlee are going to Tucson."

"Tomorrow."

"I'm expecting some medical supplies."

"I'll get them for you."

More silence. "Say, maybe I could come along, too?" he offered, as I stopped in front of my quarters.

"Why not?" I answered. "Can you get away? We're kind of short-mounted, and you'd be welcome."

"I'll go speak to the commanding officer. He'll be glad to have me off his hands for a week. There isn't anything in the infirmary the steward can't handle." His white coat flapped behind him as he hurried back across the parade ground to the admin building.

Rose was standing on the porch. "I hope he can go with you," she said as I joined her. "He'll liven it up."

We left at dawn the next morning, the nine of us . . . Sergeant Lucas Pennington, a corporal, four privates, Brownlee, Mac, and me. Bowie is situated at the eastern end of Apache Pass, and as we started through the pass, I could feel the hairs rising on the back of my neck. I couldn't see anything other than two hawks wheeling and dipping on the currents far above us, but I looked over my shoulder anyway.

Mac was slouched on his horse. He clenched his pipe tight between his teeth and hummed "The British Grenadier," while he drummed on his saddle. I leaned toward him, and even the creaking of my saddle made the goose bumps stand out on my arms.

"Do you feel it, Mac?"

He raised his eyebrows and nodded. "Arizona's a damned queer place."

Sergeant Pennington, who had been riding next to the captain, dropped back and joined us. We rode three abreast deeper into the pass. Pennington was the ranking non-com of B Company. He was a short, beefy man with the most brittle blue eyes I had ever seen. I was half afraid of him.

I did wonder what he was doing with us today. "I thought you were finishing monthly reports, Sergeant," I finally commented.

"I was, sir," he replied, "but Sergeant Quinn's daughter, Ellen, is going to meet us in Tucson. Since Quinn is laid up with rheumatism, I told him I'd come instead."

"Don't believe I've ever met her," Mac said, as he guided his horse with his knees and filled his pipe.

"She's been living with an uncle in Iowa and teaching school the past three–four years. You'd remember her if you'd met her, Captain."

"How's that?"

Like many a rough man before him, Sergeant Pennington had trouble expressing himself. "Well," he began, scratching his head, "well, she's . . . she's . . ."

"Is she pretty?" I asked.

"Yes, sir, but that's not it." He paused, thought a moment, but didn't continue.

"Guess we'll just have to meet her," Mac said, but it sounded like he was only trying to be polite.

Pennington nodded in relief. "Yes, sir, you'll just have to meet her." He spurred his horse ahead to rejoin Brownlee.

We would have made Tucson sooner than three days, but Mac had to stop at a ranch to remove some stitches the Camp Grant surgeon had put into a cowman's leg three weeks earlier on a trip of his own. The delay took us a day out of our way and off the regular route.

We sat around a little fire our last night out from Tucson, listening to Mac tell a dirty story that I knew I wouldn't dare repeat to Rose. Captain Brownlee started to launch into one of his own when I interrupted him.

"What I want to know is, what's it really like?"

"What are you talking about?" Brownlee asked.

"Indian fighting."

"It's hard to describe," Sergeant Pennington said in his usual explanatory style.

"You know, it is," Brownlee stated, leaning back against his saddle.

"It's like this, John," Mac said, hunching forward. I found myself leaning toward him like a collaborator, until our heads were close together. "It's like sex for the first time."

It was so absurd, I laughed. "What on earth are you talking about?"

"Now hear me out. Before you try out the family jewels on some willing miss, you have a pretty good idea what it must be like, but when it finally happens, it's a little different than you ever figured."

"Well, yes." I had to agree, but I was glad it was too dark for him to see me blush. My experience was limited to Rose, but I didn't see that he needed to know that.

Brownlee sat up again. He winked at Mac. "Maybe so, Mac, but I wish to hell the one would last longer and the other was shorter!"

Even Pennington had to laugh. As I lay on top of my blanket that night, I wondered all over again what an Indian attack was like. I wondered how I would act. I knew what I should do, but I wondered what I would do.

As we rode down Tucson's dusty main street toward the depot the next day, I thought about Sergeant Quinn and wondered about his daughter. Quinn was the regiment's ordnance sergeant and, as near as I could figure, had been born and raised in the army. I guess I was a little afraid of him, too. I really couldn't picture his daughter.

I met her soon enough. When we got to the depot, two women waited there. One was pacing back and forth, swirling up clouds of dust every time she moved. Her skirts swept a zigzag pattern across the platform. As we got closer, she took off a glove, and I noticed the gold band on her finger. She must be the lieutenant's wife we were to escort to the fort.

The other woman was seated on a canvas-covered trunk, leaning forward with her chin propped on her hand. She looked up when she saw our blue uniforms and smiled. Pennington had been quite right.

She was pretty, with wonderful blond hair swept up on her head and held in place with a big comb. Little ringlets danced at her temples, as if impatient with the comb's confinement. Her nose was straight and maybe too long, but I went next to her smile. It was warm and friendly and this was odd enough, because I don't believe she knew any of us except the sergeant. I realized that she was smiling at us because of our uniforms. For all my years at the academy and now on active duty, here was a woman who probably knew a lot more about the army than I did.

Then she stood up, and I understood why Pennington had been so hard put to describe Ellen Quinn. She had a magnificent bosom, the like of which I have never seen before or since. She was obviously well corseted, but as she walked toward us, her bosom had a bounce to it that I can only describe as delicious. Mac sighed as he sat next to me, and I looked over to see him take his pipe out of his mouth and put it back in. He did that several times.

We must have both dismounted as she came toward us. She was as tall as Mac, and I remember she was wearing a dark green corduroy traveling dress that nipped in at the waist and flared in smooth gores over her hips. Part of the material was drawn back tight over her knees and pulled into a small bustle. My eyes kept returning to her bosom; she looked so *soft* there. Mac whispered to me later that he had an almost irresistible urge to squeeze her.

I didn't realize I had taken off my hat until I looked down and saw it in my hand. I noticed Mac had done the same thing. Sergeant Pennington dismounted and walked to her. She grasped both his arms just below the elbows.

"Sergeant, it's good to see you again."

Mac sighed.

"And you, Ellen," Pennington replied. His face was beet red. The four troopers and the corporal just gaped at him.

She let go of his arms and stepped back. "How's my da?"

"Well enough. He would have come, but his rheumatism was acting up, so the surgeon here put him on sick call." Pennington gestured in Mac's direction, and Ellen looked over at us and smiled.

Before he could introduce us, Brownlee dismounted and spoke to the lieutenant's wife. The captain waved us over, and as we walked toward them, I could tell by her crisp speech and frown that she was irritated her husband wasn't there to meet her. I could also tell she had a lot to learn about army life.

We ate dinner that evening in Tucson's only non-Mexican restaurant. Ellen sat with Pennington, the corporal (who had cut himself shaving and sported little scraps of tissue paper on his face), and the privates. The new recruits sat by themselves. Of the eight expected, three had gone over the hill somewhere between St. Louis and Tucson. Of the five left, two spoke only German.

Mac and I sat with Captain Brownlee and the lieutenant's wife, but I noticed that Mac kept glancing in Ellen's direction. Ellen in profile was as rewarding as Ellen full front. She caught him looking at her once and smiled at him. He blushed and kept his eyes on his food for the rest of the meal.

We never did get properly introduced to Ellen Quinn. Mac complained about that to Brownlee as the three of us crawled into the same bed in the town's only safe hotel. The captain had drawn the short straw and had to sleep in the middle. The sides were better, because you could stick out your arms and legs. Besides, it was hot.

"Well, what do you think?" Brownlee asked. He put his hands behind his head and jabbed us with his elbows in the process.

Mac rolled over. "I think I feel sorry for your wife," he muttered. He pulled off the bedspread, wrapped it around himself Indian-style and lay down on the floor.

"No, no. I mean about Ellen Quinn," Brownlee said. "Isn't she something?"

"She *is* pretty," I said, already starting to itch from the bedbugs, real or imagined.

Mac didn't say anything. He shaped his pillow into a soft, round ball. As he put his head down on it and smiled, I knew exactly what he was thinking.

We left Tucson at daylight, the women riding in the Dougherty wagon along with the rations, luggage, and Mac's medical supplies. The recruits were in the saddle but just barely. I don't think more than two of them had ever ridden before from the way they clutched the saddles and jiggled and bounced like sacks of grain.

We only made fifteen miles that day because a couple of the recruits kept getting thrown from their mounts, and the inevitable finally happened. Mac taped cracked ribs, and two fresh fish got to ride with the ladies. Ellen sat on the wagon seat with the private that Brownlee had volunteered as driver. During the morning, I overheard one of the other Bowie troopers offer him two months' wages to change places. Ellen had unbuttoned the corduroy jacket, and the lace on her shirtwaist seemed to spill out like a waterfall.

The next day, we made better time. We detoured again toward the rancher's place. He had talked Brownlee into picking up a windmill part for him in Tucson, and we had to deliver it.

Toward dusk, we came in sight of the ranch house. As we looked down on the little adobe house, that same feeling I had experienced in Apache Pass came back to me—I can still feel it after forty-five years. There was no smoke coming from the chimney, and the corral that had contained a half-dozen horses was empty now.

I glanced at Mac, and he looked back at me and frowned. Ellen was leaning forward on the wagon seat and squinting into the distance. The recruits still occupied themselves with their horses, but the Bowie troopers all eyed the building below.

As we rode slowly toward the cabin, Brownlee reined in close and stopped the wagon with a motion of his hand. He whispered, "By fours," and gestured to the first four troopers to follow him. They dismounted in front of the cabin, the fourth trooper holding the horses of the other three. With his revolver in his hand, Brownlee kicked open the door and went inside. The rest of us watched from a little rise about fifty yards away. He stayed inside for a moment, then came out and motioned to Mac.

Mac cantered down to the house, dismounted before his horse stopped, and went inside with Brownlee. He came out quickly and said something to the corporal, who yanked his blanket from behind his saddle and tossed it to the doctor. They were back with us in a few minutes. Brownlee's face looked almost green under his tan, but Mac just looked disgusted.

"Damn it to hell, what a waste of good sutures," he growled. He took his hat off and slapped it on the saddle, and his horse sidestepped in a half-circle.

"What's up, Captain?" I asked, not really wanting to know.

"Apaches. Took that poor sod a long time to die."

We heard the lieutenant's wife gasp inside the wagon. Ellen clutched the board seat. Her knuckles were white, but she didn't say anything. We continued toward the cabin at a walk. Brownlee detailed two men to dig a grave near the water tank where the ground was softer, and he told the women to wait in the wagon. Ellen stayed where she was on the seat, and the officer's wife peeked out the front flap.

When the grave was ready, the soldiers carried the body out. It was covered with the army blanket, but the arms dangled down, and we could see the first joints of all the fingers had been cut off. The hands swarmed with ants. I heard a retching sound inside the wagon. Ellen still gripped the seat, her eyes on the corpse and the blood and ants as the soldiers moved toward the corral.

"Sorry, ladies," Brownlee muttered as we watched. The retching inside the wagon turned into sobs, and Ellen swung around and ducked under the canvas. We could hear her low murmuring.

Brownlee walked over to where we were standing and patted my horse absently. "How long do you figure, Mac?"

He didn't hesitate. I wish he hadn't sounded so sure of himself. "Not more than two or three hours."

"Lord Almighty." Brownlee sighed and hooked his thumbs in his belt.

The sergeant came up. "We going to camp here, sir?"

Brownlee nodded and patted my horse again. "Might as well. Don't think they'll be back here tonight."

We camped in the shadow of the adobe hut as the sun burned its way down. As soon as the coffee was lukewarm, Brownlee kicked out the little brush fire. The lieutenant's wife whimpered. Ellen sat with her back against a wagon wheel. She crunched down the hardtack with the rest of us but shook her head at the cold sowbelly Pennington offered her. The lieutenant's wife didn't eat anything. The recruits huddled together in a little bunch, whispering to each other.

As the sky turned black, Mac walked over to the wagon and hunkered down next to Ellen. "They're probably long gone, miss," he said.

"Yes," she said, "I'd like to think that, too."

Mac was silent at that. He got off his haunches, walked back to where I was lying, and puffed on his pipe until the detail was silent.

No one slept much that night. I heard hammers on carbines click back every time a coyote yelped. We were on our way when the sky was still gray and only the faintest pink outlined the eastern hills. Brownlee warned us to keep together and cautioned the recruits to lay their carbines across their laps. Ellen sat on the wagon seat again, and I noticed Pennington's big Colt resting in her lap.

We nooned in the wagon's shade, the troopers squatting on the ground as they ate their hardtack and drank from their canteens. No one said much except the German recruits, who jabbered to each other. They kept glancing over their shoulders and giggling until Brownlee told them to "Shutten ze up, damn it."

After a short rest that I don't think anyone wanted, we mounted and rode into the Arizona afternoon. The smell of sweaty wool, leather, and horses made me drowsy, and I was about to close my eyes for a moment when I heard a soft hiss. I glanced to my right in time to see a recruit jerk straight up in the saddle, then topple slowly into the dust. Before I had time to react, another private clutched at an arrow sticking out of his neck as he gurgled and choked on the blood rising in his throat.

I was fascinated. The private kept tugging at that arrow, and his blood spattered all over me in little drops. He looked at me and kept tugging, trying to say something that sounded like a foreign language. Blood ran down his chin and covered the front of his uniform. His eyes rolled back, and he was dead before he hit the ground.

"Dismount!" the captain yelled, and we were all on the ground before the word was out of his mouth. The horses pranced and stepped around us, snorting and throwing back their heads at the smell of blood and Indians.

As I looked around, twenty or thirty Apaches seemed to rise up out of the ground and come riding toward us. I couldn't imagine where they had come from. The drought-blasted bushes were even scrawnier than usual and offered no cover. There was only a slight dip in the ground about thirty yards ahead.

"Fire at will," Brownlee shouted, and he took aim across the back of his horse. The animal stood stock still as he fired, and I was so impressed

I forgot to shoot. I saw Ellen crouched down behind the wagon seat, the Colt pointing out. It took both her hands to hold the gun, and I wondered if she knew how to use it.

Before I had a chance to find out, one of the Indians threw something in the wagon and it burst into flames. The driver clutched at an arrow between his eyes, and the mules jerked the reins from between his knees and took of running. The driver fell off the wagon, and Ellen grabbed for the reins, which were already dragging under the mules.

Mac and I both jumped on our horses to head off the wagon. As we galloped toward the burning wagon, we saw the lieutenant's wife crawl onto the wagon seat next to Ellen. Her mouth was open in a scream, but I couldn't hear anything except the "huh huh huh" of our horses.

The wagon, its canvas top blazing, hurtled toward a knot of mounted Apaches which separated and grabbed for the lead mules. One of the riders swooped down, lifted the lieutenant's wife off the wagon seat as neatly as you please, and threw her across his knees. The rest of the group followed him, and Mac forced the lead mules to turn back toward the soldiers.

Ellen leaned out of the wagon. Mac slowed his horse, held out his arms, and caught her as she jumped. She wrapped her fingers in the mane of his horse as he pulled her over the saddle and swatted at the flames on the hem of her skirt.

We charged back toward the troopers, escorted from the rear by a cordon of Apaches who whooped and yelled and swore at us. One of them said something like "bugger Grant." I recall thinking that was kind of strange. I mean, Grant wasn't even president anymore.

We were almost inside the circle of troopers when my horse was hit. He stumbled and fell, rolling over on me before I could get my foot free of the stirrup. I heard my left leg crack like a dry twig, but I didn't really feel anything. As I struggled to get out from under that miserable horse, four soldiers dodged bullets and arrows to push against the carcass and then drag me to safety.

Safety isn't a very good word. We were ringed in by Apaches, with no more protection than the bodies of half the horses. I looked for Brownlee and finally picked him out lying face down in a clump of rabbit brush. Mac crouched behind the body of his horse, firing. The last thing I remember was hollering to him that he had been right about Indian fighting.

When I opened my eyes, it was quiet. My head was resting in Ellen's lap. I looked around without raising my head. We were in a shallow ravine, and the corporal and two recruits were digging earthworks with an entrenching tool and two mess cups.

I tried to raise my head, but Ellen pushed me back. She called over her shoulder, "Jesse, he's conscious."

I had never heard anyone call Mac by his first name before. He crawled over to us. His face was black with gunpowder, except around his eyes where his glasses were. He looked like a raccoon. One of the lenses in his spectacles was cracked, and he had a bruise on one cheekbone, but he still puffed on his pipe. He felt my pulse.

"Brownlee?" I asked.

"Dead. Looks like I'm commanding officer." He grinned suddenly, and his teeth shone white against his black face.

I could have argued with him that technically I was in command because he was staff and I was line, but this wasn't the time. "Some command," I tried to growl at him, but it came out in a croak. I looked down at my leg to see if there really was an elephant sitting on it.

"Don't complain," he said as he crawled away, "or I'll kick you in the leg." He was back in a moment with his saddlebags slung over his shoulder. He knelt next to me, took out a knife, and slit my pants up the outside to the belt. He worked as gently as he could, but every movement made me suck in my breath.

"Have a heart, Mac!" I gasped. "Couldn't you have done this while I was out?"

"Hell, no," he said, sounding so reasonable that I wanted to smack him. "Suppose you had died? What a waste of time that would have been."

I couldn't argue with his logic. I bit my lip through as he tried to straighten out my leg. I could see tears in Ellen's eyes. "Who died?" I managed to say, as he sat back on his heels.

"Don't you mean, 'who's left?'" he began, but Ellen put her hand on his arm. "Brownlee's gone, plus three recruits, three Bowie troopers. God knows where the lieutenant's wife is. Hope she's dead." Mac felt my leg, and as I jumped, Ellen gripped me by the shoulders.

"Anyone else hurt?" *Was that my voice?*

"Couple scratches around. One Bowie private's ankle is shattered." Mac leaned closer to my face. "John, your leg's broken in at least two places. I've got to set it." He shook his head and patted my stomach. "I'm afraid the morphine and my other supplies burned up in the wagon."

I had to say something at that news. "Are the Indians still out there?" was the best I could come up with.

"Try raising up your head, and you'll never have to worry about a bill for setting your leg." He tossed a handful of rocks in the air, and four or five guns went off. Mac called to the men scratching out the earthworks, and they crawled over to us. "Men, go over to the wagon, and find me two straight boards, about so long. Doesn't matter if they're a little charred. Just get straight ones."

As the men crawled away, he turned to Ellen. "How many petticoats do you have on?"

She blushed. "Only two. It's hot."

"John needs one of them more than you do."

She gentled my head down on the sand, unhooked her skirt, untied a cord that held up her petticoat and wriggled out of it, gazing into the distance as she did so.

"Rip it in strips," Mac said. The sound of the ripping cloth made me jump. The sergeant tending to the wounded private whirled around, his hand to his holster.

Ellen finished as the soldiers crept back with the plants. Mac padded the boards with pieces of an army blanket. Following his instructions, the soldiers held my arms and good leg, and Ellen put her arms around me and rested her head on my chest. Her hair smelled of lavender and gunpowder. Mac took hold of my left ankle and slowly started pulling. I screamed and screamed.

It was dark when I woke up. I was covered with a blanket stiff with someone's blood. My left leg felt four sizes too large and it throbbed and pounded like a drum. From what seemed like a hundred miles away, I heard Mac talking. He was sitting cross-legged with the other soldiers and Ellen around a tiny fire, and the men were going through their saddlebags.

"What do you have, Sarge?" Mac asked.

"Two days' worth of hardtack, some salt pork, and a can of goldfish." Pennington put the items in front of him and shook his canteen. "It's nearly full, sir."

The doctor went around the circle, and the men held out their supplies, mostly hardtack, salt pork, and some green coffee beans. The German recruit had a chocolate bar.

"What about you, Ellen?"

"Everything I had was in the wagon," she said, reaching into her pocket, "except these." She pulled out a handful of linty dried apples.

The only nearly full canteens belonged to Mac and the Bowie veterans. The recruits had just learned another hard lesson in a day of hard lessons. "I've got some raisins," I called out. My voice sounded far away from my mouth.

Mac turned around and smiled at me. "I've already gone through your saddlebags and pockets."

"Scoundrel!" I tried to shout at him, but it came out in a whisper. "What about Brownlee and the others?"

"Hardtack, chewing tobacco." Mac crept over to where I lay. He pulled back the blanket and ran his hand over my leg, testing the strips of petticoat that anchored the splint in place.

"Feels tight," I complained.

"I'll loosen it in a little while."

"How's that other soldier?"

Mac gestured to my right. I turned my head and saw the trooper lying near me. He was asleep, I think, but his breath came in little moans. "He's not too good," Mac said. "I may have to take off that leg, but I'm going to sit tight for a day. Maybe someone will rescue us."

"Do you really think so?"

He shrugged and turned away. "I like to think so."

He went back to the fire, sat down, and filled his pipe again. Ellen came over and gave me a sip of water.

"Poor Mac," I said. "His first command. Kind of a rough go for the world's most refined practical joker."

Ellen didn't say anything.

"Ellen, are you all right?"

"Fine, fine." She brushed the hair from my eyes. "Go to sleep."

When I woke up, it was morning. Ellen stirred something over the fire. She looked at me and smiled. "How're you feeling this morning?" She spoke so calmly and naturally, as if I had awakened in a hospital ward instead of a grubby ravine somewhere between Tucson and Bowie. She walked over to me, knelt down, and felt my forehead.

"Aren't there any Indians out there?" I asked hopefully, noting that she hadn't crawled over.

"They're out there, but no one is firing." She brought me some hardtack and coffee bean stew and held up my head while I choked down a few bites. I really wasn't very hungry.

Mac came over in a few minutes. He had taken the broken lens out of his glasses so one eye looked normal, while the other one was slightly magnified. I saw his pipe stuck in the front of his pocket and not in his mouth.

"What's the matter, Mac?" I asked, "are you out of tobacco?"

He put his hand to his pocket quickly. "No, no. I just forgot about it." He felt my leg and winced when I winced. "Guess I'm too damned tenderhearted," he said.

"How's the other trooper?"

"Not good. He's spiking a high fever and asking for his mother," Mac answered after a moment's hesitation. He loosened the strips binding the splints a fraction of an inch.

"What are you going to do?"

Mac sat back and crossed his legs. "You're the second person who's asked me that this morning," he said, and looked at Ellen. "I keep forgetting I'm in command of this miserable detail. Gives me a pain in the ass."

I waited for him to say something else, but he got up, brushed off the seat of his pants, and walked to the edge of the ravine, where he stood looking out.

The day was two years long. I was conscious most of the time, and I lay there with my hands behind my neck, counting the buzzards that flew overhead. I could smell rotting flesh to the north and west of us, but I didn't have the heart to ask Ellen about it. I watched the buzzards circle over there, drop down, squabble among themselves like quarrelsome relatives, then take off. Some of them were so gorged they could scarcely fly. A few of them flapped around me and the other soldier—a bad sign indeed—but Ellen shooed them off with a strip of her green skirt.

Ellen spent the afternoon fanning me and the trooper with a piece of partly burned canvas she had scavenged. Mac and Sergeant Pennington sat a few yards off, talking. I couldn't hear what they said, but Pennington did most of the talking, and Mac nodded occasionally.

In the late afternoon, Mac came over and relieved Ellen, who curled up at my feet and fell asleep at once. Mac fanned the three of us until the sun dipped behind the hills. When the sky was black and the moon only a slice, Mac shook Ellen awake and handed her the canvas. He went over to Pennington.

"Are you ready?"

Ready for what, I wondered, craning my neck to see what was going on.

"Guess I am, sir," the sergeant said, standing up and stretching his arms over his head.

The three horses had been left in a small dip. Pennington picked out the best one and spoke to it, nose to nose. Mac poured half of the water from his canteen into the hat and held it up to the horse. The water was gone in two swallows. One of the men saddled the animal while Pennington talked to Mac. He clapped an arm around Mac's shoulders in a surprisingly familiar gesture for a non-com, and they walked over to the horse. Pennington swung into the saddle. He blew a kiss to Ellen, which surprised me mightily, then saluted Mac and said, "Good luck, sir."

"Good luck to you, Lucas," the surgeon replied as he slapped the horse on the rump. "Write when you get work, hear?"

Pennington laughed. The horse scrambled over the lip of the ravine, staggering a little, then found its legs. We all strained for the sound of guns and other horses but heard nothing but the hoofbeats of that one horse. I let my breath out slowly.

Mac went to the wounded soldier lying next to me. He barely touched the man's ankle, but the private shrieked and grabbed at the doctor's hand. While the corporal and a recruit held down the soldier, Mac unwound the bandage and sniffed it. He dropped the bloody, yellowish strips of petticoat and took out his pipe. He filled it and tapped down the tobacco, then went over to the fire and lit it. He stood there a long time afterward.

I could almost see what was going on in his mind. The surgeon in him was telling him to hurry up and get it over with, while the soldier in him was urging him to wait a bit and trust Pennington's luck. And I think the ordinary man in him was wishing he didn't have to make any decisions at all. I was glad all the way down to my socks that it wasn't me doing the deciding.

Finally, he picked up his saddlebags and carried them over to the trooper, who was conscious and trying to raise up his head. "I've got to take off your leg just above the knee, soldier," Mac said as he squatted there and puffed on his pipe.

The soldier closed his eyes, and I could see the sweat on his forehead. "No, Doc, don't do it."

"Have to. You've got mean red streaks already running up your calf, and you smelled that bandage when I took it off, didn't you?"

The soldier whimpered and started to cry. Ellen lifted his head into her lap and hugged him to her.

Right before the Great War, Rose and I took a trip to Rome and spent a day in Vatican City. We saw a statue by Michelangelo, I think, of Mary holding Christ. Rose could tell you. I suppose most people think of religion when they see that statue, but I was struck by the resemblance it had to Ellen holding that feverish, stinking soldier. And I began to think that when Pennington had been at a loss for words to describe Ellen, he hadn't been only referring to her magnificent structure, but to the quality of caring so uniquely hers.

I dozed off then. When I woke up, the trooper was silent. Ellen and Mac were sitting by the fire, and I could see the Bowie corporal and two recruits sitting with their carbines across their laps. "I'd better get to it," Mac said to Ellen. They sat close together, and his arm was around her waist. *He must be trying to reassure her*, I thought, but when her arm went around his waist, I wondered.

"You can't wait until morning?" she asked.

"No. Damn me for waiting this long. It'll be too hot when the sun's up." Mac stood and looked at the troopers. "Anyone have any candles?"

He came back to the fire with two little white stubs and what looked like a slush lamp made out of Pennington's sardine can. "Anyone have any whiskey?" he asked next. "Come on, come on! Who could I possibly report you to?"

The corporal tossed him a small flask from inside his uniform blouse, and Mac shook it.

"Are you going to make him drink it?" Ellen asked.

Mac shook his head. "Wish I could. No, I'm going to pour it on the leg and clean my bone saw with it."

Mac motioned the corporal and two recruits over to the wounded private. The three troopers were in no hurry to get there, and if they could have found a long way around that ravine, they'd have taken it.

"That's right. Closer to the fire. Now, Corporal, you light the slush lamp, and for God's sake, hold it steady. Light the candles and set them there, and you men hold him down." He pantomimed this for the German recruit, who nodded. He sighed and turned to Ellen. "I need your last petticoat."

She slid out of it and started tearing it up, while Mac knelt by the private's head. He bent down until his lips were practically on his ear and whispered to him. I couldn't hear what he said, but the private started whimpering again and saying, "No, no, no," over and over. Mac said something else to him, then patted him on the chest until he was quiet.

Whatever you could say about Mac, he kept his surgical saws in beautiful condition, all tidy and wicked-looking in their plush case. He looked at them a long time, the way I look at golf clubs, selected one, then poured a little whiskey on it. He laid it on a strip of petticoat. He took what looked like curved needles and thread out of a little box, threaded several of the needles, and stuck them in the front of his uniform. He took other things out, but I didn't know what they were.

"Ellen, I want you to hand me these things when I ask for them. Those are clamps, those are scissors, and sponges, and I've stuck the sutures here. Can you do it?"

She nodded, and I saw how pale she was, even before the corporal lit the slush lamp. She looked into Mac's eyes, and he smiled at her and squeezed her arm. "Honeybun, I've done a hell of a lot of these," he said, which amazed me.

Mac poured a little whiskey on his hands and waved them in the air until they were dry. He poured the last few drops right above the private's knee, and Ellen coughed from the fumes. They all took their places around the soldier, and I couldn't see much else, which didn't disappoint me greatly. I heard the private take a deep rattling breath as Mac began to cut.

Let me pause here. Isn't this the place in the movies where the picture fades out, and when it comes up again, the patient is all bandaged and flirting with the nurses? The real thing isn't like that at all. Nothing fades away. In fact, the whole experience becomes so unforgettable it seems to etch itself into my brain like acid on metal. I mean, I can go to a granddaughter's piano recital, or a Bingo game, or be lathering up my hair in the shower, and that image can come back quick enough to leave me shaking, even after all these years.

When Mac started to cut, the private let out his breath in a scream I thought would never end. It rose and wavered and hung on the air until even the coyotes rimming the nearby hills were silent in tribute, I guess. One of the soldiers vomited, and someone was crying. I think it was me.

The private screamed again and again, but even above the noise, we could all hear the sound of saw on bone. The soldier finally fainted. The saw was sharp and the sound over quickly, but many a night since then I have sat up in bed, tears on my face and that whining, rasping sound in my ears.

Ellen put her hand over her ears until Mac shouted for clamps and sponges. She handed them to him, then tried to push his glasses up farther on his nose. Her hands were shaking so badly that she poked him through the empty lens instead. I don't think he even noticed. He cut and tied and sponged and wiped. I couldn't see what was going on, but Ellen said later that he covered up the stump with a large flap of skin and sewed it all in place.

"Pull the leg away, Ellen."

"I can't. Really, I can't."

"You have to. He's coming around again, and you're the only one with a free hand!"

She shuddered and shook her head, but did as he said, flinging it with both hands beyond the fire. As the leg flew in the dark, drops of blood hissed on the little fire until I thought it might go out.

I must have fainted then myself, because when I opened my eyes, the sun was up. Ellen was sitting between the private and me, fanning us. She saw me open my eyes and stopped fanning. She put her hand to my forehead and took it away quickly, a frown on her face.

"Is he still alive?" I croaked. My tongue filled my whole mouth.

"Yes. He came to about an hour ago, but he's sleeping now."

Mac came over in a few minutes to check my pulse. He couldn't find it right away and moved his fingers around my wrist until he was satisfied. He sat by me on the ground while Ellen fed me a thin broth made of that everlasting hardtack, salt pork, and dried apples with lint. It tasted better than it looked; of course, apples do compliment pork, don't they?

"When are we leaving, Jesse?" Ellen asked. She wiped my chin with her skirt.

"Soon as you're done." Mac looked at me. "John, we're pulling out."

"Surely the Indians aren't gone."

"Hell, no. In fact, the corporal nearly got his balls shot off last night when he was taking a leak." Mac glanced at Ellen, and she frowned. "Beg your pardon, Ellen." He turned to me. "I think they're just going to play around with us for a while. Besides, there's not much to do here after you've seen the sights, and we're all starting to stink." He grinned and patted my shoulder.

Mac was right. We were starting to stink. A funny thing to recall, I suppose you're thinking. Maybe it is, but remember, I was strapped in a travois when we got underway, couldn't move, and had plenty of opportunity to make observations I never would have bothered with ordinarily.

Did we stink! You won't gather this from the picture shows. Those soldiers in *Twelve Brave Men* looked liked they put on fresh, tailored uniforms every day and left their boots out in the hall for a spit shine every night. It wasn't like that. People's sweat smells different. The corporal smelled a bit like rotting hay. I guess Mac was luckier than the rest of us. A bottle of oil of cloves had broken in his saddlebags during the fight, and he was almost nice to be around. Ellen sweated like the rest of us, but her clothes still smelled a little of lavender.

I was the worst of the bunch. I hadn't moved much in three days (Ellen was enough of a lady to look away when she brought me a can to pee in). I smelled like a galley slave chained to his bench, except that I was wearing army wool and long johns. Strange for Arizona in the summer, you ask? That was the army. In 1880, we were still being issued hardtack made during the Civil War and uniform parts new at Antietam. Anyway, I'm sure that if someone had come too near me with a lighted match, I would have exploded.

Mac walked away to see about the two remaining horses. About an hour later, the horses had been fitted with travois. One side of the Dougherty wagon had been lightly burned. Mac and the corporal took two long planks, lashed them at the top over the horse's back, then wove strips of the last unused army blanket to form a webbing between the planks. They repeated the process with the other horse.

The horses might have objected under other circumstances, but they were too hungry and thirsty to care. They stood quietly while the soldiers lowered me onto a travois and tied me in with the last of Ellen's petticoat. Ellen draped the two remaining canteens around the horse's neck, and Mac secured a canvas bag with our food on the back of the other horse. He carried his saddlebags over his soldier and a carbine in one hand.

The horse lurched forward, and I braced myself, and then relaxed. The poles of the pony drag glided over rocks and small bushes, and I was more comfortable than I had been yet in this experience of pain and immobility. I swayed between the poles on the webbing and watched the clouds through the brush frame Ellen had woven over my head.

Our troubles were so huge that I tried to empty my mind of them as we came up onto the desert floor. That I succeeded in any degree is credit to how much a person can deny, if he's really serious about it. And I was. Oh, my, I was.

One thought remained to nibble at me. None of us had much experience with survival, Arizona-style. B Company had recently been garrisoned in California, Mac had spent the last four or five years in

Louisiana with another regiment, and I was from New York. The German recruit only said, "How are you? I am damn fine," when we asked him about his origins. As there aren't too many deserts between the Rhone and the Rhine, we didn't expect much.

No one said anything about our relative pea-greenness in the wilds, and since these good folk were being so kind to keep me alive, I didn't feel like complaining about the obvious. I figured that we would either develop some desert savvy quick, or it wouldn't matter, anyway.

One unpleasant thought did lead to another, before I dismissed it. Even if anyone did start out to look for us, we had detoured to take that windmill part to the defunct rancher, and they could search for days and miss us. I didn't need to be a mathematician to realize that we didn't have days. After that disturbing bit of reality, I decided to confine my thoughts to pain and Apaches. It was less agonizing that way.

Ellen walked between the two travois. She had traded her high-topped shoes for a pair of Apache moccasins, and I wondered where she had found them. She wore Brownlee's campaign hat. I noticed that the underarm of her shirtwaist had ripped out at the seam in the back; I could see the lace of her camisole through the tear. It was yellow eyelet lace, with little holes and scallops.

That's strange, isn't it? I've forgotten the names of old friends and some relatives, the capital cities of Delaware and Kentucky, but I have never forgotten what that yellow eyelet lace looked like.

As we came out of the ravine, I expected to feel an arrow attach itself to my chest and hear Apaches making merry around us. The desert floor was silent. I even began to hope they had really left us, when Ellen patted my shoulder and pointed.

About a half-mile to our rear, I could make out fifteen or twenty Apaches following us. They walked their horses, stopped when we stopped, moved when we moved. I have never heard of anything like it, and it was more unnerving than being attacked. We were being diddled by practical jokers at least as good as Mac. Obviously there wasn't much else going on that week in Apacheria.

We moved slowly and stopped every half-hour to rest. The horses drooped and bowed their heads in the heat. They stumbled often, and I would have been tipped out if I hadn't been lashed down like cargo on a ship's deck. The private on the other pony drag began to moan and toss his head from side to side. Mac checked his bandages. Ellen asked if she should give the man a drink, but Mac shook his head. "He's unconscious, and it would only dribble out. Save it, Ellen."

Mac and Ellen walked on either side of my travois in silence for a while, then Mac shifted the carbine onto his shoulder and asked, "Anything like this ever happen to you before, Ellen?"

She looked at him, her eyes wide.

"Well, you know. I mean, you've been in the army longer than any of us, I suppose."

She smiled at that, and I could watch her thinking. I could see incidents come into her eyes, and then she finally said, "I do remember a time. I was out riding with a sergeant from A Company. We were at Fort Robinson. We were chased back to the fort by some Sioux." She paused and looked around. "Of course, that was different. We had two good horses and a head start."

Mac grinned over me to Ellen. "Well, hell, we've got two good horses." He looked at the jaded remounts that were nearly walking on their knees. He glanced back at the Apaches behind us. "And a head start."

Ellen gasped, then started to laugh. It was a surprised, delighted laugh, without any trace of hysteria in it. She laughed and laughed, put her hand to her stomach and laughed some more. Mac joined in. He leaned on the travois, and the horse nearly fell down. Ellen laughed harder.

I couldn't resist all that. Even though it hurt my leg, I laughed, too. So did the corporal. The two recruits in front hadn't heard the exchange, but they laughed right along, even the German. I imagine the Indians began to wonder what kind of a vaudeville show they were trailing.

The expression has become a family joke in our house. Whenever anyone is faced with a task of doubtful outcome, the person will say, "Well, at least I have two good horses and a head start."

I have wondered many times since why the Apaches followed us like that. They obviously could have overrun us with no difficulty, then gone on to burn down a couple ranch houses, drive off the horses, capture some Mexican slaves across the border, and call it a well-rounded day. They didn't, and I have been puzzled ever since.

I have an old army friend I told most of this story to once. He had been with the Second Cav at the Rosebud Creek fight with Crook in the summer of '76, and he chuckled when I told him about those Apaches. "You know, John," he said, "we'd been pretty well stomped on by Crazy Horse that afternoon, and I guess we were waiting for that final charge that might have finished us. It never came."

"Why not?" I asked him.

He shrugged. "Don't know. We met up with some of those same braves at Slim Buttes in August, and I asked one of them that we captured why they hadn't charged again on the Rosebud. He told me that they just hadn't felt like it."

I realize this isn't much of an explanation, but I have no better one. I guess those Apaches just felt like following us.

We camped that night in the middle of nowhere. There wasn't a waterhole in sight, and we were still far from the main route, but one horse fell and would not get up, so we had no choice. The corporal started to build another tiny fire. He piled up a little greasewood, lit it with his flint, and blew on it until a slender yellow flame rose up. Mac stomped up to the corporal with an armload of tinder he had scrounged and threw it on the little fire. The twigs caught and crackled.

"What on earth are you doing, Mac?" I said.

Mac laughed and piled on some larger sticks. "Hell if I'm going to freeze again, John."

Ellen was listening. She was frowning and twisting and untwisting a strand of hair around her first finger, something I noticed she did when she was agitated.

"You've got all the blankets," Mac said, "and according to my scientific observations of the past two nights, it gets cold enough to freeze your ass off between midnight and four."

"But the Apaches," I whispered, as if I was afraid of offending company.

Mac squatted down by me. "What the hell does it matter? They know we're here, and we know they're here. Besides . . ."

He would have continued, but Ellen cleared her throat and interrupted him. "Jesse, if you don't stop using such vulgar language, I'm going to . . . to . . ." She couldn't think of anything to say, but I was sure she meant it.

I glanced over at Mac, but his eyes were on her face. I wasn't really sure what he was registering. I thought he was going to say something awful.

"I'm sorry, Ellen," was all he said. I could tell that he meant it.

I thought Ellen was through, but she went on. "And while you're at it, please quit smoking that beastly pipe. The tobacco makes my stomach churn."

Without a word, he took the pipe from his mouth, emptied out the tobacco, and put in his pocket. They were both silent, looking at each other, and I wished I could have taken up my bed and walked somewhere.

"And when we're out of this, I still don't want you to swear or smoke anymore."

"I promise I won't, Ellen."

I couldn't believe my ears.

Then the strangest thing happened. Or maybe it wasn't so strange. Ellen burst into tears. She didn't try to cover her face with her hands or turn her head, and the tears washed over her cheeks leaving clean spots. Mac made a move to put his arms around her, but she turned away and stumbled over to where the fallen horse lay. She put her face against its neck and sobbed quite audibly for a good while. The corporal shook his head, and the recruits shrugged at each other. Mac didn't say anything, but he lay back on the sand and stared at the sky.

Dinner was a little late that night. It was hardtack raisin stew made with most of the remaining water. Ellen had dried her tears and seemed her usual self. She spooned that grubby mess into my mouth and followed each bite with her eyes. She cupped her hand under my chin so I wouldn't miss a drop.

"I'm still hungry," I complained as she wiped the spoon on my shirt.

She grinned and wiped out the bowl with her finger. "So am I." She stuck her finger in my mouth, and I sucked off the rest of the gruel. Rose would have been scandalized.

The wounded private woke up, and Ellen tried to feed him, but he couldn't swallow, and the broth ran down his chin. Ellen glanced at Mac, who was watching her, and he shook his head.

The soldiers gathered more tinder, and the fire roared. The sparks danced against the dark sky, and it reminded me of a clambake back home. I remembered walking hand in hand with Rose across the sand, on the pretext of finding more driftwood for the fire. For just a moment, I could almost smell the seaweed and hear the waves lapping on the pilings.

Ellen's tears must have cleared the air. After eating, the corporal got out his harmonica and played "The Regular Army-O." The German recruit sang a song next, something none of us understood, but which must have comforted him, because he was smiling when he finished.

Mac checked me and the wounded private before he settled down for the night. He stood over the private for a long time.

"How's he doing?" I asked, craning my neck to see.

"I don't think he'll get through the night."

Mac walked back to the fire and sat down, his elbows resting on his knees and his hands making gradually smaller circles in the sand. He leaned forward with his eyes closed, and I wondered when he had slept last. I think he was asleep sitting up when the screams began.

One of the recruits leaped to his feet and fired his carbine into the dark before the corporal could get to him. Ellen crawled on her hands and knees over to Mac, who had jerked awake and was looking around him. He jumped up and nearly stepped on Ellen, who crouched by the fire, covering her ears with her hands, her forehead touching the ground.

The screams couldn't have been more than two hundred feet away. I really couldn't tell if it was a man or a woman, but whoever it was shrieked over and over, begging, pleading, screaming. I raised my head up and could see the red glow of a little fire in the distance. The occasional breeze brought us the whiff of charring flesh.

Mac stalked to the edge of our firelight and stood staring into the dark. I could tell from just looking at his back that he was really angry. He turned to me, started to say something, stopped, started again. I figured he must have been thinking about the promise he made to Ellen earlier. He took a step into the darkness. "Bunch of savages!" he finally yelled. The wind carried the sound of laughter to us, along with that indescribable smell of someone burning.

Ellen was sitting now and staring into the fire. Her eyes had the look of a fawn I shot by mistake one spring, years ago. She looked up at Mac as he stalked back to the fire. "Jesse, who is it?"

"I think they've got Sergeant Pennington. I bet they've been saving him for us."

Ellen shuddered. Mac sat down beside her and put his arm around her. The corporal and the recruits sat close by, and I wish I could have joined them. I reckon that was the low point of the whole business, having to sit there helpless and listen to Sergeant Pennington die only a stone's throw away.

When the screams stopped for a few minutes, Ellen wiped her eyes and blew her nose on her dress. "Jesse," she said, "did you know that Sergeant Pennington is my godfather?"

"Oh, Jesus, Ellen, Jesus," was all Mac said.

The screams finally stopped around two o'clock in the morning. In the silence that followed, most of us began to accept the idea that we wouldn't get out of this alive.

I woke up before anyone else. The wounded soldier next to me was dead, with his eyes wide open and staring at the buzzards that flew around us. Perhaps it was just as well, because his horse was dead, too, and already beginning to swell.

Our bonfire of the night before was only a pile of ashes. The corporal snored, and one of the recruits muttered and twitched in his sleep. Mac and Ellen slept side by side, sandwiched together for warmth, his arm thrown over her.

I raised up on one elbow and saw a small pile over a smoking fire. The buzzards flopped around it and craned their red necks at it, but Sergeant Pennington was still too hot even for them.

Mac woke up next. He disentangled himself from Ellen and slid quietly away from her. He went right to the dead soldier, knelt by him, and closed his eyes. He came over and sat down next to me. He put his hand to the pipe in his pocket, then glanced at Ellen and put his hand down. He stared at the smoldering mound for a long while.

"Well, John, what do I do now?"

I was dozing off again, but the question surprised me. "Do? Do? Mac, it's your command." It was a pretty churlish thing to say, but I was even having trouble remembering my name.

"We keep going, don't we?" he asked himself. God knows I wasn't any help. "I mean, even though it's useless, we keep going."

"I guess we do."

My eyes weren't focusing properly, because I kept seeing Rose floating toward me over the sand. No, it wasn't Rose but Ellen, who stood at an angle and brushed the sand off her dress.

Mac went over to the corporal and prodded him with his boot, then stepped back quickly, his hands up, when the soldier pulled his carbine to full cock and sat up in one motion.

"Hey, hey, Corporal, it's only me!"

"Sorry, sir," the corporal said, blinking in the bright light. "I'm a little nervous, I guess."

Mac smiled and patted his shoulder.

We left that spot quickly. No more water remained, other than a few mouthfuls in the three canteens. Ellen handed each of us a piece of hard-tack, covered the dead soldier's face with his blanket, and helped the German recruit prod my horse to its feet.

The Apaches waited to the rear of us again, but much closer than yesterday. I don't think anybody bothered to glance at them once we got underway. They had become part of the landscape, and we had seen enough of that to satisfy any curiosity.

We passed the mound that used to be Sergeant Pennington. He had been roasted alive over that little fire, and his skin was the strangest shade of pink I have ever seen. Indeed, I've never even been tempted to eat salmon from that day to this. His skin oozed oils and fat, and he looked as though he would fall off the bone if we touched him. Ellen stood there and stared at him until Mac moved her on.

She looked back over her shoulder. "Isn't there something we ought to say?" she asked him.

"I suppose there is," he replied, "but you made me promise not to use those words any more."

It wasn't much of a morning. The others fought to stay on their feet, and I had the opportunity to stare up at the sky and reflect on the nature of the Apache. I can't recall any conclusions I would repeat today, except the notion that our pursuers had a peculiar sense of humor. I thought about mentioning this to Mac, but the look on his face told me his sense of humor had probably melted away the night before, along with Pennington.

He didn't look much like the man who had painted the commanding officer's chicken coop blue a month ago. I think if I had mentioned that incident to him, or any of fifty others, he would have stared at me and crammed a sedative down my gullet, if he'd had one. I pitied him because he was in charge, but I was glad it was his responsibility and not mine.

At one point before noon, Ellen just sat down on the ground. Mac put his arm around her and hauled her to her feet. She looked surprised, as if she didn't recognize him at first. Then she smiled and put her arm around him.

"Jesse, what keeps you going?" she asked.

He looked at her. As I said earlier, she was the same height as he, so they were nearly eye to eye. I thought at first he might grin at her and give some casual reply, but as I said, he was beyond that. He touched his forehead to hers. "You do."

She didn't say anything else.

After the noon stop, where we sucked on hardtack, we pushed on again. After an hour's travel, Ellen flopped down and lay still. Mac tried to hurry over to her but his steps took him in a zigzag course. He dropped down by her, and turned her over. The corporal handed him a canteen. He forced her mouth open with his fingers and poured the last of the water down her throat. Her eyes opened then and she just lay there and looked at Mac.

"Get up, Ellen. We're not through yet."

With the corporal's help, Mac stood up, then slung Ellen over his shoulder. Her arms dangled down his back. Her hair had come partly undone and hung down to his feet. He staggered under her weight, and we started forward again.

He carried her for nearly an hour, before we stopped. Ellen was conscious now and protested until Mac set her down. "I'm so sorry," she said over and over.

Mac tried to smile at her. "Don't worry. It was a pleasure." It took him an age to get that out. I think he almost forgot what he started to say even before he finished.

We sat there for an hour, and the Apaches crept closer. As much as I hated them, I had to admire their endurance. They had been following us for four days and probably weren't even tired. I would gladly have given them the whole stinking desert and every miserable spot of land between here and Atlantic City, if I could have.

Finally, Mac got to his feet and pulled up Ellen. She sagged against him for a moment, and they both nearly toppled; then she straightened up and raised her chin. "I'm all right," she insisted and started walking in the wrong direction. Mac turned her around, and she kept going.

The afternoon wore on. Ellen walked beside the travois and leaned on the poles. The recruits held each other up, and the corporal and Mac took turns carrying the saddlebags and the carbines. My leg boomed and thundered until I was sure the others could hear it. The pain began to worry me. When Mac groped around for my pulse during a rest, I asked him about it.

He tried to wink at me, but both his eyes opened and closed and opened. "Don't worry about it, John," he said. "I can't even find your pulse right now, so I can't see how it matters." He stared at me until he figured out who I was. "John," he began carefully, "I hate to hurt your feelings, but you stink."

We started again, the sun at our backs. We had traveled less than a quarter-mile when the horse pulling my travois dropped down between the poles. The corporal drifted over and prodded it, but the animal was dead.

Mac cut the lashing on the poles with his knife and motioned to the steadier of the recruits, who picked up the two front poles. Mac staggered around to the back and picked up the others and we continued on.

Now isn't this the spot in the silent pictures where the wounded man begs the others to leave him behind so the rest can save their own lives? Not me. Blamed if I wanted to be left behind to be roasted or toasted or shortened or lengthened by those comedians following us.

We had stopped for the fifth or sixth time in an hour, when the corporal suddenly got up and started walking north, away from us. Mac watched him a few moments, then got to his feet and followed him. I heard him arguing with the trooper as they lurched toward a slight rise. Then they stood still, staring at each other. The corporal went on, and Mac shambled back to us.

"A waterhole! There's a waterhole!"

Actually, it didn't sound like that. He moved his mouth as though it were numb, but we got the gist of it. The recruits got up, and each grabbed an end of my litter. Ellen hung onto my hand. She was crying, but her eyes were dry and red.

It seemed to take hours to reach the waterhole. I felt as though we were moving in a dream, taking two steps backward for each one forward. The Apaches were still behind us, and as we crept toward the water, a thought kept running through my brain like ticker tape that something was wrong. If that really was a waterhole, why were the hostiles still following us? Wouldn't they have circled in front and taken it for themselves? I tried to voice this skepticism to Ellen, but it just didn't seem polite.

The waterhole was in the middle of a small depression, with a few scraggly cacti growing nearby. When we got there, Mac and the corporal were sitting by the little pool. The recruits dropped the stretcher with a thump that made me cry out and stumbled toward the water. As the first man tried to throw himself down and drink, Mac stopped him.

"Don't, trooper," he said. "It's salt."

Ellen dropped to her knees beside me. "It can't be."

No one said anything. The corporal looked around, his eyes traveling over the hollow we sat in, and he saw the cactus at the same time I did. They were greener and healthier than those we had seen on the desert floor, as if the ravine had sheltered them from the drought around us. He took out his knife.

Mac must have thought he was going to kill himself, because he started to crawl over to him. The corporal was too fast. He half-ran, half-crawled to the nearest cactus, stuck his hand in among the thorns, and pulled off a green bulb. As his knife slashed into the spiny lump in his hands, Mac crawled up and wrenched off another one with his bare hands. I don't think either of them noticed the little needles. They peeled off the outer layer and I could see the red pulp beneath.

Mac cut his in half and brought it over to Ellen and me. I grabbed mine and stuffed it in my mouth. The fruit of that cactus was tasteless, but I don't believe I ever ate anything as good as that dirty little lump. I felt my throat opening up. I had trouble swallowing because my tongue got in the way, but I stuffed in another piece as soon as Mac handed it to me. The five of them sat around my stretcher, slurping and chewing on the fruit.

Mac looked over at the corporal, who was slicing another bite. "Corporal, if we ever get back to Bowie, I'm going to write you the damnedest commendation!"

"Jesse, you promised," Ellen reminded him.

"I'm sorry."

I think we all remembered the hostiles at the same instant. The corporal unslung his carbine and stretched himself out until he could peek over the rim of the waterhole. Mac joined him, flattening out and pulling his gun forward until the muzzle was even with the ground. He and the corporal fired at the same time. Ellen jumped and put her hands over her ears.

"Did you get one, sir?" the corporal asked, when the smoke cleared.

"Nah. I can't shoot worth sh . . . shoe leather. But you got one."

I heard the Apaches riding a little west of us. Mac and the corporal stayed where they were a few minutes, then slid back down the slope.

"Well, this looks like the end of the line," Mac said as he rested his carbine across his knees. He put one of the recruits on watch and told Ellen to make something out of the cactus fruit and the rest of the hardtack.

She unloaded one of the guns and pounded the hardtack with the butt until it was powder. She chopped some of the fruit and mixed the hardtack flour with it. The corporal built a small fire, and she put the mixture in the one remaining mess plate, stirring it with forceps from Mac's saddlebags. I found a couple coffee beans in my pocket, and she added those to the stew, along with the last quarter-inch of the chocolate bar, which had melted all over the wrapper.

We wolfed down our food and finished off dinner with a half a piece of cactus fruit each. The corporal belched and lay back on the sand. Ellen and Mac sat back to back, leaning against each other. They slept that way until the fire died down, then Mac got up and slowly laid Ellen down. He came over to me and checked my leg.

"Hey, Mac," I said, putting a hand on his arm as he started to rise. "Thanks for all you've done. I really appreciate it."

He smiled at me but didn't say anything. He shook my hand formally, then walked over to the sentry and lay down next to him, watching the Apache campfire a quarter-mile off. He came back down and sat by me.

Ellen woke up. She sat cross-legged by the fire and took the pins out of her hair. She plunked the pins in her lap and pulled out the tortoise-shell comb. It was the kingpin that tumbled down the rest of her hair around her shoulders. She tried to tug the comb through her tangled nest of hair. Several of the teeth snapped and she frowned at them in her hand.

"Oh, the dickens!"

Mac clucked his tongue and wagged a finger at her; she ignored him. She dragged the comb through her hair again, using her fingers to help. I saw tears come to her eyes, but I don't think it was because it hurt her. We were all pretty close to the surface.

Mac watched her. He lay on his side, pitching bits of rock at the fire.

"Say, Ellen, will you marry me?" He went on pitching gravel, and I wondered if my mind had drifted away for good.

She paused, her hands in her hair. The rip in her shirtwaist had traveled around to her armpit by now, and I saw that yellow eyelet lace again.

"No." She put her arms down and rested her hands in her lap, where she fingered the hairpins.

"Why not?"

"Two reasons." She flipped some of the hairpins out on the sand.

We were all listening now. I saw the corporal lean forward, a smile on his face. Even the German recruit who spoke no English was listening. I don't think Mac or Ellen were even aware of us.

"Well?" Mac sat up, facing her across the fire.

"Well, you're a captain, and my pa's a sergeant." She watched him through the flames.

He thought about that. "What's the other reason?"

"You're a captain."

Mac rose on his knees so he could see her better. I tried to raise my head and lean on my elbow, but I couldn't find either elbow.

"I don't understand. You already said that," Mac stated, as he peered at her.

Her hands were still now. She wasn't even breathing hard. It was as if she held all the right cards. "You're a captain, and you ought to be a major by now."

"I see." He got back up and started toward the rim of the waterhole. He looked back. "But do you love me, Ellen Quinn? Better than anyone else? I'd like to know that."

We all strained to hear her quiet answer.

"Yes, I do. Very much, in fact."

Mac took the eight-to-midnight watch. The recruits and the corporal slept close to the fire. I was about to close my eyes when Ellen got up and tiptoed over to Mac, who lay against the embankment, watching the Apache fire. She knelt down beside him and rested her head against his back. He rolled over and put his arms around her.

She said something to him, but I couldn't hear it. He whispered back, and it sounded like a question. When she said yes distinctly, I knew I should look away, but I had no urge to do so. Please don't think of me as a voyeur or a Peeping Tom. I knew we were all going to die tomorrow; I guess all I wanted was the comfort of knowing that we six, inside the waterhole, were still human, even if it was only for a few more hours.

Ellen shucked off her underdrawers pretty quick, then simply lay back on that incline and raised her knees. She looped her arms pretty tight around Mac after he pulled down his trousers and mounted her. He didn't take his trousers off all the way. I wanted to tell him to go ahead, by all means, because it would be less constricting, but didn't think any commentary from me would be appreciated.

He appeared to be kissing her pretty thoroughly, but when her legs came around his, I knew that events had progressed rapidly beyond the playful stage. She ran her hands up and down his back over his shirt, and then under it, and then she pressed hard on his butt when he began to breathe hard.

I never told Rose anything about this, because I can imagine what she would have thought about me, and maybe even about Mac and Ellen. I didn't want her to remind me that they weren't married and it was scandalous, or ask, where were their morals, when none of that mattered to me. As Mac and Ellen clung together making those wonderful motions, I only wanted them to be happy with each other. I just didn't care about anything else. I still don't.

Then a funny thing happened. I'm still not sure how I kept from laughing. Mac didn't move off Ellen, but he raised up slightly on his elbows and kissed her. She unlimbered herself but kept her knees raised on either side of Mac. As I watched, her knees relaxed and then splayed out. Her hands slid off his back at the same time I heard her breathing evenly and deeply. She had fallen asleep, in what could only be called a vulnerable position.

I saw Mac's shoulders start to shake. He removed himself carefully from Ellen, sat back on his haunches and pulled down her dress. He tugged up his pants, then lay back and laughed softly. He must have remembered what he was really supposed to be doing then, because he grabbed his gun and peered over the waterhole's rim. His shoulders started to shake again; I guess he was imaging what a sight the Apaches would have seen, had they chosen to stroll to our waterhole a minute earlier.

He sat beside Ellen again, resting his arms on his knees. God knows what he was thinking. In another moment, he noticed her drawers beside him on the sand, and figured he'd better get her back into them before the watch changed. Now, I've never tried to do what he did. Getting drawers on a cooperating women probably isn't a hard task, but Ellen was sound asleep, and Mac seemed disinclined to wake her. His task was probably comparable to stuffing a marshmallow up a straw.

Laughing softly, he guided her drawers up one leg a little at a time, obviously trying to keep as much sand as he could out of the process. I think he even fell asleep once. He did spend a few moments kissing the inside of her thighs. I looked away then, mainly because I was getting a little too involved personally, if you know what I'm saying. My God, I am astounded at people. I was nearly dead on that stretcher, and you'd have thought I was a whaleship captain coming off a three-year voyage, all randy and ready to go. I guess the instinct to survive trumps everything else.

Then Mac was laughing again. When he finished the impossible task, he pulled Ellen's skirt down once more, straightened her legs into a more dignified posture, and lay down beside her. I think I can say without argument that he was the most contented man at the waterhole.

When I woke in the morning, Ellen was squatting by the fire and stirring a plate of cactus cuisine. Mac sat halfway up the embankment, gazing at her. He ran his hands up and down his carbine, but I don't believe he was thinking about the gun, particularly.

While a recruit kept watch, the rest of us ate breakfast, scooping the red pulp and juice into our mouths as fast as we could. Ellen was dipping out a cup to carry to the man on watch when he hollered down to us, "Herr doctor, Indian de komm!" He was learning English fast.

Mac wiped his hands on his uniform and grabbed his carbine. The corporal and recruit bellied down next to each other on the rim of the waterhole and took aim. Ellen crawled to me, and we gripped hands. I had a revolver in my other hand. We waited for the firing to start. The hoofbeats grew louder and louder, but still Mac was silent.

"Fire!" he yelled finally, and the four guns roared almost at the same time. As I looked over Ellen's shoulder, several of the hostiles leaped their horses over our heads and soared halfway across the waterhole, then circled back and came at the soldiers again.

They charged once more, then we heard hoofbeats clattering away. Mac slid down to us. "Are you all right?"

I almost said yes, then saw he was asking Ellen. "I'm fine," she said through chattering teeth, "but I'd rather be up there with you."

He gripped her hand and mine for a moment. "Ellen, we've got a couple more rounds each, then I'll come get you."

We heard a shot, then, "They're coming again!"

Mac scrambled up the slope and dug in with his boots. We heard the Indians coming. Although the sound was still frightening, I was sure there were fewer horsemen than before. The soldiers fired, and again, the Apaches circled around us, with one difference. This time they drew a little away in the distance.

The corporal had been hit by an arrow in the fleshy part of his arm. Mac walked him over to the saddlebags and made him sit down. He got what looked like pliers, quickly pushed the arrow the rest of the way through, then snapped off the head and pulled the shaft out. Mac bound the arm with a hunk of his shirttail, and the men walked back to the firing line.

Mac stopped and turned to Ellen. "Honey, if I got a promotion, would you marry me?"

"Yes." Tears streamed down her face.

"Nice to know," he said and blew her a kiss before he hunkered down again.

It was a breathtaking moment. I couldn't think of anything to say to the good woman next to me. All I knew right then was that I didn't want to die flat on my back.

"Ellen, help me. I've got to sit up."

She pulled me into a sitting position. When the thunder in my head receded, I knew this would be better.

They came again. The screaming and yelling got louder and louder; then we heard the guns and whiz of arrows. They roared over us as we fired, then circled. We waited for them to charge one more time.

Mac crawled down the slope. "I'm on my last round, Ellen." He separated our hands. "I want her with me, John. I'm sorry, but I do." He surprised me then by kissing my cheek. "You know what to do, don't you?"

I nodded. I couldn't speak. I wanted to tell him he was the best officer I had ever served under, but I believe he saw it in my eyes.

Mac pulled Ellen up the incline and handed her a revolver. "One round left in here, m'love. When you see them coming this time, put the muzzle in your mouth and pull the trigger. For God's sake do it, because I can't."

The corporal pantomimed to the German recruit what was to happen next. The man grinned and nodded, so I'm not sure he really grasped the situation in its entirety. The corporal and the other soldier lowered their carbines to their sides, their fingers on the triggers. I pulled the hammer back on my weapon and stuck the muzzle in my ear.

Hampered briefly by our remaining mortality, we waited for the Apaches to come back again. I've never been so ready for anything in my whole life. A minute passed, then two or three, then ten. Nothing. I pointed my gun away and eased the hammer down.

They didn't return. Ellen put her gun down and leaned her forehead against Mac's shoulder.

"Why?" the corporal asked of no one in particular.

We didn't know. Perhaps it was the ultimate practical joke. We stayed there watching the horizon until late afternoon, when a puff of dust appeared in the east. It was C Company, searching for a long overdue patrol.

When we got to Bowie, I was transported directly to civilization and a hospital, where I spent the next six months in traction. A couple of visitors from Bowie came by to see me while heading for other duty, and one of them told me that Mac had been promoted to major. Two weeks later, I got a short note from him saying he and Ellen had been married the week before. He was sorry I couldn't be best man, but the commanding officer had filled in.

I never saw Mac again. I was transferred back East a year after the incident, resigned my commission, and became a stockbroker. Mac resigned his commission when the regiment was reassigned and set up a private practice in Tucson. Rose, John, Jr., our two daughters, and I moved here to Carlsbad when the Great War started. Over the years, we've exchanged Christmas letters, birth announcements, graduation cards, wedding announcements, more birth announcements.

I really don't know why we never saw each other again. We tried a couple of times, but Mac had to perform some emergency surgery and cancelled our plans, and another time Rose had a miscarriage, so we pulled out. It wasn't that we didn't want to. I don't know.

I suppose that is the end of the story. Since I don't know you, I am not aware of your usual standard of entertainment. At least you didn't have to pay a dime like you do for the silent pictures. Besides, it was all true.

About the Author

Carla Kelly is the author of sixteen novels and a ranger for the National Park Service at Fort Union Trading Post National Historic Site, located on the Montana-North Dakota border. Much of her inspiration for the stories in her collection came from her experiences in Fort Laramie National Historic Site's living history program where she wore period clothing and assumed various personae, as she offered visitors a glimpse into history. She divides her time between Fort Union in the summer, and Valley City, North Dakota, the rest of the year, where her husband teaches at Valley City State University, and she writes.